"I found myself in need of something,"

Cole said.

"What?" Kelsey asked, confused by the sudden change in his voice.

It took him only three steps to reach her. Only a moment to draw her into his arms. "This," he murmured.

"This" was a kiss that nearly short-circuited her body's life-support systems. She was clinging to his forearms when he finally raised his head, and she wasn't at all sure that she'd remain upright if he released her.

"You—" She had to clear her throat to speak clearly. "You came all the way across town for a kiss?"

Even his smile was dangerous—very male, very predatory, very much satisfied with her reaction to his kiss.

She was in a whole lot of trouble, she thought again, but this time with a fatalistic awareness that it was already too late to pull back.

"Since you went to all that trouble..."

Dear Reader,

Welcome to Silhouette **Special Edition** . . . welcome to romance. Each month, Silhouette **Special Edition** publishes six novels with you in mind—stories of love and life, tales that you can identify with—romance with that little "something special" added in.

And may this December bring you all the warmth and joy of the holiday season. The holidays in Chicago form the perfect backdrop for Patricia McLinn's *Prelude to a Wedding,* the first book in her new duo, WEDDING DUET. Don't miss the festivities!

Rounding out December are more stories by some of your favorite authors: Victoria Pade, Gina Ferris, Mary Kirk and Sherryl Woods—who has written Joshua's story— *Joshua and the Cowgirl,* a spinoff from *My Dearest Cal* (SE #669).

As an extraspecial surprise, don't miss *Luring a Lady* by Nora Roberts. This warm, tender tale introduces us to Mikhail—a character you met in *Taming Natasha* (SE #583). Yes, Natasha's brother is here to win your heart—as well as the heart of the lovely Sydney Hayward!

In each Silhouette **Special Edition** novel, we're dedicated to bringing you the romances that you dream about—the types of stories that delight as well as bring a tear to the eye. And that's what Silhouette **Special Edition** is all about—special books by special authors for special readers!

I hope you enjoy this book and all of the stories to come.

Sincerely,

Tara Gavin
Senior Editor

GINA FERRIS
Prodigal Father

Silhouette Special Edition

Published by Silhouette Books New York

America's Publisher of Contemporary Romance

With special thanks to Vicki O'Connor-Davis,
founder and volunteer administrator of
Arkansas Children's Dreams, Inc.

And to the thousands of volunteers nationwide
who give of their time and resources
in service for others.

SILHOUETTE BOOKS
300 East 42nd St., New York, N.Y. 10017

PRODIGAL FATHER

ISBN: 0-373-09711-5

First Silhouette Books printing December 1991

Printed in the U.S.A.

Books by Gina Ferris

Silhouette Special Edition

Healing Sympathy #496
Lady Beware #549
In From the Rain #677
Prodigal Father #711

GINA FERRIS

declares that she is Southern by birth and by choice, and she has chosen to set many of her books in the South, where she finds a rich treasury of characters and settings. She particularly loves the Ozark mountain region of northern Arkansas and southern Missouri, and the proudly unique people who reside there. She and her husband, John, live in Jacksonville, Arkansas, with their three children, Courtney, Kerry and David.

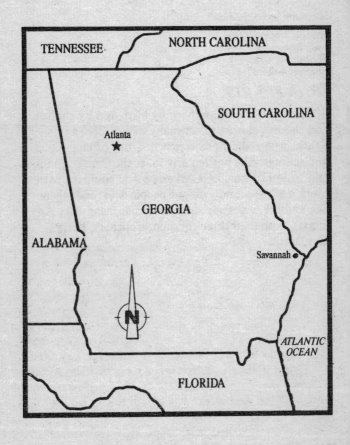

Chapter One

"Look, I've told you this is very important. I need to see Mr. Saxon as soon as possible." Kelsey planted her hands on the secretary's desk, scowling in her effort to look intimidating.

Having handled much more daunting unscheduled callers, the secretary was unfazed by Kelsey's vehemence. "I'm sorry, Ms. Campbell, but, as senior vice president for this company, Mr. Saxon is extremely busy. Mondays are always very hectic. He can't possibly spare you any time today. If you'll tell me the nature of your business with him and leave your card, I will see if he wants to schedule an appointment for next week. I'm afraid that's the best I can do."

Kelsey straightened and impatiently shoved a hand through her short dark hair. "My business with Mr. Saxon is personal. It won't wait until next week. Tell him I'll only take a few minutes to explain—"

"Mr. Saxon will be leaving very shortly for a meeting downtown. He hasn't even a few minutes to spare today. I really must insist—"

Their stubborn standoff was interrupted by the opening of the heavy paneled door beside the secretary's desk—the door marked with a discreet brass plate bearing Cole Saxon's name. The man who stepped through was tall, broad shouldered, brown-haired and impeccably dressed in a tailored gray suit worn with a crisp white shirt and dark tie. His head was lowered, attention directed to the sheaf of papers in his hand, so Kelsey caught only a glimpse of his face when she whirled to look expectantly up at him. She moistened her lips, prepared to launch into a rapid request for his attention.

His secretary spoke first. "You're leaving for your meeting now, Mr. Saxon?"

"Mmm." The distracted murmur was obviously an affirmative. "Call Parker for me, Alice. Tell him I may be a few minutes late this afternoon. Tell him to wait for me."

"Yes, sir. Anything else?"

Without looking up, he headed for the outer door. "No."

Kelsey knew it was now or never. "Mr. Saxon."

The secretary spoke warningly. "Mr. Saxon is in a hurry, Ms. Campbell. He doesn't have time—"

Kelsey ignored her, hurrying after the man stepping into the hallway. "Mr. Saxon."

The man flicked her a glance without slowing on his way to the elevator. "Yes?"

"I need to speak with you. It's very—"

He punched the call button. "I'm running late for a meeting. Leave your card with my secretary and I'll—"

"Mr. Saxon, I really need to talk to you soon. Perhaps later this afternoon?"

The elevator doors slid open. "Not possible, I'm afraid. Talk to my secretary." He stepped into the car with an air of finality.

Resisting the impulse to stamp her foot in exasperation, Kelsey followed him into the otherwise-empty elevator, slipping through the already-closing doors. "I've talked to your secretary, Mr. Saxon. I've tried calling, but she won't put me through to you and I can't explain my business to her. Only to you. She keeps putting me off with excuses about how busy you are."

He turned a page of the report he'd been studying, obviously hoping Kelsey would disappear if he ignored her. "She's right. I am busy."

"Yes, I know you are and I'm sorry to bother you, but this is important. Too important to discuss in an elevator. Couldn't we—"

The elevator bumped gently to a stop, interrupting her yet again. Saxon stepped out the moment the doors opened, leaving Kelsey glaring after him in frustration. "Damn it," he muttered, pressing determinedly after him. "Mr. Saxon, please. I wouldn't be such a nuisance if it wasn't very important. I really must speak to you."

His hand was already on the revolving door that led out of the office building. For the first time, he looked directly at her. She caught her breath. Cole Saxon was a handsome man in his thirties, but it wasn't just his attractiveness that startled her. She knew only two other people with eyes that exact silvery-green, one of them a fifty-six-year-old man, the other a three-month-old infant.

Saxon frowned at something he saw in her expression. And then he turned away. "Some other time perhaps." He pushed through the revolving doors without looking back.

This time Kelsey did stamp her foot, just before launching herself into the door behind him. "Mr. Saxon!"

Her quarry slid into the back seat of a limousine, beside which a uniformed chauffeur stood at almost-military attention. "Let's go, Fred, I'm in a hurry."

"Yes, sir, Mr. Saxon." With barely a glance at Kelsey, Fred started to close the door.

Kelsey hovered on the curb, hoping for any sign of en couragement. "Mr. Saxon, please. It's about—"

The door closed with a conclusive snap, leaving Kelsey staring at her own reflection in a tinted window. Fred climbed briskly behind the wheel and closed his door, and then the long gray car pulled away, merging smoothly with the traffic on the busy Savannah, Georgia, business ave-nue.

"—your father." She finished the sentence with a sigh, conceding defeat. For the moment.

A professional fund-raiser for a perpetually struggling charity organization, she was accustomed to being snubbed and avoided by wealthy businessmen. Cole Saxon would simply have to learn that Kelsey Campbell wasn't one to give up easily once she'd set her mind to something. One rue-fully resigned industrialist had likened her to a deceptively innocuous-looking toy poodle with the tenacity of a pit bull.

Settling her oversize leather purse more comfortably over her shoulder, Kelsey whirled and headed for her car, her mind already busy with alternative plans for making Cole Saxon listen to what she had to say.

Kelsey swept into Saxon's secretary's office early the next morning. Her rakish green dress sported military epaulets and a bold brass belt buckle, chosen deliberately to empha size the not-to-be-trifled-with expression she wore as she approached the desk. "Good morning. I'm here to see Mr Saxon."

The secretary took one look at Kelsey and drew her ele gant eyebrows into a frown. "Ms. Campbell."

Kelsey smiled. "I'm pleased that you remember my name. Please announce me to Mr. Saxon."

"Mr. Saxon is not to be disturbed. If you'll tell me the nature of your business and leave your number, I'll—"

Kelsey broke into the memorized spiel with a bright dangerous smile. "I'll just have a seat here until he has a minute to talk to me." She chose a chair from the four available in the waiting area and settled into it, crossing her legs to look as though it wouldn't bother her to wait all day. And then she focused on the woman seated behind the wood desk, blinking as infrequently as possible. Kelsey's stares had gotten her past more than one dauntingly efficient secretary.

The other woman returned the stare with an icy one of her own. "This won't do you any good, Ms. Campbell. Mr. Saxon is even busier today than he was yesterday. He won't be able to see you—not even briefly."

"Oh, I'm sure he can arrange a few minutes with me," Kelsey replied without looking away. "Particularly when you tell him how important it is."

"I'm sorry, I can't do that. I've been instructed to screen all callers today so that Mr. Saxon is not disturbed. Now if you'll excuse me, I have work to do."

"Go right ahead," Kelsey urged magnanimously. "I'll just wait here quietly." She smoothed her skirt over her knees and stared even harder at the secretary.

Her professionally impassive face going taut with displeasure, the woman turned to her keyboard, her back to the unwelcome caller. Kelsey wasn't fooled. She knew the secretary was well aware that Kelsey was still watching her. It had to be uncomfortable. She wondered how long it would take to break the woman whom Saxon had called Alice. She hoped when that time came, Alice would ask her boss to talk to Kelsey for a moment just to get rid of her. Kelsey intended to make good use of that opportunity.

But some thirty minutes later she had to admit that Alice was good. Better than most. The woman hardly seemed aware of Kelsey's presence as she went about her work with brisk competence. Kelsey wished fleetingly that she'd chosen another chair. This one wasn't as comfortable as it had looked. But she couldn't be shuffling around or the secretary would assume that she had no staying power. She'd be wrong, of course.

Another five minutes passed before Alice's telephone buzzed. She picked up the receiver. "Yes, Mr. Saxon?"

Kelsey perked up abruptly, hope flaring.

"No, Mr. Saxon.... Yes, Mr. Saxon.... All right, I will.... Yes, sir. I'll see you in the morning." Alice hung up the phone with a quick glance toward Kelsey, then turned back to her work.

The hint of smug satisfaction in that brief look made Kelsey suspicious. A moment later she heard the sound of a door closing out in the hallway. "There's not another door out of your boss's office, is there?" she demanded, half-afraid she already knew the answer.

Alice looked at her with a rather feline smile. "Perhaps you'd like to leave your number with me now?"

"Damn it!" Snatching her purse, Kelsey leapt from the uncomfortable chair and threw herself toward the door. She made it to the hallway just in time to see the elevator doors close behind Cole Saxon. If he saw her, he gave no indication.

Cursing steadily beneath her breath, Kelsey shoved open the door to the stairway and barreled through it. Three flights, she thought, groaning. Praying she wouldn't trip and land in a broken heap at the bottom of those stairs, she hurried down them as quickly as safely possible.

Fred was just closing the door of the limousine when Kelsey stumbled out to the street, panting and disheveled. "Mr. Saxon!"

The man in the back seat glanced through the smoked window, knowing he was safely shielded behind it. Her, again. The woman who'd followed him out of his building yesterday. She was persistent, he'd give her that. But then, salespeople and fund-raisers generally were. "Drive on, Fred."

"Yes, sir, Mr. Saxon." The powerful vehicle slid smoothly away from the curb.

Glancing over his shoulder, Cole took one last look at the woman glaring angrily after him. Something about her interested him. Maybe it was the way she carried herself, her shoulders braced and head high as if she stood six feet rather than her no more than five feet two inches. Maybe it was something about her enormous brown eyes or gaminely cut, short dark hair. Cole usually preferred statuesque blondes for his occasional social companions, but this woman intrigued him. Not that he intended to do anything about it, of course. It was obvious that she wanted something from him. But he simply didn't have time to deal with her.

At that thought, he opened the briefcase resting on his knees. He was immersed in the papers within it before the limo had traveled another mile, the woman already pushed to the back of his mind.

Listening to the telephone ringing at the other end of the line, Kelsey cleared her throat nervously, hoping her next ploy would work. Outright deception wasn't something she'd ever tried before. She didn't like it, but her situation was getting desperate. It seemed that Cole Saxon was never going to talk to her unless she took drastic steps. Telling his secretary the truth would probably guarantee that he'd never listen to anything Kelsey had to say. Kelsey knew that Saxon wanted nothing to do with the father who'd abandoned him some twenty-six years earlier. If only he'd give her a chance to talk to him about Paul....

"Cole Saxon's office. Alice speaking. May I help you?"

Alice's tone was as clipped and unencouraging as the woman herself. Kelsey cleared her throat again, and when she spoke, her voice came out husky and hardly recognizable. "Hi. Is Cole in?"

"Mr. Saxon is out of the office. May I take a message?"

"I feel so silly," Kelsey murmured with a nervous titter. That much was true, anyway. She felt *very* silly. "I've completely forgotten the name of the restaurant where I'm supposed to meet him tonight for dinner. We talked about several and I simply can't remember which one we finally decided upon. I don't suppose you made reservations, did you?"

It was a desperate effort, Kelsey had to admit. Ever-vigilant Alice would probably see right through it. Oldest trick in the book. It would never work. She closed her eyes and prepared for a brush-off.

"Did you say tonight?" Alice asked instead, sounding puzzled.

"Um . . . yes," Kelsey affirmed, remembering at the last moment to alter her voice. Was it possible that Cole Saxon was known to have a weakness for fluffy females?

"Could it be that you have your dates mixed up as well as your restaurants? I made reservations at Brandreth's for six-thirty this evening, but I'm sure he said he was dining with his attorney."

It was all Kelsey could do to keep from shouting, "Yes!" Instead, she feigned embarrassed confusion. "Oh, dear. Maybe it was tomorrow night? Or Friday? Honestly, how silly of me. Heavens, I hope it wasn't last night!"

"Why don't I have Mr. Saxon give you a call?" Alice suggested, sounding almost kind.

Kelsey began to feel guilty. "No, thank you. I'll be seeing him soon anyway and I'll ask him then. You've been very helpful." She disconnected the call as quickly as possible.

Brandreth's. Taking a deep breath, she looked across her living room to the portable crib in which lay a tiny, sleeping duplicate of the man she intended to corner that evening. "Well, Jared, this is it," she murmured. "You and I have an appointment for tonight. We'd better make the most of it."

* * *

A flower-lined veranda circled the front of Brandreth's, a popular Savannah restaurant converted from an antebellum mansion. Small benches sat among the hibiscus and periwinkles lining the brick walkway that led to the entrance. Kelsey chose a bench with the best visibility and settled down to wait for Saxon's arrival. Jared squirmed in his carrier at her side, his tiny little face screwing up in discontent. Gingerly Kelsey unsnapped the restraints that held him in the seat, lifted him to her shoulder and patted his back. She'd had very little experience with babies—just three months, to be exact.

At least the weather was nice, she thought absently. Under any other circumstances she would have thoroughly enjoyed sitting outside with her nephew on this warm, beautiful evening in late July, the scent of flowers surrounding her. Unfortunately, her anxiety at the upcoming confrontation with Cole Saxon ruined her pleasure in the scenery.

She recognized the limo that pulled up in front of her even before Fred got out to open the back door. The first man who stepped out wasn't Saxon, but an older man with a shock of white hair and a hint of a paunch. Saxon slid smoothly out after him, his own seal-brown hair gleaming in the waning sun, his body athletically lean.

Kelsey surged to her feet. "Mr. Saxon."

He turned automatically at the sound of his name. His eyes went first to Kelsey's face and then to the baby in her arms. His jaw hardened. "What the hell do you want? Why are you following me around?"

She swallowed, startled by his expression. Kelsey had never been easily intimidated, but she sensed that she'd never met a man quite like Cole Saxon before. Not the kind of man she'd want for an enemy. There wasn't even a hint of softness in his ruggedly attractive face. For the first time she began to wonder if her mission was destined to failure from the onset. "I only want to talk to you for a few minutes, Mr. Saxon. Please, I'm getting desperate. I didn't know how else to get your attention."

Saxon's companion—his attorney, Kelsey remembered—stirred uneasily, his gaze locked on the baby. A baby whose striking resemblance to the lawyer's client would have been apparent to anyone. "Uh, Cole, maybe you'd better let me handle this."

Saxon's frown deepened. "No. We're having dinner. Now."

Clutching her courage, Kelsey stepped in front of the two men, blocking their way. Aware of the obvious confrontation, other restaurant patrons walked warily around them. Kelsey ignored them, as did the men in front of her. "Why are you being so difficult?" she demanded. "Why can't you give me even a minute to explain my business with you?"

Saxon didn't answer. Instead, the older man moved forward, smiling placatingly. "I'm Bob Herrington, Mr. Saxon's attorney. I could give you a few minutes tomorrow if you'd care to come by my office. The address is—"

Genuinely confused, Kelsey tilted her head in question. "That's very nice of you, Mr. Herrington, but I really need to speak to Mr. Saxon, not his attorney." And then a ripple of annoyance at the way she'd been treated made her glare at Saxon and add, "You could learn something in manners from your lawyer."

As if disturbed by the tension in the air around him, Jared stirred against Kelsey's shoulder and whimpered. Automatically, she turned her attention to him. "It's okay, sweetie," she murmured, settling him into the crook of her arm. He peered myopically up at her, seemingly looking for reassurance in the smile she gave him.

Herrington shoved a hand through his white hair. "Hell, would you look at those eyes," he muttered. "Cole—"

Saxon stiffened and turned incredulously to the other man. "Surely you don't think—"

"You mean it's not..."

"It's not mine," Saxon growled flatly. "Until a couple of days ago, I'd never seen this woman in my life."

The attorney slumped in visible relief.

Kelsey had had enough. Her quick temper ignited into full flame with this last indignity. Her eyes locked with Saxon's, her voice deepening with her fury. "Why, you arrogant, egotistical, ill-mannered jerk. You honestly think I would claim to have been indiscriminate enough to go to bed with *you?* Give me credit for taste, would you? I have never once implied that this baby is your son."

Herrington spoke quickly, before his obviously angry client could retort. The attorney seemed more aware than the others of the public setting of the confrontation. "Maybe we should find someplace more private to discuss this."

Saxon took a step closer to Kelsey, looming over her as he glared down at her temper-flushed face. She tilted her head back defiantly to return the stare, knowing he'd been infuriated by her deliberate insults. "What, exactly, is it that you want to discuss, lady?"

"The name is Campbell. *Ms.* Campbell to you," she added cuttingly. "And I want to talk to you about your father."

He obviously hadn't been expecting that. His eyes widened perceptibly in surprise. "My father?"

She nodded. "Paul Saxon."

"Look, *Ms.* Campbell, I haven't seen my father in twenty-six years and I don't particularly care if I never see him again. I don't know why he sent you after me, but—"

"Paul didn't send me. He doesn't even know I'm here," Kelsey interjected. "But there are a couple of things I think you need to know."

"All I'm interested in right now is having my dinner before I lose my reservation," he replied dismissively, stepping around her. "Come on, Bob."

Kelsey turned to look after him. Raising her voice to carry clearly, she announced, "This baby is your brother, Mr. Saxon. Paul Saxon's son. And your father is dying."

She had never intended to blurt out the news so precipitously. But the response was immediate. Cole Saxon froze, then turned slowly to look at her. He searched her face for a long moment as if to test the truth of her words. Something he saw must have convinced him that she meant what she said. "Well, hell."

Looking beyond her, he made a motion with his hand. Fred, who'd been waiting in the limousine during the brief episode as if to be available if needed, immediately leapt out. "Yes, Mr. Saxon?"

"Open the door, Fred. We won't be dining here tonight." Saxon turned back to Kelsey. "Get in."

She looked from the limousine to the hard, tense man in front of her. "But—"

"I said get in. You want to talk, we'll talk. Now."

She hesitated only a moment longer. Then, deciding this was the only opportunity she'd probably have, she strapped the baby into the carrier, balancing him awkwardly in one arm as she reached for her purse and the diaper bag. Saxon beat her to them, somehow managing to look all-male even with her purse and the yellow-and-white gingham tote dangling from one hand. "Just get in the car," he repeated. And then he looked at Herrington. "You coming?"

The attorney was already halfway to the curb. "I wouldn't miss this for the world."

Kelsey took a deep breath and slid into the seat, beginning to wish she'd never heard Cole Saxon's name.

Chapter Two

Kelsey had just settled into the plush seat of the limo and was trying very hard not to look as though it were her first time to sit in one—which it was—when Cole Saxon leaned his head in the door and glared at her. "Did you drive your own car to the restaurant?" he demanded.

"No," she answered equally curtly, not bothering to add that her tired old sedan had died quietly in its sleep during the night. "I—we came in a cab," she added, groping for a seat belt to secure the baby's car-safe infant carrier.

"Where do you live?"

She gave her address grudgingly, knowing better than to waste time arguing with him. She had the duration of the short trip to talk to him about his father, she reminded herself, though she'd already half decided she'd wasted her time contacting him in the first place. She hadn't expected Paul's son to be so cold, so hard, so intimidating, despite what Paul had told her about him. She heard him repeat her address to the chauffeur, and then he climbed into the limo to sit beside his attorney. Both of them looked at Kelsey. She couldn't help but compare their expressions. Herrington's was kind, sympathetic, curious; Saxon's annoyed, suspicious. She swallowed hard.

Cole crossed his arms over his chest and leaned back against his seat, his narrowed eyes never leaving her face. "All right," he began coolly. "How much do you want?"

The attorney shifted and cleared his throat.

Kelsey frowned. "I beg your pardon?"

"It's obvious that you've gotten yourself into trouble with my father and now you've found out he's not one to stick around and take care of his responsibilities. So you decided to try your luck with me, instead. Did you think I'd pay to avoid scandal, Ms. Campbell? Maybe you should know that nothing my father can do could possibly embarrass me."

She hadn't really believed she could get any angrier than she'd been. It seemed she'd been wrong. Her cheeks burning, temper narrowing her eyes, she sat as straight and tall as possible, hoping her voice was as icily precise as his when she responded. "You, Mr. Saxon, are the rudest, most unpleasant man I have ever met and I regret that I ever made the effort to meet you. I felt sorry for Paul because he wanted so much to see you one more time before he—"

Her voice broke slightly, but she forged on. "Anyway, now I can see I was wasting my time. It's quite apparent that you care nothing about anyone but yourself. You haven't even asked if it's true that he's ill. You simply assumed that I was here because I want something from you. Tell me, is it something I've done or do you always leap to the conclusion that everyone you meet wants your money, Mr. Saxon?"

His brow lifted slightly. "Everyone does," he answered simply.

For just a moment, she could find it in herself to feel sorry for him. And then she remembered Paul lying helplessly in a hospital bed asking for his son, and she hardened her heart. "Not everyone," she told him with a defiant toss of her head.

Herrington must have decided it was time for the calming voice of reason to intervene. "Perhaps we should start from the beginning, Ms. Campbell. You say Paul Saxon is ill?"

She looked at him gratefully, clearly turning a cold shoulder to Cole. "Very ill," she confirmed quietly. "It's his heart. He had an attack last week. The doctors say there's a chance he could be helped with surgery, but they're having trouble stabilizing him enough to give him a chance to survive the operation."

"Aren't you rather young to have become involved with a fifty-six-year-old man?" Cole interrupted, his expression showing no reaction to her words. "What are you, twenty-three? Twenty-four?"

"Twenty-four," she answered crisply. "And your father is my brother-in-law, not my lover. He married my older sister, Lauren, eighteen months ago. They've been very happy together." She waited defiantly for a scornful comment.

Instead, Cole nodded toward the infant carrier beside her. "And the baby?"

Her hand went automatically to the sleeping child. "My nephew. And your brother," she couldn't resist adding.

"Half brother," he murmured.

She swallowed back an angry retort. "I've been watching him in the evenings so my sister can spend as much time as possible at the hospital," she explained instead.

"What made you decide to contact Cole, Ms. Campbell?" the attorney asked, interceding again.

"I'm very fond of my brother-in-law, Mr. Herrington," she explained with a brief, challenging look at Cole. "I was concerned at first when my sister married a man twenty-five years her senior after a whirlwind courtship, but he's been wonderful for Lauren. She...hasn't always had an easy time of it, and she needed someone like Paul. Someone loving and patient and caring and gentle."

Cole snorted.

Herrington placed a restraining hand on his client's arm. "Go on, Ms. Campbell."

"I work for the Children's Dream Foundation of Georgia. It's an organization dedicated to granting wishes for children with life-threatening diseases," she added, in case either of the men hadn't heard of it. "Maybe that's why it seemed important to me to try to fulfill Paul's, in case he... Because he's so ill." She still couldn't accept the fact that Paul might die, leaving her sister devastated and little Jared fatherless.

Blinking back unwanted tears, she cleared her throat and went on. "Paul told me last week, just after his attack, that the one thing he regrets is his alienation from his elder son."

She turned to Cole then, pleadingly, hoping to touch some hidden softness within the stern-faced exterior. "He only wants to talk to you—just once—to explain why he left when you were a child. He says he's tried repeatedly to contact you in the past few years but you refused to see him. He doesn't ask for your forgiveness or your understanding, just a few minutes of your time so that he can tell you his side of what happened."

"I know what happened, Ms. Campbell," Cole answered flatly, his silvery-green eyes bleak. "He left. He walked away from me, from my mother, from his family, from his business. He had responsibilities and he wasn't willing to honor them."

She held his gaze with her own. "Maybe that is what happened. I don't know. He and I have never discussed it. But can't you at least give him a chance to tell you if there is another side of the story?"

Cole looked away first, his jaw rock hard, his expression unreadable. "Look, I don't owe my father anything. He was never there when I needed him. Why should I do anything for him now?''

Something inside her mellowed at his words, despite her best efforts to prevent it. She was just too softhearted for her own good, she told herself in exasperation even as she suggested quietly, ''Maybe you owe yourself this meeting. If nothing else, it will give you a chance to tell Paul exactly how you feel about him before it's too late.''

His eyes turned back to hers, and she could tell that she'd gotten through to him. She wasn't so sure she'd convinced him. ''I'll think about it,'' was all he said.

''Do that. But...don't wait too long,'' she added bleakly, thinking of the way Paul had looked the last time she'd seen him, only a few hours earlier.

The limousine slid to a smooth stop in front of her modest apartment building. Kelsey tried not to think of her neighbors' reactions to seeing her emerge. She'd be in for some teasing tomorrow, she thought absently, turning one last time to the sympathetic attorney. ''Talk to him, will you?'' she asked, jerking her head toward Cole. ''Maybe you can convince him he should do this.''

Herrington gave her one of his kind smiles. ''You're obviously very sincere, Ms. Campbell. Paul Saxon is fortunate to have you for his friend.''

He may as well have patted her on the head and told her she was young and hopelessly naive, Kelsey thought with an inward sigh. ''Thank you, Mr. Herrington. I'm sorry I spoiled your dinner.''

''Not at all,'' he assured her courteously. ''I can have dinner with Cole anytime. It's not often I get to meet a beautiful young woman.''

She smiled faintly and slid out of the limo, pulling Jared's carrier with her. Cole stood beside the door, still holding her purse and the diaper bag. Balancing her nephew in one arm, she reached for them. He stepped back. ''I'll help you to your door.''

"Thank you, but—"

He turned away before she could finish the sentence. "Which way?"

She sighed. "Second door on the left, upper level."

He glanced at the stairway leading up to her apartment, then back to the baby in her arms, sleeping in his molded plastic carrier. "Is that heavy?" Cole asked awkwardly. "I'll carry it, if you'd rather take these things."

That. Not *he.* Not *the baby.* Just *that.* "Thank you, but I can handle him," she replied coolly. She didn't look at him again as she headed for her apartment door, though she knew he followed close behind her.

She had her key out of the pocket of her short-sleeved jacket by the time she reached the door. She wasn't particularly surprised when Cole took it from her and slid it into the lock. The man was arrogant even when he was being polite, she thought resentfully. She tried to ignore the warmth of him as he leaned over her. She was much too aware of his closeness. Beneath her navy jacket and jade knit dress, her skin felt suddenly . . . tingly, sensitized, as if she'd passed too closely to an electrical charge. She told herself that it must be a reaction from an overly emotional evening and a long, tiring week.

Cole followed her into the apartment. Depositing the baby carrier on the couch, she was aware that her uninvited guest was looking around, classifying the apartment and its owner. She wondered what conclusions he would come to from her eclectic decor. That she liked bright colors and unusual designs, obviously. That she had her own sense of style combined with a talent for combining unusual, diverse elements into an oddly harmonious whole. He could probably tell that she had a strictly limited budget with which to work. She'd never expected to get rich in her charity job. Would a man like him understand that wealth had never been one of her goals? Probably not.

She turned to him, her hands in the pockets of her jacket, her lower lip caught between her teeth. His gaze searched her face for a moment, and then he dropped her things on a striped chair and glanced toward the door. "Was there anything else you wanted to say before I go?"

She shrugged. "I don't think there's anything left to say."

He nodded and turned away. Impulsively she stepped forward, detaining him at the door with a hand on his arm. "Mr. Saxon—Cole—please think about what I said. I know he hurt you, but . . . Paul needs you. If you could only . . ."

"I said I'll think about it." His gaze fell to the hand that rested on his arm, looking small and pale against the dark, obviously expensive fabric.

Her eyes following his, Kelsey pulled quickly away. "That's all I can ask," she murmured, locking her suddenly unsteady hands behind her back. "Again—I'm sorry I ruined your evening."

Unlike his attorney, Cole made no efforts to soothe her with polite disclaimers. He only nodded and reached for the door. A moment later he was gone.

Running both hands through her short, thick hair, Kelsey turned away from the door with a muttered string of curses. She'd failed, she thought glumly. Not only that, she'd made an utter fool of herself.

Cole was too cold, too unaccommodating to be swayed by her—or anyone's—pleas. She found it hard to believe that anyone who looked so very much like good-natured, caring, always upbeat Paul Saxon could be so very different in personality. She also found it incredible that, despite her annoyance with the man, she could still have been so attracted to him. It was probably a good thing he had refused her request, she decided ruefully. Paul wouldn't enjoy a visit with his unforgiving son, and Kelsey would just as soon not spend any more time with the man who'd disconcerted her so thoroughly, seemingly without any effort on his part.

She wouldn't tell Lauren or Paul that she'd met Cole, she decided abruptly. Paul would only be hurt that Cole had refused yet again to see him, even after hearing that Paul was very ill, possibly dying. And Lauren would be embarrassed that Kelsey had made such a nuisance of herself on their behalf.

No, better all around if she just forgot she'd ever spoken to Cole Saxon. It wouldn't be easy, but she could do it. She'd start by concentrating on Paul's other son, who was probably in need of a change. She reached for the diaper bag, but was unable to stop herself from remembering Cole's large, tanned hand clasped around it. Yes, she decided, it was probably just as well that she wouldn't be seeing him again.

"So, are you going to do it?"

Cole looked up from his steak, thinking that it wasn't as good as the dinner he'd anticipated at Brandreth's, but at least this restaurant didn't require reservations. "Do what?" he asked in response to Bob's unexpected question.

The attorney cut into his own steak, eyeing Cole intently. "Are you going to see Paul?"

Cole scowled. "I doubt it."

"Sounds like he needs you, Cole."

His knife cut savagely through the thick steak. "Yeah, well, what about all the times I needed *him?* Where was he then?"

"Why don't you ask him that?"

"Because I quit caring about the answer a long time ago."

Bob, his longtime friend as well as his attorney, only looked at him.

Cole concentrated on his dinner.

They ate in silence for a time before the attorney spoke again. "She's quite persuasive, isn't she?"

Cole swallowed a bite of baked potato and reached for his iced tea. "Who?"

"Ms. Campbell. I'll bet she's good at what she does."

Cole nearly choked on his drink. Bob surely didn't realize how provocatively his words could be taken. Cole was annoyed that he had immediately envisioned several things Kelsey Campbell probably did very well.

What was the matter with him? She detested him, and he didn't particularly approve of her. He wasn't sure what her game was with his father—either she was after something from Cole or she was incredibly naive to think that one meeting would erase twenty-six years of hurt and bitterness. Either way, he had no intention of being taken in by her big brown eyes or husky, musical voice.

"Cole?"

"Yeah?" He blinked, realizing he'd drifted into his own thoughts.

Bob eyed him speculatively. "Pretty little thing, isn't she?"

"She's okay," Cole agreed indifferently. "If you like that type." Without even trying, he could clearly envision her delicate features, picture the banked temper in her chocolaty eyes. The image made his pulse race, and made him swear silently at the unwanted reaction.

"Can't imagine why anyone would like that type," Bob agreed with a thread of amusement lacing his voice. "Pretty, well built, bright, sincere. Nope, no reason to like that one."

Cole sighed gustily. "Eat your dinner."

Bob chuckled. "All right. We'll consider that subject closed, too. So, would you like to talk about your new brother?"

It suddenly occurred to Cole that he didn't know the baby's name. He wished he'd asked—just for the sake of idle curiosity, he assured himself. And then his mouth quirked into a wry smile as he remembered the way Bob had looked at him earlier. "You really thought it was my kid?"

The older man shrugged. "Well, he does have your eyes."

"I thought you'd credit me with more sense. You know I've always been careful in my . . . relationships."

With a snort of often-expressed disgust, Bob set down his fork. "Relationships? That's not what I'd call them. A series of fleeting liaisons, perhaps. And if you ask me, it's about time you had yourself a kid. A man needs to think about the future when he gets to be your age. Hannah and I had all three of our girls by the time I was thirty."

"Find me someone like Hannah and I'll consider it," Cole retorted, as he had many times before. "Which means I'm safe, because Hannah's one of a kind."

"She is that," Bob admitted with a fond smile. "But Kelsey Campbell reminded me of Hannah at the same age."

"We're not talking about her, remember?"

Bob chuckled. "I forgot. You know, I believe I'll have some dessert. That cherry cobbler looks too good to resist."

Sternly dragging his thoughts away from Kelsey Campbell and her unwelcome request, Cole nodded. "Yeah, I'll have some, too." He'd think about Ms. Campbell later, he told himself. Not that he had any intention of changing his mind about seeing Paul Saxon.

Even as he cut into his cobbler, he found himself wondering fleetingly if Paul really was going to die. And wondering why the thought left him feeling oddly hollow inside if it was true that he had no feelings left for his father.

Still smarting from her failure with Cole Saxon, Kelsey went to work Thursday morning with a renewed determination to help "her kids" see their last dreams come true. She'd been working for the Children's Dream Foundation of Georgia for nearly three years at a barely-get-by salary, but she loved her job, which had quickly become her obsession.

She had an interview scheduled this morning with a reporter from a local newspaper for an article to run the following day. She welcomed any opportunity for media exposure, seeing each one as another chance to solicit funds for the foundation. As she'd showered earlier, she had rehearsed her planned appeal for public donations.

"Good morning, Jessie," she said as she entered the reception area of the foundation offices. The office space was donated by a Savannah oncology clinic.

Jessie, the retired volunteer receptionist who came in every Tuesday and Thursday, looked up from her hunt-and-peck typing with a warm smile. "Good morning, Kelsey. You look great today."

"Thanks. I have a newspaper interview this morning. The reporter said he'd be taking pictures."

The older woman eyed Kelsey's cheery red dress with approval. "That'll show up real nice. Don't forget to tell him we still need fifteen hundred dollars for the Graceland trip."

Kelsey smiled indulgently. "Would I forget that? That's the main purpose of this interview. I'm hoping it will bring in a flood of donations. Kyle Foster is a very talented feature writer. I'm sure he'll do a good job."

Jessie didn't need to ask why Kelsey would be interviewed, rather than Dr. Dylan Stafford, the founder of the organization. Dylan avoided the media whenever possible, despite his dedication to the foundation's cause. He had chosen Kelsey as his administrative assistant primarily because of her outgoing personality. Not to mention her willingness to work for peanuts, she thought with a rueful smile as she entered her tiny, cluttered office.

She had just sat behind her paper-littered desk when the telephone rang. At least she'd had time to put her purse away this time, she mused, reaching for what would be the first in an almost endless string of calls. "Kelsey Campbell."

"Hi, Kelsey, it's Liz. Guess what."

Hearing the smug undertones in the woman's voice, Kelsey tensed in anticipation. "You found it?"

"I found it!" One of the most active of the Dream Foundation's volunteers, Liz had been determinedly tracking down a rare toy, no longer in production, for a young boy with cystic fibrosis. "A friend of a friend bought one two years ago for her son, who has had it out of the box only once since. It turned out he didn't care for it as much as he'd thought he would. His mother asked if he'd like to donate it to a very sick boy, and he said he would. The woman said the toy is still just like new."

"Oh, Liz, that's wonderful. Brian will be thrilled. He wanted one so badly."

"I'll have it to you by this afternoon."

"Thanks, Liz. I don't know what we'd do without you."

The other woman laughed softly. "You'd just go out and find someone else to talk into doing this."

"You're probably right," Kelsey agreed with a chuckle. "But you're terrific, anyway."

The next call wasn't as encouraging. A child who was scheduled for a wish the following week had been hospitalized during the night. "But he was doing so well," Kelsey exclaimed, when a nurse who was also a good friend called with the news. "I just talked to him yesterday."

"It was totally unexpected," Annie replied. "He seemed to be improving lately."

Kelsey took a deep breath and made a note to reschedule the child's wish, a postgame, locker-room meeting with a local sports celebrity who'd generously given his time in the past. She told her friend that she was sure the kindhearted minor-league baseball player would visit the child in the hospital when he learned what had happened. "Would that be okay?" Kelsey asked.

"Of course. But he should probably come as soon as you can arrange it," Annie answered quietly.

Kelsey closed her eyes in mute protest of the nurse's meaning. Stevie's prognosis was very poor. "I'll take care of it," she murmured huskily. Immediately after disconnecting the call, she pressed the intercom button and asked Jessie to attempt to get the athlete on the phone for her. She had learned not to waste precious time when it came to her kids.

A small stack of new applications sat at one corner of her desk. She dove into them immediately after her conversation with the cooperative athlete. Children served by the Dream Foundation were required to have a doctor-verified life-threatening illness and to come from families whose income fell below a certain level. All the requests were carefully verified, but Kelsey had rarely found it necessary to refuse an application.

She glanced at the first neatly filled-out form, usually supplied by doctors, nurses or social workers to the families of the gravely ill children. This one concerned a twelve-year-old girl whose dream was to own a horse—not just any horse, Kelsey noted with a wry smile. A black horse with a white star on its forehead. She sighed and began to make a list of the things she'd have to check into before beginning a search for the requested horse. It never once crossed her mind that she wouldn't be able to find one. Kelsey had a phenomenal record of success in arranging wishes.

Except when it came to her own family, she thought glumly, her thoughts inevitably turning to Paul Saxon and his stubborn, unforgiving son. Damn the man. Why couldn't she put him out of her mind? And how badly would he disrupt her life if she persisted in her efforts to convince him to see Paul before it was too late?

"Kelsey, Mr. Foster is here for your interview," Jessie announced through the intercom system. "Shall I send him in?"

"Yes, please." Kelsey made a hasty attempt to smooth her hair and straighten her desk before the door opened and the young reporter entered, notebook and camera in hand. She smiled at him, automatically pushing her troubles to the back of her mind. She had a job to do.

* * *

"Kelsey, you look so tired." Lauren spoke anxiously,
hovering in front of the door to her sister's apartment. "Are
you sure you're up to watching Jared tonight? If not, I could
always—"

"What?" Kelsey asked matter-of-factly. "Stay home,
when Paul needs you to be with him? Take a tiny baby to the
hospital with you again? Don't be ridiculous, Lauren. Of
course I'll watch him. It's not as if he's any trouble."

Her anxiety making her look older than her thirty-one
years, Lauren wearily pushed a lock of brown hair away
from her face and tried to smile. "I know that's not exactly
true," she reproved her younger sister. "Three-month-old
babies aren't exactly a snap to take care of. Especially since
he's started teething."

"We'll be fine," Kelsey assured her. "I love having him
here. And you need to be with Paul."

She tried to hide her own worry about her sister's husband. She'd seen Paul only hours earlier and had been disturbed by his appearance. He was losing ground, she'd
thought in dismay. He would never be able to survive the
surgery he so desperately needed if his condition didn't start
to improve—soon. She knew Lauren wanted to spend as
much time as possible with her husband and her tiny son,
and that she was being torn apart by the multiple responsibilities.

Kelsey was determined to do all she could to help her sister through the ordeal, whatever the outcome. After all,
there wasn't anyone else to turn to just now. Their mother
had died several years earlier. Their father, an engineer, was
working on a major project in South America. Their
brother, Dale, was in the service, stationed on an aircraft
carrier in the Middle East. Lauren had friends who helped
whenever possible, but no one could take the place of family, Kelsey reflected. "You'd better go," she urged her sister. "Jared and I will be fine."

Jared wasn't in a particularly good mood, Kelsey discovered almost immediately after Lauren left. His gums were sore, his diaper was wet and he was sleepy. Kelsey changed him quickly, then rubbed teething gel on the tiny gums exposed by his open-mouthed wails. By the time she'd rocked him to sleep, they were both exhausted. She laid him carefully in the portable crib she kept for him, then stood watching him for a moment. Fiercely working his pacifier, the baby frowned in his sleep, as though he were still thoroughly disgruntled with life in general. Kelsey bit her lower lip against a smile when it occurred to her that the tiny scowl made Jared look even more like his older brother.

"But don't think," she warned in a whisper, "that I'm going to allow you to turn out like him." She refused to believe that her nephew would become a cold, bitter, hardhearted man like Cole.

Both Jared and Kelsey started when the doorbell rang suddenly. Relieved that the baby hadn't wakened, Kelsey threw herself at the door. Intent on preventing the caller from ringing the bell again, she hadn't given a thought to who she would find when she opened the door. She certainly hadn't expected it to be Cole Saxon.

He wore casual clothing as elegantly as the expensive suits she'd seen him in before. He lifted an eyebrow at her obvious surprise, as though she should have expected him. "Did I come at a bad time?"

Kelsey moistened her lips, acutely aware of the dribble of regurgitated baby formula on the front of her hot pink T-shirt and the ragged condition of her threadbare jeans. She curled her bare toes into the worn carpet. "No, of course not," she lied.

He looked expressively at her hand on the doorjamb, barring his entrance. "Then may I come in?"

"Oh. Yes, of course." She stepped back, watching numbly as he strolled inside.

Why was he here? Had he changed his mind about seeing Paul? She closed the door behind him, pleased with the thought that her efforts to contact him might not have been in vain, after all. And then she turned to face him, wishing futilely that she hadn't changed out of the snappy dress she'd worn earlier for the newspaper interview. For some reason, she would have liked to look her best for this meeting with Cole Saxon.

Chapter Three

"Would you like a drink?" Kelsey asked, when Cole stood silently in the center of her living room, obviously waiting for her to speak first.

He nodded. "Scotch, if you have it."

"I don't. I have cola, fruit juice or wine."

"What vintage?" he asked suspiciously.

She flashed a cocky grin, hoping to hide her unexplainable attack of nerves. "Last Monday."

"Cola will be fine," he assured her. Though he didn't smile, his eyes glinted with what she could almost believe was humor.

A forced smile lingering on her lips, she turned toward the kitchen. She waited until she was out of his sight before pressing one hand to her quivery stomach, her other going automatically to smooth her hair. The man was dangerous, she thought weakly. How else could he turn her to oatmeal with nothing more than a gleam in his silvery-green eyes?

Cole was standing by the crib when Kelsey carried the tall glass of iced cola to him. She studied his face as he looked down at the restlessly sleeping baby, but his expression was unreadable. What was he thinking? she wondered.

He turned to take the drink from her. "Thanks."

"You're welcome." She gestured toward the couch. "Please, sit down."

He nodded, but waited until she settled into the rocking chair before seating himself. She thought he'd probably been drilled from childhood in the manners of a refined Southern gentleman. According to Paul, Cole was a true representative of the Saxon family—arrogant, powerful, ruthless, but rigidly proper to the end.

Kelsey wondered if Cole ever had the urge just to cut loose and do something crazy. Or had Paul been the only Saxon driven to rebel against his family's expectations?

Cole sipped his cola, his eyes turning back toward the crib. "When I was a kid, my nanny would always make me say my prayers before I went to sleep," he murmured, almost as if to himself. "The one thing I prayed for every night was a brother."

Looking back at Kelsey, he shrugged rather self-consciously and added, "That was before Paul walked out on us, of course."

She noted the rather defiant use of his father's first name, as well as the pain that still lingered in his eyes after so many years. Her throat tightened for him. "Prayers have an odd manner of being answered at the most unexpected times," she said quietly, her own gaze turning toward the crib.

Cole agreed dryly. "But I think it's a bit too late for playing ball or going fishing with my brother."

"Not necessarily. I'm sure Jared would love to play ball or go fishing with his big brother. That's entirely up to you."

Cole frowned and looked away from the baby. "Has anyone ever pointed out that you're a bit naive, Kelsey?"

At least he hadn't called her Ms. Campbell in that condescending tone he'd used before, she thought. "Yes, they have," she answered candidly. "But I think they're wrong. Just because I think hard work and determination can make dreams become reality doesn't mean I'm naive. I know happy endings aren't always possible."

Cole drained his glass, then set it on a plastic-and-cork coaster on an end table. "You said the baby's name is Jerry?"

"Jared," she corrected.

He nodded. She couldn't tell if he liked the name or not. She decided abruptly that it was time to find out the purpose of his unexpected visit. "Have you thought about what I asked you last night? About visiting Paul, I mean."

Again, he nodded. "I've thought about it."

"And?" she prodded impatiently.

"And I've decided to refuse," he answered without apology. "I can't see that such a meeting would accomplish anything. There are too many years and too many bad feelings standing between me and my father. I really can't see us staging a touching deathbed forgiveness scene," he added impassively.

Kelsey gasped. "That's the most unfeeling thing I've ever heard!"

Cole only shrugged.

Leaning forward in the rocker until her bare feet were planted firmly on the floor, she tried again. "You know, it's possible that Paul will survive this. But if he doesn't, can you ever forgive yourself if he dies longing for one last look at his firstborn son?"

"Very touching phrasing," he commended her dryly. "But I'm afraid it doesn't change my mind. I spent most of my adolescent years longing for a father's guidance, something that was denied me after Paul went off to 'find himself.' You probably think I'm being vindictive to deny him what he wants now, but that's really not my intention. I simply think it would be hypocritical of me to pretend to have any feelings left for a man who is virtually a stranger to me."

"Cole, he's your father."

"He was my father for seven years. I've lived twenty-six years without him. I can't even remember what he looks like."

"Look in the mirror," she advised him. "Or look in that crib. You're both very much like him."

"A fact that is easily explained by genetics."

She clenched her fingers in her lap. "You're a very hard man."

"Only as hard as I have to be," he replied tonelessly.

She might have argued further, but the conversation was interrupted when Jared awoke with a cry.

"What's wrong with him?" Cole demanded, watching as the baby squirmed and fussed.

"He's probably hungry." Kelsey bent over the crib. Jared jammed his fist into his mouth, sucking noisily on his knuckles, the pacifier shoved to one side. He let out another furious squeal when his tiny hand failed to provide the formula he wanted. "All right, sweetie, I'll get the bottle," she promised, lifting the baby into her arms. "It will just take a minute."

"Your sister isn't breast-feeding?" Cole asked, sounding disapproving.

"She was," Kelsey answered defensively, "until Paul's heart attack. She wasn't able to continue and still be with Paul as much as she needs to be."

Cole didn't respond.

Kelsey had stocked up on prefilled, disposable bottles. She pulled one out of a kitchen cabinet and peeled the plastic cover from the attached nipple. Jared quieted in midbellow when she placed the nipple into his open mouth. He was already sucking noisily when she carried him back into the living room.

Cole had risen from the couch while she'd been out of the room. He roamed restlessly around the room, studying the mementos she'd arranged casually on available surfaces. He turned when she walked in, but he didn't say anything.

Feeling the need for conversation—anything to reduce the tension hovering between them—Kelsey settled into the rocker and looked down at the baby. "He can be a bit demanding," she commented, without bothering to add that she sensed it was a trait the brothers shared in addition to eye color.

"Obviously."

"Would you like to feed him?" She made the offer impulsively, looking up at him as he hovered beside her.

Cole shook his head. "I've had no experience with babies," he explained.

Kelsey smiled faintly. "I hadn't either before Jared. The children I work with are usually over three."

Cole returned to the couch and watched in silence as Kelsey finished feeding Jared and then burped him. She was rocking him back to sleep when Cole spoke again. "Is your sister a good mother?"

"Lauren's a wonderful mother." The reply was immediate, even as Kelsey wondered if he would ever stop surprising her with his out-of-the-blue questions. "It's tearing her up to have to spend so much time away from him now. She'd quit her job as a legal secretary just before he was born, because she wanted to be a full-time mother for the early years of his life.

"Paul has been a good father, too," she added, unable to resist the pointed comment. "He helped Lauren a great deal during the first days home from the hospital."

"It's ridiculous for a man of his age to be fathering babies," Cole said, grumbling, his attention focused on Jared.

Kelsey's chin lifted. "Older men have started families. Paul said he'd made many mistakes with his first child, and he intended to do better with this one. Until last week, he

was in excellent health. There was no reason then not to
think he would live for another thirty years, at least."

Growing angrier by the minute by Cole's attitude, she finally dropped the polite facade and let her irritation show.
"Why did you come here tonight, anyway? You said you
haven't changed your mind about visiting Paul and all
you've done is criticize him to me."

Cole lifted his gaze from the baby to Kelsey. "I came to
tell you that I'm setting up a trust fund for your nephew, to
ensure that the child is cared for after Paul's death. Though
I don't intend to play an active role in the boy's life, I believe it's my duty to make sure that your sister and her child
aren't victims of my father's irresponsibility."

Mentally counting to one hundred, Kelsey looked down
to find that Jared was asleep. She rose and settled him back
into the crib, covering him with a duck-print flannel blan-
ket. Only then did she turn to Cole.

"I suppose I should thank you for your offer, even if it
was made out of nothing more than a misdirected sense of
duty," she began coolly. "However, you needn't worry
about Lauren and Jared. Paul has seen that they will be well
cared for in the event of his death. Even if it were otherwise, my sister has too much pride to take the grudgingly
offered money of a stranger.

"The only thing I've asked of you," she reminded him,
her voice rising a bit despite her efforts to hold it down, "is
a brief visit with your father. Since you've refused, you can
rest assured that you will not hear from me or from any
member of my family again. When he's old enough to understand, someone will tell Jared of your existence. I suppose it will be up to him, then, if he wants to try to make
contact with the older brother who wanted nothing to do
with him earlier. Frankly," she added, "I can't imagine that
Jared will care to know such a cold, arrogant, unfeeling man
once he hears the entire story. Now, if you don't mind, I
have a lot to do. I'd like you to leave."

"You're angry," Cole observed unnecessarily, rising slowly to his feet.

"How perceptive of you. Goodbye, Mr. Saxon." She motioned toward the door, her other hand clenched at her hip.

Obviously stung by her words, Cole turned to go, scowling. He opened the door. Then, as if he felt the need to make one last effort on his own behalf, he looked over his shoulder when she approached to lock it behind him. "I was only trying to do the right thing. I think my offer was quite generous."

"You know, I feel sorry for you if money is the only thing of value to you. I, on the other hand, place more value in people—family, in particular. I would certainly never turn my back on a brother I'd once prayed for every night!" she finished curtly. And then she firmly closed the door behind him, certain she'd never see him again.

She didn't even try to analyze the vague depression his departure left within her. Instead, she kept herself very busy for the remainder of the evening, determined not to think about Cole Saxon.

Though hospital rules had relaxed considerably during the past decade, Kelsey knew that finding Lauren and Jared in Paul's room the next morning was only more confirmation that Paul's condition was still critical. The staff was being very lenient in allowing Paul to visit with his infant son— probably, Kelsey thought with a pang, because no one expected him to live to see the boy grow.

"He really doesn't need the excitement of another visitor right now," his nurse explained apologetically, when Kelsey asked whether she could go into the room. "Maybe you'd better wait until later."

Kelsey nodded her understanding. Of course she'd never do anything to endanger Paul's recovery. "Would you tell my sister I was here? And that I'll call her later?"

The nurse readily agreed. "Oh, and Miss Campbell—"

Kelsey turned back curiously. "Yes?"

The woman's smile was tremulous. "Thank you for what you did for my brother's boy. It meant the world to him to go to Walt Disney World with his folks. And my brother said Tony felt better during those three days than he has in months."

"I only made the arrangements," Kelsey replied gently. "Your gratitude should go to the people who donated the money to make Tony's trip possible."

With a stubborn shake of her head, the woman persisted. "It's easy to give money—for a lot of people, anyway. It's the time and effort you and Dr. Stafford put into your organization that make the dreams possible. I want you to know that there are a lot of us who appreciate your work. Whatever happens with Tony in the next few months, we'll always remember how happy he was getting to go to Walt Disney World when it didn't look like he'd ever get to go."

Touched, Kelsey could only smile and squeeze the woman's hand. She was just turning to leave when the sound of her name brought her back around. This time it was her sister behind her. Looking tired and rather pale, Lauren clutched her son tightly as she walked down the hallway from her husband's room. "Did you come by to see Paul?"

Kelsey nodded, waiting for Lauren to stop close beside her. "How is he this morning? Did you and Jared enjoy your visit with him?"

Lauren looked down at the soundly sleeping baby in her arms. "Jared slept through it, I'm afraid."

"And Paul?" Kelsey was almost afraid to ask.

Lauren sighed dispiritedly. "He's very weak. He's trying so hard to regain his strength, so determined not to let this beat him. But—" Her voice broke.

Kelsey could only chew her lower lip, wanting so badly to reassure Lauren that everything would be all right, that Paul would recover, and yet unwilling to make promises she was afraid wouldn't come true.

Lauren took a deep breath, reminding Kelsey that her older sister had always been strong. A survivor. "Why don't you go on in and tell him good morning? He always looks forward to your visits."

"I don't want to overtire him."

"I think it would do him good. Just for a few minutes, of course."

"Of course. I'll talk to you later, okay? And bring Jared over around five-thirty. I'll be home by then."

"Kelsey, you know I appreciate it, but don't you want to spend some time with your friends this evening? After all, it's Friday night. You—"

"I want to spend the evening with my nephew," Kelsey broke in flatly. "And you will be here with your husband, where you belong."

Lauren surrendered, her brown eyes gleaming with a film of tears. "I don't know what we would do without you."

Kelsey kissed her sister's cheek. "Go home and get some rest. I'll see you later."

She checked to make sure Paul was awake before entering his room. Seeing her peeking around the edge of the door, he motioned her in. The weakness of the gesture from this man who'd always been so strong and exuberant nearly broke her heart. She stepped to the side of his bed, her smile feeling unnaturally stiff. "Good morning."

"Hi, Kelsey. It's good to see you."

She found his hand beneath the many tubes and wires connected to him and closed her fingers around his. "You, too. I saw Lauren and Jared leaving."

"Did you?" He smiled. "The boy's growing like a weed, isn't he?"

"Looking more like his father every day," she replied. *And his brother,* she could have added, but didn't. She still had no intention of letting Paul know that Cole had rejected him yet again.

Paul grimaced. "Maybe he'll grow out of it," he quipped.

"If he's lucky," Kelsey agreed teasingly, giving his hand one last squeeze before pulling hers away.

"He slept the whole time he was here. Didn't even know his old man was in the room with him."

"That's what Lauren said. But don't take it personally. Babies sleep a lot."

"I know." He exhaled gustily. "I hate being cooped up here like this. I hate missing these weeks watching him grow. I hate being so much of a burden to Lauren—and to you."

"Paul—"

He interrupted her with a partially raised hand. "Never mind. I know it's useless to bemoan my fate. I just have to get it off my chest every now and then."

"I understand," she assured him, knowing that he would hold the feelings inside for Lauren's sake. If nothing else, maybe she could help him just by listening, by allowing him to not have to be strong and courageous all the time. "It's only natural."

"It's just so damned unfair," he complained bitterly. "For once in my life, everything was going so well. I've been successful doing something I enjoy, I'm married to a woman I love with all my heart, I have a new son, a chance to be a real father this time. And now this."

"You're going to beat this thing, Paul. I know you will." Kelsey heard the defiance in her words, her challenge to fate to correct this terrible mistake.

"I'm going to try," he confirmed, nodding his slightly grayed head. The determined set of his strong jaw reminded her forcefully of Cole, despite her efforts not to think of Paul's infuriating elder son. "Lauren needs me—and so does our son. I want to do it right this time. For once in my generally worthless life I want to be there for those who need me."

Kelsey didn't answer. Again, her thoughts were on Cole. What would he think, she wondered, if he could hear his father's words? Would he understand the regrets, or would his resentment only be compounded by Paul's resolve to do for his youngest son what he hadn't done for Cole?

Paul's eyes were distant, focused on something that only he could see. Scenes from the past? she wondered. Was Cole's image invading Paul's thoughts as well as her own?

"I'd better get to work," she said after a moment, tactfully avoiding mention of his pallor or obvious weariness. "I just wanted to stop by to see how you're feeling this morning."

He nodded against the pillow. "Thanks for coming by, Kelsey. And for listening."

"I only wish there was more I could do."

"Are you kidding? I don't know what Lauren and I would do without you," he said, unconsciously repeating his wife's sentiments. "Thank you, Kelsey."

"You're welcome." She leaned over to drop a kiss on his hollow cheek. "See you later."

"Yeah. Later." His eyes were already closed when she straightened.

Kelsey tiptoed out of the room, then paused for a deep breath to regain her composure. *Damn you, Cole Saxon. How can you be so heartless?*

Cole usually read the business section of the newspaper first and then scanned the front-page headlines when he had the time. He never read the feature articles in the Lifestyles section. So it was coincidence when he dropped the newspaper and bent with a muttered curse to recover it—only to find himself staring at a grainy photograph of Kelsey Campbell—the woman whose face he'd been trying unsuccessfully to forget.

He straightened slowly in his chair, pushing away his emptied breakfast plate. Lifting his freshly refilled coffee cup to his lips, he devoted his attention to the article accompanying the photograph.

"A dauntless dynamo in a petite package," the article called her. Cole's lips twitched at the accuracy of the description. He thought of Kelsey's persistence in getting him to listen to her request. Like the interviewer, Cole suspected that not many people would be able to turn Kelsey Campbell down when she set her mind to something.

"The foundation is wholly funded by donations," Kelsey had explained to the interviewer concerning her obviously beloved Children's Dream Foundation. "We receive no government assistance. And yet we have served over four hundred children in just under three years."

Cole suspected that Kelsey's never-take-no determination had played a major role in raising the funds to fulfill those four hundred wishes. He remembered her apartment and his impression that her money was limited. Obviously she couldn't draw a very large salary from her charity-organization job. So why did she do it?

As if the writer had anticipated the question, the next section of the article dealt with Kelsey's reasons for working for the foundation. It had all begun with the child of a friend, she'd explained. A single mother with whom Kelsey had worked during her senior year of college had a three-year-old daughter who'd been diagnosed with cancer. The child had desperately desired to visit Walt Disney World. Wanting to help out, Kelsey had organized a fund-raising drive at the department store where they worked and, when that had failed to raise sufficient funds, had expanded the drive to include the local community.

By the time she'd finished, there'd been enough money to send the little girl and her mother to Orlando—and enough left over to send a second child, a six-year-old leukemia patient whose financially drained parents had given up on such nonessentials as family vacations.

After hearing of Kelsey's involvement with his tiny patient's wish-fulfillment, Dr. Dylan Stafford had approached her about organizing the Children's Dream Foundation of Georgia, promising that he'd support her wholeheartedly. "He told me that I'd never make much money but that I would be richly rewarded in other ways," Kelsey had told the interviewer with what was described as "an easy laugh."

"And he was right," she'd added. "I'd rather have the smiles and hugs and creatively spelled thank-you notes from my kids than have all the money in the world."

Cole turned the page to finish the article, his brows drawn together in a suspicious frown. Come on, he thought cynically. No one was that noble. There had to be something in it for Kelsey. Maybe she was just one of those people who thrived on publicity, on the fawning admiration she must receive for her work.

The interviewer had asked how many of the over four hundred children served by the foundation were still living. "Forty-one," Kelsey had replied. "Forty-one children have beaten the odds, at least for now. And medical breakthroughs continue to provide hope for them and the ones I've yet to meet."

How did she cope with those losses? she was asked. Did she look at each child as a work case, maintain her distance by reminding herself of the gravity of the prognoses?

"Of course not!" Kelsey had answered with well-described indignity. "My kids aren't 'cases.' They're children—very sick children who have hopes and dreams and fears just like all other children. It breaks my heart each time we lose one. But at least I know that we—the organizers and contributors—did all we could to make their last days as happy and normal as possible under the circumstances."

The article concluded with a plea for donations from the readers, along with an address to which contributions could be mailed.

Cole cleared his throat and folded the newspaper, setting it on the table beside his plate. And then he admitted, if only to himself, that Kelsey Campbell had fascinated him from the moment he'd first seen her.

He simply couldn't figure her out. It had been his experience that everyone—particularly women—wanted something from him, something for themselves. Yet Kelsey claimed that she wanted nothing, either on her behalf or her sister's. She'd immediately refused his offer of a trust fund for her nephew, to whom she seemed genuinely devoted. She worked for a charity organization and seemed surprisingly genuine in her dedication.

So what did she want from him?

Either she was a consummate actress with an angle he hadn't caught on to yet, or she really was as naively unselfish as she appeared. If the latter were true, he thought cynically, then it wouldn't be long before the realities of life rid her of her illusions. It would be a shame, of course, but inevitable.

Paul must have found wide-eyed young Kelsey easy prey for his play for sympathy. If Paul were genuinely ill—and Cole suspected that he was, if Kelsey were to be believed— then he must be broke. Paul probably needed money for medical care, not to mention money to support the young family he'd foolishly founded.

Chewing thoughtfully on his lower lip, Cole stood and headed for a telephone. Though he'd avoided it as long as he could, it was time to find out exactly what was going on with Paul Saxon.

And then he intended to find out more about Kelsey Campbell. A great deal more.

Chapter Four

Kelsey entered the amount of the check into the aging calculator and punched the total button. She swore beneath her breath when she read the results—the third different total she'd gotten after adding the stack of checks three times. "Honestly, Kelsey," she scolded herself aloud, resignedly turning the thick stack over to begin again. "Concentrate on what you're doing, would you?"

"Or you could concentrate on me, instead," a smooth male voice said from the doorway.

Kelsey looked up with a gasp to find Cole Saxon lounging against the doorframe, looking as if he'd been there quite awhile. Unfortunately, none of the regular volunteers had been available to serve as a receptionist that day, which explained how he'd entered without her knowledge.

"What are you doing here?" she demanded, telling herself her suddenly racing pulse could be attributed only to surprise at his unexpected appearance. She'd brought her unwanted attraction to the man firmly under control—right?

Wrong, she thought with a mental groan when he gave her a slight smile that curled her toes. Moving with the natural grace she envied, he crossed the room to stop beside the desk, looking down at the paperwork scattered in front of her. "Problems?"

"Only in my utter incompetence with numbers," she answered, falling back on a quick quip to hide her shock at seeing him. She had no intention of letting him know how much she'd thought about him since he'd left her the night before. She hadn't expected to see him again, especially not so soon.

He nodded toward the stack of checks, his dark brown hair gleaming in the light above his head. "Are those donations to your foundation?"

"Yes." She lifted the top check so that he could read the amount. Three dollars. "Every little bit helps."

"So I see." He settled one hip on the corner of the desk, so close to her she could almost feel his body heat.

She dropped the check on the floor, and bent to pick it up, muttering an oath. "This bank deposit has to be made by one o'clock. Is there something I can do for you?" she asked coolly, when she'd retrieved the check as well as most of her dignity.

"I saw the article in the newspaper this morning. I thought I'd take a look at your organization. I'm always investigating charities to contribute to—tax purposes, of course," he added blandly.

She eyed him suspiciously, knowing full well that he wasn't particularly interested in the foundation. She'd like very much to know exactly what he *was* interested in. "Is that right?"

"Mmm. Perhaps you'd have lunch with me to discuss your operation?"

"Look, Cole—"

Her not-particularly-gracious refusal was forestalled by the arrival of Dr. Dylan Stafford. Tall, lean and heartbreakingly handsome, Dylan could have stepped out of any 1950s nurse-and-doctor romance novel. Kelsey had always found it amusing that serious, dedicated, deeply intense Dylan had no idea of the effect he had on women. The word around the hospital was that one had to be under the age of twelve and diagnosed with a life-threatening disease to capture Dr. Stafford's attention.

"Ah, Kelsey, there you are. I have another application for you. A new arrival at the hospital—a little boy with cancer. Family's in bad shape financially, but he— Oh, hello." He looked at Cole with interest, his golden-brown head tilted.

"Dr. Dylan Stafford, this is Cole Saxon," Kelsey said, resigned to satisfying Dylan's curiosity. And then something made her add, "He's—um—interested in making a contribution to the Dream Foundation."

Dylan's sober brown eyes lit up with unconcealed avarice. "Did you say Cole Saxon?"

It was obvious that he'd recognized the name. Sometimes Kelsey, like others fooled by Dylan's habitual abstraction, forgot that very little escaped the sharp-witted doctor. "Yes."

Smiling broadly, Dylan pumped Cole's hand. "Nice to meet you, Saxon. And we appreciate your interest in our organization. You can rest assured your contribution will be put to good use. Has Kelsey shown you our scrapbook of photographs and news articles?"

"No, she hasn't."

"You must get her to do so. The looks on those kids' faces—well, they're enough to melt the hardest heart. Not that yours is, of course," Dylan amended hastily, looking uncomfortable. "At least, I assume, since you're here—"

"Cole was just leaving," Kelsey broke in, taking pity on her socially awkward administrator.

"Actually, I had just invited Kelsey to join me for lunch," Cole explained smoothly. "To tell me more about your organization, of course. I have a great many questions."

"I'm sure you do. And Kelsey would be happy to answer them." Dylan gave her the genial, benign smile that meant he fully intended to have his way on this one.

"But, Dylan, I have to make this deposit by one o'clock and I still haven't gotten a correct total for the contributions."

"Then go ahead and add it up. I'll get the scrapbook. I have a few minutes to spare—if that's agreeable?" He looked at Cole for confirmation of his solution.

Cole smiled. A shark's smile, Kelsey thought irritably. She wished again she knew just what game he was playing.

"I'd like to see the scrapbook," he assured Dylan graciously. "I like to know as much as possible about any situation before I become involved," he added, and Kelsey wondered why it seemed that the words were directed primarily to her.

"Very wise. Come, have a seat in the reception area. We'll leave Kelsey in peace to finish her calculations. I'm sure it won't take long, will it, Kelsey?"

Meeting Dylan's eyes, Kelsey swallowed a sigh. "No, Dylan. I'll hurry."

He smiled. "Thank you."

With only a quick, resentful glance at Cole, Kelsey bent over the calculator one more time. It wasn't easy to concentrate on entering the correct numbers when her mind was whirling with questions. What was Cole doing here? He couldn't possibly have developed a sudden interest in gravely ill children, so what did he want?

It occurred to her that he was still suspicious of her motives in contacting him about Paul. *I like to know as much as possible about any situation before I become involved,* he'd said. And yet he'd already said that he had no intention of changing his mind about visiting Paul, that he had no real interest in becoming a part of Jared's future. So what, exactly, was he expecting to become involved in?

It couldn't possibly be that he was interested in her.

The thought crossed her mind only fleetingly, almost making her laugh. She and Cole Saxon had nothing in common, other than a connection to his father that he'd already rejected. And, though she knew herself to be passably attractive, she couldn't imagine that Cole had seduction in mind. It didn't seem his style to pursue a woman who'd shown no interest in him, particularly a woman who came with connections that could prove uncomfortable, to say the least. So what did he want?

The only answer seemed to be that he still thought she wanted something from him, that he didn't trust her to keep her word and stay out of his life. He was obviously spying on her, trying to find out more about her and her sister, looking for evidence against them.

Her chin firmed even as she punched the calculator buttons more violently. How dare he make such unfounded assumptions about her! Though she'd felt rather sorry for him before for believing that everyone wanted something from him, her sympathy was beginning to wear thin. She'd told him she wanted nothing from him for herself, assured him that Lauren wouldn't bother him, promised to leave him in peace. If he didn't believe her, that was his problem. She had more important things to do than to waste her time trying to convince him of her sincerity. There were more deserving people to spend her energy on.

Now if only she could get through this lunch without attempting to strangle him, she thought with a grimace, hitting the Total key for the fourth time. She was relieved when the amount displayed was exactly the same as it had been the time before. Neatly filling out the deposit slip, she bundled the checks and reached for her purse, settling her mouth into her practiced professional fund-raiser smile.

Cole Saxon said he wanted to hear more about the foundation. Fine. She had facts, figures, statistics and anecdotes always ready for presentation. By the time lunch was over, he'd know more than he'd wanted to know about her organization. Maybe she'd even hit him up for a nice, fat check, she thought with a smug grin.

Kelsey had never believed in wasting time or effort. And she didn't intend to start now.

"And, of course, everyone expected the child to be deliriously excited about being on a plane bound for Walt Disney World. Her mother couldn't understand why Tammy seemed so worried and tense. Finally she asked her what was wrong. Do you know what Tammy said?"

Cole murmured a negative—the first sound he'd been allowed to make since he and Kelsey had been seated at the restaurant table half an hour earlier, after making a stop by the bank for her deposit.

"She tilted her bald little head, looked up at her mother with huge, nervous blue eyes and asked, 'Will there be needles there, Mommy?'" Kelsey's voice trembled just a bit as it always did when she told that particular story. There was nothing artificial in the emotion behind her voice. She'd never been able to fake emotion, and would have scorned anyone who'd accused her of doing so.

Cole only looked at her over his coffee cup.

Kelsey moistened her lower lip, which had become dry from all the chattering she'd been doing for the past half hour, and continued. "Anyway, her mother assured her that there were no needles in The Magic Kingdom—no doctors, no IVs, no treatment tables or nauseating medicines. Tammy immediately brightened and from then on she had a wonderful time. Her mother said she loved every minute of the trip."

"Is Tammy still living?" Cole inquired, setting his cup down and pushing away his empty plate.

Her lashes shielding her eyes for a moment, Kelsey shook her head. "No. She died earlier this year. But for that weekend, at least, she was just a normal, happy child on vacation with her mom."

"Do you send entire families on these trips or just the sick kids?"

"The sick children and one or both parents. We really don't have the money to include healthy siblings, and besides, the parents need the opportunity to spend that time in a somewhat normal setting with their ill children. You see, they fall into routines of treatments and doctor visits and worrying about money and medical crises, and sometimes they forget their children still have normal dreams and pleasures. Just as doctors and nurses sometimes start seeing the children as so many textbook cases unless they pull back and remind themselves that each child is an individual."

"I understand you have a financial requirement for the children whose wishes you grant?"

Vaguely surprised that Cole really was asking questions about her work, Kelsey nodded. "Yes. The family income must fall below a certain level before we agree to help. Obviously, if the family is able to provide the wish, then we save our limited money for those who cannot. Of course, medical expenses, even with insurance for those lucky enough to have it, are so astronomical that families who start out comfortably end up in serious financial straits. Luxuries, such as vacations and expensive toys, are the first thing to go from the family budget."

"Do you provide funds for medical treatment? Food, clothing, living expenses?"

She shook her head, toying with her half-eaten salad. "No. We exist only to grant one wish from each seriously ill child—you notice that we don't say dying children. It's our hope that each child will survive whatever life-threatening illness has developed. The wish may be frivolous or seri-

ous, big or small, as long as it's something the child truly
wants and something the family is unable to provide without assistance."

"And have you ever failed to provide a wish? Been unable to acquire what the child asked for?"

"Only a time or two," she admitted. "Sometimes the kids
ask for something that simply isn't possible because of their
physical condition. Usually they have a second choice that
we can provide. And once a dying boy wanted very badly to
receive a telephone call from his hero—a celebrity who has
become known for working with children with the particular disease the boy had. The time was getting very short and
I was sure the man wouldn't mind making a quick telephone call. I was wrong. When I finally reached him, I was
told quite curtly that he couldn't be bothered making telephone calls to every dying kid in the country."

It always made her angry to remember that call. She took
a sip of tea to remove the bitter taste from her mouth.
"Anyway, it turned out the guy wasn't quite as noble as he
likes to appear to the public. That child died, still longing to
hear from the jerk."

"Maybe he really doesn't have time to make all the calls
he's probably asked to make," Cole suggested with the air
of a man whose time is always in demand.

"You're not telling me he couldn't have taken five or ten
minutes to talk to a dying boy. No one's that busy," Kelsey
argued. And then she shrugged somewhat self-consciously.
"As you can tell, I get pretty intense about my kids. I don't
like to fail."

"Yes, I see." Cole looked at her a moment, then asked,
"Don't you think the money you spend on wishes could be
put to better use? What good is a trip to Walt Disney World
or a video-game machine to a child whose family can't afford medicine?"

She'd heard the question before, many times. Somehow,
it seemed especially important to make this hardened, cyn-

ical man understand. Leaning forward, she clasped her hands on the table and met his eyes. "Cole, these children are very, very ill. No matter what we do for them, most of them are going to die. They have to have the medicine, they have to have the treatments, and there are programs that take care of those necessities, one way or another.

"But these wishes, these dreams—they're the bright moments in young lives that are filled with the darkness of pain and fear and confusion. The illness will still be there when the vacation is over, or when the computer is turned off for the night or the toy put away. But these memories can't be erased, not even by death. The memory of the smiles and laughter linger on, easing the pain of those left behind, helping them cope with their grief through the knowledge that their loved ones' last days weren't all unhappy. I know research foundations need funds, government assistance programs are sometimes strained to the limits, that there are hundreds of charities equally worthy of donations from the public. But even if we make only a few sick children happy for a few hours—isn't that worth something?"

Cole's left eyebrow rose slowly. "It isn't my place to judge whether your efforts are worthwhile. I simply asked a question."

She sighed and sat back in her seat. "What is it you want from me, Cole?" she asked then, silently conceding that her efforts to bore him with details of her work had failed. He seemed perfectly willing to listen to her stories all afternoon. And still he'd given no hint of his reason for pressuring her into having lunch with him. "I really thought we'd settled everything between us last night, when you told me you had no intention of changing your mind about visiting Paul."

"I haven't changed my mind," he replied. "That's not why I looked you up today."

"Then why did you?" she asked again. "And don't tell me you're investigating our foundation as a potential charity contribution. I just can't believe that."

"No."

Frustrated by his smoothly affable concession, she frowned. "So?"

He leaned back in his chair and fumbled inside his jacket. She recognized the gesture as a habitual search for cigarettes. He frowned and dropped his hand, giving her a look that would have been sheepish coming from anyone else. From Cole, it was merely ironic. "I quit smoking a year ago and still do that after nearly every meal," he complained.

She nodded coolly, though she didn't speak as she waited for him to explain his confusing actions.

A waiter approached the table with a steaming carafe of coffee. Cole motioned for a refill. When they were alone again, Cole looked at her across the table. "I did some research this morning. I found out what Paul's been doing for the past few years. As well as how successful he's been at it."

Genuinely surprised, Kelsey cocked her head. "You didn't know?"

"I haven't been interested enough to ask before," he replied in a deceptively mild tone.

Kelsey scowled. "And now you know Paul's made quite a bit of money developing computer software. That Lauren and Jared will be very well cared for in case of his death. Is that why you came to see me? To rescind your offer of a trust fund for them?"

"The offer still stands."

She nodded. "Ah, yes," she murmured, faintly mocking, rather surprised at her own temerity. "That overdeveloped sense of Saxon responsibility. Always live up to your obligations, despite your distaste for doing so."

His mouth hardened, and she could tell he was biting back a furious retort. "Maybe I thought you deserved an apology for my earlier suspicions about your motivations," he said instead.

She didn't believe that any more than she believed he'd been interested in her work. "Yes, I do. But I don't expect to receive one."

Cole sighed and ran a hand through his sable hair. "Look, maybe I just wanted to see you again."

That startled her. Her eyes wide, she asked blankly, "Why?"

His gaze met hers. For the first time she saw masculine speculation there, the way a man looks at a woman he wants. It stunned her all the way down to her toes. "You interest me. I'd like to know what makes you tick."

"Why?" she asked again, more forcefully this time, already afraid she knew the answer.

"Call it curiosity. You're a very unusual woman. I've never met anyone who dedicates so much energy on behalf of others. It intrigues me."

She thought he'd probably intended it as a compliment, of sorts. She couldn't imagine why it suddenly made her so furious. "I think you should take your curiosity and—"

"Now, Kelsey." He smiled then, and the unexpected softening of his usually unyielding expression took her breath away. "Would Dr. Stafford want you to be so rude to a potential contributor?"

"I was going to say," she began, making a desperate grab for dignity, "that I am really much too busy to indulge your curiosity. I have a very demanding schedule this afternoon—as I'm sure you do—and I need to get back to it. If you're truly interested in making a contribution, I'll give you my card and you can have your secretary mail a check. I assure you it will be greatly appreciated and put to good use. There's a thirteen-year-old boy who wants to visit Graceland, Elvis's home in Memphis. We need the money to send him and his parents."

"Consider it done."

Again, he'd caught her by surprise. "You mean you want to contribute toward the trip?" she asked carefully.

"No. I mean I'll pay for the trip. And I want you to have dinner with me this evening."

Temper mounting, perhaps fueled by a touch of panic, Kelsey reached for her purse and stood, her voice deliberately icy. "You insulted me with your assumption that everyone has an angle, that all good deeds are motivated by an ulterior desire for personal gain. It seems you were basing that assumption on your own behavior.

"My work and my kids are very important to me, Cole. I'd do just about anything to see that their wishes are granted. I stop short of selling myself for contributions. We'll find the money for the Graceland trip from other sources."

Cole shoved himself out of his chair, opened his mouth to speak, then glanced around at the surreptitiously interested onlookers at surrounding tables. His mouth snapped shut. He dropped some money onto the table and took Kelsey's arm. His fingers weren't gentle. "Let's go."

She allowed herself to be led out of the restaurant only because she, like Cole, wanted to avoid a scene.

He'd driven his own expensive sports car, to her earlier relief. He'd explained that he used the limo primarily when he was working, to avoid the hassle of finding parking places and to give him time to go over paperwork as he was driven from one place to another. She didn't care why he hadn't used the limo this time; she was only glad that he hadn't. She'd been uncomfortable enough when they'd started out. Having his chauffeur watching them would have only made it worse. Especially now that Cole was obviously furious with her.

He waited until they were in the car, seat belts snapped, powerful engine running, before he turned to her, white-lipped with anger.

"First," he said coldly, "I offered to pay for the kid's trip and I will. Make the arrangements and send me the bill. Second, I said I wanted to have dinner with you only because it was true. Then. I never said, never implied, that one was contingent on the other. That, Ms. Campbell, was a deduction you made all on your own—after lecturing me on the evils of being overly suspicious of generous gestures, I might add."

He shoved the car into gear. "The offer to fund the trip is still open. Even if you choose to turn it down, I doubt that Dr. Stafford will. As for the dinner invitation, you can consider that withdrawn. I have no interest in dining with a woman who thinks I'm buying her time with contributions to sick kids."

The short trip to her office was made in silence. He didn't waste time—or speed limits—getting her there. Kelsey turned tentatively to face him when he stopped at the door to the clinic, leaving the car engine running. He obviously had no intention of walking her in. "Cole—"

"We're blocking the driveway. There are cars waiting behind me."

She sighed and reached for the door handle. "I'll be in touch about the Graceland trip."

"Talk to my secretary."

He barely waited for her to close the door behind her before he pulled away.

Looking after him, Kelsey realized with a pang that she'd hurt him as well as angered him.

It shook her to realize that the seemingly invincible Cole Saxon was a man who could be hurt, just like anyone else. Her hand wasn't quite steady when she reached out to open the door to the clinic.

Alice approached her employer's desk, her arms loaded, her expression guarded. Noting her caution, Cole tried not to scowl. He knew he hadn't been the easiest person to work with—or to be around, for that matter—for the past few days. Four days, to be precise. It had been four days since that disastrous lunch with Kelsey Campbell. "What is it, Alice?"

"I have these letters ready for your signature, Mr. Saxon. And here is your mail—two envelopes are marked Personal, so I didn't open them. Also, Mr. Herrington is holding on line two and you have that meeting with your department heads in fifteen minutes."

Suppressing a sigh, Cole nodded. "Leave the letters on the corner of the desk. I'll sign them after I've looked them over. Tell Bob I'll get back to him immediately after the meeting."

"Yes, Mr. Saxon."

He took the stack of mail she handed him. "Thanks, Alice."

There was nothing of particular interest in the pile of letters. He automatically divided them by order of importance. Slitting the first envelope marked Personal, he grimaced when a diamond pendant fell into his hand. No note accompanied the necklace, but then it really wasn't necessary. He realized it had been at least a month—no, more like six weeks—since he'd called the recipient of this particular gift. The lovely Deirdre must have tired of waiting for him to remember her.

It really hadn't been necessary for her to return the necklace—he never expected his gifts back with the inevitable end of his liaisons—but, since she had, the least she could have done was been more careful in its delivery, he thought with a grunt. He slipped the necklace into his pocket, remembering the cost with wry acceptance. He usually ended his relationships with more finesse. It made him rather uncomfortable to realize that this one had, quite literally, slipped his mind. He wasn't proud that he found people so easy to forget.

He couldn't help picturing the one person he was having the devil of a time putting out of his thoughts. Kelsey. Just thinking of her made him furious all over again—with her, for assuming the worst of him, and with himself, for still wanting her anyway. No matter how often he'd reminded himself that she wasn't his type, that she'd probably want more than he had to offer, that she was involved in a close relationship with the father he'd chosen to reject, he still thought of her and wanted her. Damn her.

He froze when he pulled the photograph out of the second envelope he'd just opened. Only one person could have sent it.

Kelsey.

The boy in the picture was thin to the point of emaciation. His eyes were watery and weak, his skin pale, almost translucent. A battered cap covered his head, which was nearly bald from radiation treatments. But his smile was heartwarming. Wearing a white satin jumpsuit and carrying a photo of Elvis, he was shown being escorted through an airport terminal in a wheelchair embellished with a whimsical sign reading Graceland Or Bust. Several well-wishers stood on the sidelines of the photograph, waving him off.

The note accompanying the photograph was brief, handwritten in a feminine scrawl.

Aaron and his parents left for Memphis yesterday morning. He was thrilled to be visiting the home of his idol, Elvis. You made this possible for him. Thank you.

Kelsey

A postscript had been written at the bottom, the writing smaller, a bit shaky, as if she hadn't quite known what to say. "Cole—I'm sorry. Please accept my apology."

Cole groaned. He'd felt like a heel opening Deirdre's delivery, and he felt doubly so now.

Kelsey was sweetly apologizing for doing no more than he'd done from the beginning with her. She'd questioned his motives in doing something nice, something unselfish. Though he'd done the same with her, on more than one occasion, he'd still been furious when the situation had been reversed. Why? Because he wasn't accustomed to having his actions questioned? Because he'd wondered, himself, why he'd made the uncharacteristically generous gesture?

Or because he'd wanted Kelsey to look at him and see something that no one else would see—something he wasn't even sure was there? Because he'd hoped maybe she'd find something in him to admire, though he was fully aware that he hadn't a fraction of her obvious goodness inside him?

His fist clenched futilely. And then he realized he was still holding her note.

Very carefully, refusing to question his own actions, he smoothed the sheet of paper on his desk, then folded it along the original lines and slipped it into his breast pocket.

He looked down at his desk, wondering with uncharacteristic illogic if there was something symbolic about the placement of envelopes there. Deirdre exiting his life—Kelsey entering? He pushed that thought aside, finding it uncomfortable.

And then he looked at the photograph again. He couldn't help smiling at the boy's obvious excitement. He had been responsible for that pleasure, Cole realized in wonder. It was a heady feeling. For the first time, he could understand a little why Kelsey was so totally dedicated to her work.

And then his smile faded when his intercom buzzed, reminding him that he had his own work to do. Work he'd always considered vitally important, totally demanding.

Glancing one last time at the photograph, he wondered why shipping schedules and tariff increases suddenly seemed so trivial.

Chapter Five

Her arms loaded with paperwork, Kelsey ducked out of the clinic in a hurry, hoping to catch the next bus. A last-minute telephone call had held her up, so she was concentrating on nothing but getting home in time to meet her sister. She was caught off guard when Cole Saxon stepped in front of her, blocking her way. "Hello, Kelsey."

It briefly occurred to her as she blinked up at him that she'd seen him quite often since she'd stopped looking for him. What was he doing here now? "Cole," she said warily. "What do you want?"

His eyebrow lifted at her less-than-gracious wording. "You were the one who apologized," he pointed out mildly. "I'm here to accept. And to take you to dinner."

What had happened to that supposedly hectic schedule of his? she wondered. It hadn't seemed to interfere when he wanted to see her, for whatever his reasons. "Thank you for the invitation," she replied, though they both knew he hadn't exactly invited her to dinner. "But I can't. Lauren's due at my place with the baby soon and I have to catch the bus home or I'll be late.''

He frowned. ''You keep the baby every night?''

''Yes.'' She tried hard not to sound defensive, though she wasn't sure she succeeded. ''Someone has to, and he's too young to leave with strangers.''

''Why are you taking the bus? Don't you have a car?''

''It's in the shop,'' she answered shortly. ''Look, Cole, I really have to—''

He took her arm and her words died in her throat. ''Come on. I'll drive you home.''

''That's really not—''

''Kelsey. Get in the damned car.''

The words were said without heat, but she found herself instinctively following his order. Only after she'd snapped her seat belt and arranged her papers in her lap did she realize how very good he was at giving them. Did everyone always do what Cole wanted? She decided immediately that she wouldn't always comply so easily.

''I still don't understand what you want from me,'' she complained. ''If you don't want to see Paul, why—''

He glanced away from the road ahead to look at her when he interrupted. ''This has nothing to do with Paul. It has to do with you.''

''Me?'' she murmured weakly. ''But why?''

He turned back to concentrate on his driving, his hands relaxed on the leather-covered steering wheel. ''I've made it a practice not to dwell on questions that have no clear-cut answers,'' he said philosophically.

Kelsey sat back in her seat with a little huff. ''I don't understand you,'' she told him, shaking her head in bewilderment.

His faint smile did dangerous things to her already unsteady heart rate. ''Join the club.''

Her eyes focused on the long slash of dimple in his right cheek, she wisely decided not to say anything else just then. She wasn't at all sure she could trust her voice.

Cole opened the door and slid out from behind the wheel as soon as he'd parked in front of her apartment. Kelsey followed suit, clutching her things as she looked up at him. "You—uh— Are you coming in?"

"Yes." And then he grimaced ruefully and ran a hand through his hair. "If that's okay with you," he added.

At least he was making an effort, she decided, and immediately nodded, ignoring a mocking voice inside her head that accused her of clutching at straws.

Once inside the apartment, Kelsey was relieved to drop her stack of papers on a table. And then she glanced at her watch. Lauren was due soon. "I don't suppose I could talk you into hiding in the bedroom while my sister's here?" she suggested only half-teasingly, glancing up at Cole.

He looked surprised. "Now why would I want to do that? And why would you want me to?"

"I haven't told her I contacted you," she admitted. "Lauren is very proud. She wouldn't like it that I interceded with you on Paul's behalf. And I was afraid it would hurt her—and Paul—if they found out you'd refused again to see him, even knowing how sick he is. Cole, couldn't you—"

"No, Kelsey."

She sighed at his uncompromising tone. She had hoped his continued appearances signaled a desire—perhaps even a subconscious one—to follow his father's progress, maybe even to allow himself to be persuaded to change his mind. She'd had some experience with male pride and had hoped Cole's pride was the only thing standing between them on this issue. Now she was beginning to doubt that theory. The more she saw of him, the less Cole appeared to be the type to allow himself to be persuaded to do anything without his full cooperation.

Which, of course, brought her back to the question of why he kept popping up in her life when she least expected him.

Turning away from the appeal that must still be in her eyes, Cole wandered around the living room, examining the bits and pieces that made up her life. He studied her bookshelf for a long time before looking up at her with a quizzical expression. She knew her choice of reading material surprised him, but he didn't comment just then. Instead, he turned his attention to the top shelf, which held a collection of framed photographs. "Your parents?" he asked, pointing to the first one.

She moved to stand beside him. "Yes."

"Are they still living?"

"My mother died in an accident several years ago. My father's an engineer, currently working in South America. We're not very close," she admitted grudgingly. "He was never around much when I was growing up, though my mother seemed happy enough with him."

Cole picked up the next photo and scowled down at it. "Who is this?" he demanded too abruptly, studying the handsome uniformed sailor in the photograph.

"My brother, Dale," she answered, wondering why Cole seemed so displeased. "He's on an aircraft carrier somewhere in the Persian Gulf. We don't hear from him very often. I'm afraid he's much like my father—a confirmed gypsy with very loose ties to home."

Cole's brow cleared. "Oh. He's older than you?"

"Yes, he's twenty-eight. Lauren's the eldest, at thirty-one."

"Quite a few years between you."

She shrugged. "Dad wasn't home much."

With visible reluctance, Cole turned to the next frame, though he didn't pick that one up. She didn't have to ask if he recognized the man in that shot. His expression made it clear that he did, despite his one-time claim that he couldn't even remember what his father looked like. "This must be your sister," was all he said, ignoring Paul's presence in the photo.

"Lauren. I suppose you'll be meeting her in a few minutes, if you still refuse to hide in the bedroom."

He threw her a look that told her he wasn't in the habit of hiding from anyone. "You once said she'd had a rough time before she met Paul. What did you mean?"

She was surprised that Cole had more or less remembered Kelsey's words from the time when she'd explained her reason for tracking him down. She wondered whether it would make any difference to him if he knew more about Lauren, then decided she might as well tell him. "Lauren married very young, when she was eighteen and I was only eleven. She thought she was desperately in love and her boyfriend was pushing her to marry him, so she ignored Mother's pleas that she wait and Lauren eloped with him. It turned out to be the worst mistake she's ever made."

"He treated her badly?"

Kelsey nodded, looking away to hide the old fury. "He abused her for four years before she found the courage to leave him. They lived in another state, so none of us knew what was going on until she showed up on the doorstep in the middle of the night without a change of clothes to her name. She was bruised and haunted and had no self-esteem left, but she'd found the strength to break away from him.

"Dale was only eighteen, but he tracked Tom down and beat him up. Dale joined the service right after that. Lauren divorced Tom and moved back in with my mother and me—and our dad, when he was home. Our mother died when I was seventeen. Though he sent money for my education and support, Dad hardly ever came home after that, so it's been just Lauren and I for a long time—until she married Paul, of course."

Cole had been watching her with shadowed eyes, concealing his reactions to what she'd told him. "When was that?" he asked now.

"Eighteen months ago." She pushed her hands into the pockets of her full-skirted red dress, wondering if there was any way to make Cole understand what Paul had done for her sister. She'd told him before how long Paul and Lauren had been married, but he'd obviously not been listening then. "They met through a mutual friend. Lauren hadn't been involved with anyone since her marriage and was still wary of men. Paul says he fell in love with her as soon as he saw her. He courted her with so much patience and gentleness, she couldn't help but love him back. He has made her very happy, Cole. He was just what she needed."

Again, Cole turned away. She didn't know what he would have said, if anything, had Lauren not arrived just then.

Unnoticed in the initial flurry of arrival and greetings, Cole watched silently as Kelsey hugged her sister and relieved her of some of the items necessary when leaving home with an infant. Though he'd seen her photograph, it still startled him that Lauren was so very different from her sister. She was several inches taller, more classically beautiful, he noted dispassionately. Her hair was a lighter brown, cleverly cut to sway enticingly at her shoulders, in contrast to Kelsey's short, sporty cut. Her brown eyes were as large and rich as her sister's, but glowed with a gentle warmth rather than Kelsey's spirited fire.

Of the two, Lauren was the one he would once have considered more his type. But now, having met Kelsey, he found it hard to concentrate on anyone else for more than a moment. Already his gaze was turning back to Kelsey, studying the pleasure on her face as she smiled down at her nephew. Such a transparent face, he mused. It would be a pity if she ever learned to mask her emotions, a skill most people acquired at a much younger age.

And then Lauren looked up and saw him. Cole met her widened gaze with a bland smile, wondering if she'd recognize him. Was he really so much like his father in appearance, or had Kelsey exaggerated?

Noticing Lauren's sudden silence, Kelsey looked up and followed her sister's gaze. Cole watched her moisten her lips nervously. The resulting sheen on the mouth he'd hungered for since he'd first seen it had his hands clenching behind him. He tried to concentrate on the sister—for now.

Kelsey broke the silence with a rush of words. "Lauren, this is...Cole. He's—uh—he's a new contributor to the Dream Foundation."

She made a lousy liar, Cole noted with almost fond amusement. Another skill she'd probably have to acquire to survive in the real world.

"You're Paul's son, aren't you?" Lauren's words proved there was nothing wrong with her powers of observation.

He nodded. "Yes." He saw no need to elaborate, assuming she knew the entire story—or at least Paul's side of it.

Lauren looked accusingly at Kelsey. "You called him?"

"I met him recently," Kelsey prevaricated, her guilty expression causing a smile to tug at the corners of Cole's mouth. "He very generously sponsored a child's wish this week."

Her chin lifted, expression clearly skeptical, Lauren turned to Cole. This was the woman who'd allowed herself to be abused for four years? he found himself wondering. Had she developed this nerve on her own in the years since or—he added the possibility grudgingly—had Paul been the one to help her find her own strength?

"Kelsey has told you about your father, Mr. Saxon?"

He nodded, watching her warily. "Yes. And call me Cole."

Ignoring the latter part, she continued to look at him. "He wants very much to see you."

"I've explained to Kelsey that I think it would be better for everyone if I stayed away. I have a lot of hard feelings toward my... toward your husband, Lauren. His condition sounds much too grave for a confrontation over old wounds."

Though her mouth quivered, Lauren spoke calmly. "Yes, I agree. He's not strong enough for that now. Must there be a confrontation? Couldn't you just put the past behind you for one brief visit?"

"I'm sorry." He was—for her sake. He spoke as gently as possible. "That's not possible."

"I see." For just a moment the raw anger that burned in her eyes made her look more like her younger sister. And then she sighed and turned away, her composure restored. "I didn't realize you had plans for tonight, Kelsey. I'll take Jared with me, of course."

"You will not," Kelsey refuted immediately, glaring at Cole. "I have no plans for this evening. Cole was just leaving."

He wasn't, but he saw no need to argue with her in front of her sister. His stepmother, he thought with a grim attempt at humor, glancing back at the woman who was three years his junior.

Lauren looked uncertainly from Kelsey to Cole and back again. "I—"

Shifting Jared to her left arm, Kelsey touched her right hand to her sister's shoulder. "Lauren. Go. Paul will be waiting for you."

Lauren sighed again and nodded. Cole thought she suddenly looked very tired. He could imagine how hard it must be for her, taking care of a tiny baby during the day, spending her evenings with her critically ill husband, then nights again with the baby. From what he'd heard, babies weren't exactly conducive to a full night's sleep.

"Lauren," he said impulsively, "if you or your son ever need anything—financial help or whatever—Kelsey has my number."

The signs of weariness vanished when her chin went up. "Thank you for the offer," she said, her voice icy. "But Jared and I will be fine, whatever happens. Paul has seen to that."

He'd rarely felt so thoroughly rebuffed. Kelsey and her sister seemed to share a talent for taking what he considered to be generous offers and making them sound less than honorable. He nodded to Lauren, his hands going into his pockets.

Lauren left without saying anything else, pausing only long enough to nuzzle lovingly her son's soft cheek in reluctant farewell.

Clearing his throat in the awkward silence that followed, Cole turned to Kelsey and found her looking at him with a mixture of anger, accusation and . . . sympathy, he noted in surprise. Why would Kelsey feel sorry for him? Or was he mistaken about the emotions mirrored in her lovely eyes?

"I don't think I made a big hit with your sister," he commented unemotionally.

"Lauren's first loyalty will always be to her husband. She'd have a hard time liking anyone who hurt Paul."

"I suppose that's understandable."

The anger spilled into her voice; gone was whatever sympathy she may or may not have felt. "You don't give an inch, do you?"

"Look, what do you want from me?" he demanded, suddenly angry himself. "I've done everything I can do for them short of seeing Paul. I've tried to prove to you that I'm not quite the villain you thought me originally. But you're not going to be satisfied until I do exactly what you want, are you?"

"You've offered money!" she shot back heatedly. "Sometimes that's enough—with Aaron, for example. Your money was all that was necessary to send him on his trip with his parents. But there are times, believe it or not, when your great wealth is totally irrelevant. This is one of those times. All Paul or Lauren or I have asked of you is a few minutes of your precious time. And *that* you're not willing to give."

"It's more than a few minutes of my time," he replied grimly, his hands clenching in his pockets. "It's a hell of a lot more than that."

She studied him in silence for so long that he became uncomfortable. "Well?" he snapped finally.

"It would be that hard for you to see him?" she asked, her tone much less heated now.

He swallowed. "Yeah. It would."

"Cole—I'm sorry."

He turned away. Her pity was the one thing he didn't want from her. "Forget it. You don't know anything about it."

"Then tell me."

"No. It's old news. I put it behind me a long time ago. I made it without him for most of my life. It's too late to dredge it all up again now." Resentfully, he glanced over his shoulder. "Hell, even his own parents won't talk to him—won't even talk *about* him. I don't see you nagging at them to forgive him."

"He didn't ask for their forgiveness," she answered quietly. "He hasn't even asked for yours."

"He's still asking more than I can give."

"More than you *will* give, you mean."

"Whatever." Inhaling deeply, he took one hand from its pocket to shove it through his hair. He was aware that Kelsey had moved to lay her sleeping nephew in his crib. He waited until she was finished before turning back to her.

Taking her by surprise, he caught her forearms in his hands, holding her in place as her face turned up in question. Suppressing an ill-timed urge to crush that sexy mouth beneath his until all the questions, all the demands were forgotten, he held her eyes with his own, refusing to allow her to look away. "You know why I'm here," he said roughly.

Her eyes grew impossibly wider. "No."

"I think you do." He lifted one hand to stroke the soft line of her jaw with his thumb. "I can't stop thinking about you, Kelsey. No one's ever done that to me before. I want to see you—without this other thing between us. Can we do that?"

Again, she moistened her lips in her habitual reaction to nerves. This time he almost groaned. He kept his eyes resolutely on hers. "Well?" he prompted.

"Cole, I—" Her voice died. Her eyes pleaded with him to back off.

He couldn't, not now. "Do you find me unattractive? Do you honestly dislike me?"

"No, of course not," she answered, the speed of the denial pleasing him. "But—"

"Is my refusal to see Paul the only thing standing between us?" he persisted.

"It's certainly the main thing," she admitted. "Though I'm not sure we have much in common even without that complication."

"So let's find out," he urged. "Go out with me."

"I can't just forget about Paul! I can't simply pretend you're not involved in that part of my life."

"So what do you want me to do?" he demanded. "Go see him just for you? Be a spineless hypocrite by seeing him just because I hope it will increase my chances of getting you in bed? Would that really make you respect me more, Kelsey?"

She paled. "Of course not! How could you ask that?"

"Because that's what I would be doing if I agreed to see him now," he answered evenly. "If you admire the type of man who'd go to those lengths to have you, then maybe I *am* wasting my time."

She jerked away from him and he made no effort to detain her. "Damn you, Cole," she breathed, raising unsteady hands to her temples. "You have a real knack for twisting everything your way, don't you?"

"I'm only pointing out the facts, Kelsey. I want you. I don't have a lot of time to waste on pretty speeches or catering to women's fantasies of romantic courtship. If the attraction isn't mutual, tell me now. I won't bother you any further."

She cleared her throat, avoiding his eyes. "I...it..." And then she whirled away, shoving her hands through her short hair to make it stand up in appealingly disheveled spikes around her face. "You're giving me a headache," she muttered.

He couldn't help chuckling. What was it about this woman that he found so utterly delightful? Even as he asked himself the question he warmed to the realization that she hadn't been able to tell him the attraction was all one-sided. "Kelsey—"

Jared's quavering cry interrupted. Cole exhaled and watched as Kelsey immediately responded. "Is he hungry?" Cole asked.

Lifting the baby into her arms, Kelsey nodded, still not meeting Cole's eyes. "Yes."

"What were you planning for dinner tonight—for yourself, I mean?"

She shrugged, trying to momentarily appease her nephew with his pacifier. "I was thinking about ordering a pizza."

He shrugged out of the jacket to his suit and slung it over a chair. "Make it big enough for two. My treat."

He'd half expected her to argue. She opened her mouth as if to do so, then seemed to accept the futility of the effort. Her chin went up in a gesture very similar to the one he'd noticed from her older sister. "Fine," she said shortly. "Here. You take him. I'll call in an order and prepare a bottle."

Cole had his arms full of baby before he could move away. "No, wait, I—"

She only threw him a look that very clearly told him he could go along with her or get lost. He closed his mouth and looked warily down at the squirming bundle in his arms.

Finding himself looking up at a new face, Jared stopped fussing for a moment to study the stranger. His round, surprisingly green eyes nearly crossed as they focused somewhere in the vicinity of Cole's nose.

"So, uh, how's it going?" Cole asked, feeling the need to say something but not quite certain how to converse with a preverbal person.

In response to Cole's voice, Jared smiled—a wide, toothless, slobbery grin that made Cole's throat tighten.

"Hell," he muttered, though he couldn't have explained why.

And then the novelty of the new person wore off and Jared remembered his hunger. He squirmed restlessly in Cole's awkward grip, sucked furiously on his knuckles for a moment, then wailed irritably. Cole noted with what felt suspiciously like a faint glow of pride that there was no pleading in the cry—more an arrogant demand for attention. Immediately.

"Uh—Kelsey?" Cole jiggled the baby cautiously, though he knew that nothing short of formula would successfully end the crying.

"Coming," she called back. He scowled as he recognized the smug humor in her voice. So she found her subtle revenge funny, did she? Little did she know that Cole's philosophy had always been Don't Get Mad, Get Even.

His smile would have made more than one worthy opponent justifiably nervous. He carefully suppressed it as Kelsey walked back into the room, carrying the bottle.

A day—even a few hours—earlier, Kelsey never would have believed she'd find herself sharing a pizza-with-everything-on-it on the floor of her living room with Cole Saxon while her nephew slept peacefully in his crib. She was even more surprised to find herself actually enjoying the meal. It turned out that Cole could be quite charming when he put his mind to it, as he obviously had tonight.

She'd wondered if Cole would ever mention the book collection in the corner that he'd seemed to find so interesting. He brought it up quite casually. "I would have thought," he said, "that you'd be the type to read romance novels and those inspirational self-analysis books."

She wrinkled her nose. "I like an occasional romance, but those others always make me feel insecure. Like I should be doing things I'm not."

"But still, I'm surprised your taste leans to horror and police drama. Rather violent fiction, at that. You must have everything Stephen King and Quinn Gallagher ever wrote."

She nodded. "I adore them," she said simply. "Lauren can't understand it, either. I suppose my life is so unexciting that I get my adventure vicariously through action fiction."

"I'd hardly call your life unadventurous."

"I didn't say I don't accomplish anything," she answered somewhat defensively. "Only that my routine is usually pretty much the same. I enjoy what I do, but I enjoy the adventure I find in my books, too."

"Have you noticed a change in Quinn Gallagher's work lately?" Cole asked without commenting further on her tastes.

Pleased, she smiled. "Yes, I have. His last few books aren't quite as grim as his earlier ones, though they're still as intensely written. You read him, too?"

"Yeah. I've met him a couple of times. Interesting guy."

"You've met him? Gosh, you're lucky. So why do you think his style has been changing?"

Cole's mouth twisted wryly. "He fell in love and got married. I guess marriage and babies have softened him up."

Chewing her lip, Kelsey considered that, but Cole changed the subject before she could say anything further on it. They talked about her for a few more minutes, and then she smoothly brought the conversation around to him.

They talked of his work with the lucrative shipping company that had been founded by his maternal great-grandfather. Cole, it seemed, had been given the option very early of working with that company or going into the Saxon family's long-established law firm, as his paternal grandfather and uncles had done before him. As his father had done years earlier, Cole had chosen to train in the shipping business, having decided he wasn't cut out for the practice of law.

"You're very young to be second in command of such a large corporation," Kelsey commented, picking green peppers off a third slice of pizza and laying them in a neat pile on her paper plate.

Watching her, Cole shrugged. "The presidency was supposed to have been my father's when my grandfather retires. He was training for it when he chose to bail out. My grandfather has stayed in the president's chair for longer than he may have chosen otherwise, giving me time to gain the experience and training necessary for the position. He'll probably retire in the next year or two. He's been hinting that he'd like to take some time to travel and work on his golf game."

"No one protested your youthful promotions? Wasn't there anyone else in the family who wanted the presidency?"

She noticed that he looked a bit uncomfortable at the question. "My mother has a brother—Edward," he said. "Before Mother married Paul, the family had hoped Edward would someday take over the business. By the time he was in his late twenties, it was obvious that he had no natural leadership ability. He's still in the business, but it's been quietly accepted for years that he'd never be at the helm. Paul would have been good at the job, if he'd wanted it badly enough to hang around. From what I've heard, he had the qualifications. My mother tells me I inherited his business skill. I hope to God that's all I got from him."

And then, before Kelsey could follow up on Cole's feelings about Paul, he abruptly changed the subject again.

"Thanks for sending me the photograph," he said. "The boy looked very excited to be going on the trip."

"Oh, he was. His mother called from Memphis to say they were having a wonderful time."

"I'm surprised a boy that young should be so excited about seeing the former home of a singer who died before the kid was born."

Kelsey took a sip from her soda before answering. "Aaron's parents were big Elvis fans during the early sixties. They even named him Elvis's middle name, though they spelled it differently. Aaron got hooked on old Elvis movies during one of his long hospital stays. Though his parents had toured Graceland once, Aaron never had. It was something he wanted very much to do."

"Then I'm glad he had the chance to do so."

"Thanks to you," Kelsey pointed out, watching him through her lashes.

He shrugged, though he seemed pleased by her words.

Jared squirmed in the crib, making both of them look that way, but he was only shifting to a new position. Both adults let out sighs of relief when the baby continued to sleep contentedly.

"Your nightly baby-sitting must be playing hell with your social life lately," Cole remarked. He leaned back against the sofa behind him, drawing one leg up to wrap an arm around it in a casual pose that made Kelsey's mouth go dry.

She cleared her throat and concentrated on gathering the remains of their dinner. "I don't really have much of a social life," she admitted. "My work takes up so much of my time and energy that I have little time left for dating."

"I find it hard to believe an attractive young woman like you spends all her evenings alone."

She was annoyed to feel herself flushing. "I have friends," she answered defensively. "I like to go to movies and out to eat—all the usual things people do. I just haven't been involved with anyone in particular."

"Until now," Cole murmured, lifting his own soft drink to his lips. The look he gave her over the rim made her heart rate speed into double time.

Chapter Six

Kelsey decided the safest thing to do was to ignore his words, whatever he'd meant by them. And she knew she'd spend several uncomfortable hours wondering about *that* later.

She turned the conversation back to him, instead. "So what do *you* do for fun, Cole? You surely don't work all the time, either."

He lowered the soft drink can and looked at her blankly. "Fun?"

"Yeah. You know—fun? Frivolity? Cutting loose? What do you do?"

"I go out," he answered with one of his characteristic shrugs. "Dinner, theater."

Thinking of the success she'd had with his secretary by pretending to be a bubbleheaded date of Cole's, Kelsey frowned. If going out with bimbos was his only idea of fun, then she had little hope for any sort of relationship between them. Not that she expected anything serious to develop, anyway, she reminded herself quickly. "That's all? No hobbies? Sports?"

"I like to fish—deep-sea fishing," he admitted. "I don't get time away very often, but I enjoy it when I do. As a matter of fact, I have a boat and guide chartered for this weekend."

Her head came up abruptly. "You're going deep-sea fishing? This weekend?"

"Yes." Suspicious of her sudden interest, he eyed her cautiously.

Her smile would have melted asbestos. "That's wonderful!"

He knew immediately that he wasn't going to like the reason for her delight in his plans. "Why?" he demanded.

"Well, there's this boy—"

Uh-oh. Cole held up a hand, palm outward. "Kelsey—"

"He's twelve years old—"

"No. Absolutely—"

"His family just moved here from Oklahoma, so he's never been deep-sea fishing."

"—not. This is the first chance I've had in—"

"He's very sick, Cole. His dream is to catch a sailfish."

"I am *not* taking a sick kid on my fishing trip. What if something happened to him?"

"His father would go along, of course, though Al has said he's never done any saltwater fishing. They couldn't possibly afford to charter a boat themselves, with Ronnie's medical expenses being so high."

Cole was beginning to panic. The blissful look in Kelsey's big brown eyes suggested that she already considered the matter settled. "Kelsey, you aren't listening to me. I said no."

Her eyes turned to liquid chocolate. "But, Cole..."

Tugging at his collar, he tried again. "Even if I agreed, there's no way I could guarantee a trophy catch," he pointed out desperately. "I've come home with nothing, more than once."

"Ronnie is aware of that, of course," Kelsey assured him. "He only wants the chance to try. I would have arranged something sooner but he had surgery recently and wouldn't have been strong enough to go before now."

Cole groaned. "Look, I sent the other kid to Graceland, didn't I?"

She sighed and seemed to concede defeat. "You're right, of course. That was very generous of you. I shouldn't even ask you to—"

He cursed fluently beneath his breath. "All right. Damn it, just be quiet. He can go."

Her face brightened immediately. The glow in her eyes made him have to fight an almost overwhelming urge to reach out and pull her into his arms. He wanted to taste her smile. He reminded himself sternly that he had too much to lose by rushing things now.

"He can go?" Kelsey repeated, as if afraid she'd misunderstood him.

Exhaling deeply, Cole nodded. "I said he could, okay? On one condition."

Some of the delight faded from her expression, to be replaced by suspicion. "What condition?"

"You go, too. If anything happens, it's your responsibility."

"I think I should point out that I've never been deep-sea fishing in my life."

He was beginning to see the possibilities in the plan. Why hadn't it occurred to him sooner? He smiled. "I'm not expecting you to fish. Just to go along to oversee the boy's welfare. That's not too much to ask, is it?"

She seemed to look right through him. He was fully aware she knew he'd somehow twisted her request to suit himself. Backed into a corner, she could only agree. "All right. I'll go. And thank you, Cole. Ronnie will be thrilled."

"I hope so. Remember, no guarantees."

"No, no guarantees," she agreed, and he wondered why he suddenly had the impression that she was no longer talking about the fishing trip.

"Cole's gone?"

Kelsey nodded as she stepped back to let Lauren enter the apartment. "Yes."

He'd stayed only a few minutes after they'd finished the pizza, telling her he'd be in touch about the arrangements for the fishing excursion. He hadn't touched her, though for a moment just before he'd left she'd thought he was going to kiss her. She wasn't sure how she would have responded if he hadn't pulled away at the last moment. She secretly suspected that she wouldn't have resisted at all. May even have cooperated fully. She'd have to think about that later, when she was alone.

"You've been trying to get him to visit Paul, haven't you?" Lauren accused.

Kelsey nodded. "Yes, I have," she admitted. "I'm sorry, Lauren, I haven't been successful. I'm afraid he's still hurting very deeply over what he considers to be his father's defection when he was a child."

Lauren sighed dispiritedly. "I suppose we shouldn't really blame him. Paul told me that he made a lot of mistakes with Cole. Still, I wish . . ."

She stopped and pushed her hair away from her face before looking sternly at her sister. "I don't want you to nag him about this, you understand? I appreciate your effort, but I'm sure Paul would prefer that Cole make the gesture on his own, not because you've coerced him into it."

"Believe me, Lauren," Kelsey said dryly, "no one coerces Cole Saxon to do anything."

Well, there had been the fishing trip, she added silently, but she hadn't exactly coerced him into agreeing to her suggestion. Rather she'd persuaded him. Just as she intended to do eventually in the matter of visiting his father. She tried to tell herself that was the main reason she'd agreed to spend Saturday with him, that and the possibility that Ronnie would have his wish. She knew even then that there was a lot more to it than that. The simple fact was that she wanted to spend more time with Cole. He fascinated her in ways she couldn't have explained had she tried.

Studying the expressions crossing Kelsey's face, Lauren frowned. "There's not anything going on between the two of you, is there?"

"Of course not," Kelsey denied too quickly. *Not yet.* Pushing that errant thought away, she changed the subject, asking about Paul's condition that evening, which was still unchanged.

"The doctor said that if there isn't significant improvement within the next week, they're going to have to risk the surgery, anyway. He can't last much longer without it."

Kelsey bit her lip in distress. "Shouldn't they go ahead, then? Operate before he deteriorates any further?"

Both hands held palm upward in a bewildered gesture, Lauren shook her head. "They say it would be better to continue his treatments for a few days and hope he gains some strength first. They're... afraid he wouldn't survive the surgery if they operate now."

Kelsey caught her sister's hands in her own, holding them tightly. "Oh, Lauren."

Lauren took a deep breath and attempted a smile. "I have to believe he'll be all right. I have to."

"I know." Kelsey ached to do something, feeling more helpless than she'd ever felt before. So often she wished there was more she could do for the children she worked with, yet she found it so much more frustrating when her own family was involved. Had she so successfully learned to insulate herself from her work, as the newspaper reporter had suggested? She hoped she never got to a point where the children she worked with became just a series of "cases," a job to do. She promised herself she'd always remember how it felt to be this personally involved in a medical crisis.

Lauren gave Kelsey's hands a final squeeze, then pulled away. "I'd better go. It's getting late."

"All right. I'll help you get Jared's things together."

Fifteen minutes later, Kelsey was alone, her concentration split between the paperwork she needed to do, her concern about Paul and her confusion about her feelings for Cole—and his for her. She found herself looking forward to Saturday with a mixture of dread and reluctant anticipation.

As had been arranged, Cole was waiting on the dock beside the chartered fishing boat when Kelsey arrived with Al and Ronnie MacKenzie at nine o'clock Saturday morning. With Ronnie's thin, cool hand gripped tightly in hers, Kelsey tried not to stare at Cole as they approached him, but it wasn't easy.

He looked wonderful. He wore white jeans that hugged him as any healthy woman would silently long to do herself, and a red crewneck shirt that delineated every well-formed muscle of his chest and upper arms. The man was gorgeous, in jeans or in the suits she was more accustomed to seeing him wear. She was suddenly conscious of her own appearance, though she hadn't been particularly concerned about it earlier when she'd dressed and donned only a minimum amount of makeup.

Cole didn't speak as they approached him, though he watched Kelsey intently. If he found any fault in her appearance, it wasn't evident in the way his eyes traveled from her face to her snug-fitting striped knit shirt and faded jeans.

Trying not to blush at his attention, she managed a bright smile. "Good morning, Cole. I'd like you to meet my friends, Ronnie MacKenzie and his father, Al. Guys, this is Cole Saxon."

Al MacKenzie was a blue-collar worker in his early thirties who'd been struggling to make ends meet since the oldest of his four children had been diagnosed with the tragic illness. Kelsey knew the man hadn't finished high school and wouldn't earn in a week what Cole had spent chartering the boat and fishing guide for the day. Yet it was with easy dignity that Al held out a hand to Cole.

"Nice to meet you, Cole. And I want to thank you for letting us come along today. Ronnie's been after me to take him deep-sea fishing since we moved here from Oklahoma earlier this year. To be honest, I've only fished in the lakes and rivers back home. Crappie and bass, mostly."

Cole smiled and shook the man's hand. "I enjoy freshwater fishing, myself. You ever fish for trout?"

"Got a brother who lives on the Little Red in Arkansas. I spend a weekend camping out on the river with him whenever I get a chance. There's some great trout fishing there."

"Really? I'll have to try there sometime. There's nothing quite like fresh trout fried over an open fire for breakfast, is there?"

Al grinned. "You got that right."

Pleased that Cole had put the other man so quickly at ease, Kelsey nudged Ronnie, who was rather shy, forward. Tugging at the baseball cap he wore to hide his pitifully thin hair, a common side effect to chemotherapy, Ronnie looked up at Cole. "Thank you for taking me today, Mr. Saxon," he offered tentatively.

Cole smiled, and Kelsey suspected she was the only one who could read the pity in his eyes. Funny how she was beginning to read his expressions when he was so very good at masking them, she mused.

"Call me Cole," he urged the boy. "And maybe you'd better not thank me yet. You may not catch anything, you know. We're going to try, but there are no guarantees about fishing."

"I know, sir. But there's always a chance, isn't there?" Ronnie sounded as though he'd used the words often lately.

Cole cleared his throat quietly. "Yeah, Ronnie. There's always a chance. Let's go give it a try, shall we?"

He glanced at Kelsey as he spoke. Her heart in her throat, she smiled at him. *Why, Cole Saxon,* she thought in pleased surprise. *You're a pretty nice guy after all, aren't you? So how come you try so very hard to hide it?*

As if reading her thoughts, Cole immediately turned away. He led them to the boat, conversing quietly with Al on the differences between freshwater and saltwater fishing. But Kelsey sensed that he was as aware of her following him as she was of him. And a tingle of excitement rippled down her spine with the thought. Her excitement had nothing to do with the fishing excursion, but everything to do with the man who was leading it.

A tired, giddy, rumpled group stood on a dock late that afternoon, congratulating themselves on a delightfully successful outing. Kelsey and Cole had been as surprised as Ronnie and his father when the boy had caught the nice-sized sailfish he'd hoped for. They stood contentedly to one side as Ronnie posed for a photograph beside his catch. The boy was obviously exhausted, but the pride and happiness shining from his brown eyes brought a lump to Kelsey's throat—a typical reaction to seeing the successful fulfillment of one of her children's dreams.

Tears shining unashamedly in his eyes, Al pumped Cole's hand, disconcerting him with his gratitude—both for the trip and his help with the catch. It had been Cole who'd spent hours patiently showing Ronnie what to do and then helping him land the fish, neglecting his own line, lending his strength when Ronnie's had waned. Somehow he'd managed to land the great fish without once usurping Ronnie's part in the catch. Watching intently throughout the process, Kelsey had been delighted by the unshadowed excitement and pleasure on Cole's usually stern face.

She watched now as Ronnie shyly approached Cole for his own expression of thanks. His usual distance returning now that the excitement had passed, Cole extended his hand to the boy, as he had to the father. Ronnie gravely shook hands, then hesitated only a moment before throwing his skinny arms around Cole's waist.

"Thanks, Cole. You're really terrific," he murmured.

Cole shot Kelsey a startled look, then awkwardly patted the boy's thin shoulder. "You're okay yourself, Ronnie. You did well today."

"Thanks to you," Ronnie returned sincerely.

Cole cleared his throat and murmured something unintelligible. Her throat growing tighter, Kelsey noted with weak humor that Cole was almost shuffling his feet in embarrassment. What had begun as a mild attraction for Kelsey was rapidly becoming a heavy infatuation, and she was fully aware of it. She decided to worry about it later.

Cole announced that he'd be taking Kelsey home. He hadn't bothered to clear it with her first, but she only nodded, not wanting to make a scene in front of Ronnie. Besides, she admitted secretly, she wanted to spend more time with Cole.

Father and son left with another round of thanks—and an impulsive promise from Cole to have the sailfish mounted for the boy. He watched the departure in silence. Her own attention on Cole, Kelsey wondered why he suddenly looked so severe.

He turned abruptly, catching her looking at him. "How long does he have?" he demanded. It wasn't necessary for him to clarify the question.

Kelsey's smile faded. "Not long," she replied quietly, without attempting to soften the inevitable, unpleasant reply.

Cole cursed savagely and shoved a hand through his wind-tossed hair. "How can you do this all the time?" he asked in bewilderment. "How can you spend so much time with these kids? What's in it for you?" he asked one more time, still trying so hard to understand Kelsey's motives.

Her heart twisting at his genuine confusion, Kelsey entwined her arms at her waist and looked up at him. "The only thing in it for me is the pleasure I receive when I see their happiness at having that one big dream fulfilled. Didn't you see how happy Ronnie was today?"

He nodded shortly. "Yeah, but—"

"Children aren't going to stop getting critically ill because it's too uncomfortable for us healthy adults to think about," she continued evenly. "Someone has to care, to be willing to risk getting close to them to make sure they're taken care of, that their short lives are as happy and normal as possible. Would you have had Ronnie die without ever knowing the joy he experienced today in catching the fish?"

Sighing, Cole shook his head. "Of course not. I'm glad the trip was a success. I didn't want him to be disappointed. Still, it takes a special person to do this all the time," he added.

Without warning, he stepped closer and cupped Kelsey's face between his hardened palms. "It takes a very special person," he repeated in a rough murmur. "Like you."

And then, finally, he kissed her, right there on the busy dock with people all around them, the smell of fish and saltwater surrounding them, the raucous clamor of sea gulls above them. It was probably the most romantic moment of Kelsey's life.

She closed her eyes and lost herself in the pleasure of his kiss, her lips softening, then parting for him. He kissed her slowly, thoroughly, almost reverently. And then he kissed her again, less gently this time, with less finesse but with a growing heat that had her reacting with unprecedented hunger.

It was with some effort that Kelsey finally pulled away. "We have to go," she managed to say, her voice barely recognizable. "I'm going to be late."

"Have dinner with me tonight." His own voice was raw edged.

Wistfully, she shook her head. "I can't. I—"

"We'll take him with us," he cut in, anticipating her excuse. At her questioning look, he attempted a crooked smile. "We'd stay at your place, but I don't trust myself to keep my hands off you if we do. And I know you have to concentrate on taking care of your nephew—at least until he goes home."

And after that? Kelsey wasn't ready for the message she read in Cole's eyes. But would he understand that she had a great deal to consider before going to bed with him? That it wasn't as easy for her as it was for him to forget that the most important thing standing between them was his refusal to come to terms with his past, with a much-loved member of her family?

"All right. If you're sure you don't mind taking Jared with us, I'd love to have dinner with you," she murmured.

She told herself she'd agreed because the evening would be yet another opportunity to try to convince him to give in to Paul's request.

She told herself that she'd be giving Cole a chance to spend time with the younger brother who would need a male role model in his life if he lost his father so early.

She told herself she was a liar. The real reason she'd agreed to have dinner with Cole was that he'd kissed her and made her want him as she'd never wanted anyone before. And she was terribly afraid that what she felt for him was much more than desire.

"Oh, what a beautiful baby! How old is he?" The waitress crooned as she leaned over Jared in his infant seat, which rested on a chair at the table where Kelsey and Cole had been seated a few minutes earlier.

"Three months," Kelsey answered, uncomfortably aware that they gave the appearance of a family.

The waitress smiled at Cole as she straightened. "He looks just like his daddy," she commented. "That's unusual in one so young. Usually I never think they look like anyone that early." She glanced at Kelsey, taking in the snug fit of her royal-blue knit dress. "Gosh, you sure look great. I'm still trying to lose the extra weight I gained with my son and he's nearly two now."

Kelsey squirmed in her seat. "Well...um..."

Cole's toe pressed firmly down on hers.

"Thank you," Kelsey told the waitress, and buried her face in the menu until after the orders had been placed and the waitress departed. She glared across the table. "You didn't have to squash my foot."

He was unperturbed. "Sorry. But it really wasn't necessary to make awkward explanations to our waitress."

"She thinks Jared's ours."

Cole nodded. "An understandable mistake."

Kelsey scowled. "That's the second time someone's mistaken me for an unwed mother. You and Jared are ruining my reputation and I've never even—" She stopped with a gulp, realizing what she'd almost said.

Cole's brow shot up in interest. "You've never what?"

"Oh, nothing," she muttered, and quickly changed the subject. "Aren't you tired this evening? You worked that fish for so long, your arms must be sore."

"I stay in pretty good shape," he replied, obviously amused.

She couldn't help eyeing what she could see of him above the table. He looked trim and fit in his beautifully tailored dark suit. Memory whispered that the part of him beneath the table was equally attractive. "Yeah," she agreed on a longing sigh. "You do."

Cole's amusement faded abruptly. "Damn. Don't do that while we're out in public, will you?"

Her eyes widened. "Do what?"

He frowned. "Never mind. So what about you? Are you tired?"

She recognized the abrupt change of subject for the diversion it was. She decided it would be wise to go along with him. "A little. But it was worth it. Another successful dream fulfilled."

Cole shook his head, making a wry face. "I never would have believed the kid would have caught a sailfish on his first time out. You must use magic to make sure your plans work out."

Kelsey chuckled. "No magic. Unless you count permanently crossed fingers."

"Maybe that's it." Cole sipped his wine and nodded toward the infant seat. "Looks like we're going to be allowed to eat in peace."

Kelsey smiled when she saw that Jared had gone to sleep. "Let's hope so."

Still looking at the baby, Cole cleared his throat and asked offhandedly, "So how's Paul doing?"

Kelsey looked at him in surprise. "That's the first time you've asked me that."

He frowned. "It's only natural that I'm curious. After all, it's important to you."

"Oh. Of course."

"So how is he?"

Kelsey watched for his reaction as she answered, "Still very weak. The doctors have said that even if he doesn't regain his strength, they'll have to operate soon. They're afraid to wait much longer."

Though Cole's expression didn't soften, he reached across the table and touched her hand. "Kelsey—for your sake and your sister's, I hope he'll be okay."

"Thank you, Cole. I hope so, too."

Their dinners arrived. She waited until they were served before asking something that had been bothering her for several days. "Cole, is it true that Paul's parents won't even discuss him?"

He nodded, his attention seemingly focused on his plate. "Yeah. He hurt them pretty badly when he cut out the way he did. Not to mention what he did to my mother and me."

"Did your mother love your father very much?" she whispered sympathetically.

Cole winced and squirmed in his seat. "My mother...isn't one to show her emotions," he said bluntly. "I'm sure she was very fond of my father. I know she wanted the marriage to work."

Kelsey couldn't help thinking of the deep love Paul shared with Lauren, the spontaneous gestures of affection they often displayed around Kelsey. She would never use such bland terms to describe their marriage as Cole had just used in reference to that earlier union.

"Paul must have been desperately unhappy," she suggested carefully. "He must have had very compelling reasons to give up his son and all ties to his family."

His jaw hardening, Cole gave her one quick, seething look. "Regardless of his dissatisfaction with his life, he had responsibilities—to his family and to the business he entered when he married Belinda Grayson. The same responsibilities I've prepared for since I was just a kid."

"But are you really happy with your life? Do you like your work?"

"I like my work," he assured her evenly. "I enjoy the challenges of running a business empire that has been in my family for generations. I had a choice, you know. I could have gone into the Saxon law firm. I was never pushed into Grayson Shipping."

"But you were expected to do one or the other," she commented.

"I suppose. I don't regret my choice."

"Was there ever anything else you wanted to do?"

He shrugged. "I wanted to be a policeman when I was a kid. Most boys do at some point in their lives. I outgrew that fantasy very early. I like my job, Kelsey." He seemed compelled to repeat his sentiments.

"I can see that you do." And she could. It was obvious that Cole thrived on the challenge of being a young vice president of a major corporation. "But what would you have done if you hadn't outgrown that dream? If you'd always known that you'd never be happy in the family businesses?"

He set down his fork. "Look, I'm not going to sit here and have you ruin my dinner by pleading Paul's case while we eat. Let's change the subject, all right?"

"I'm not pleading Paul's case. Not exactly," she hedged. "I was only presenting another side."

"How's your fish?" he asked abruptly, nodding toward her barely touched dinner.

She sighed and picked up her fork as he did the same. Cole Saxon was the most stubborn man she'd ever met, she fumed silently as she ate. Too bad he was also the most interesting.

When the silence had stretched long enough, Cole renewed the conversation by asking if she'd seen a recently released movie that was receiving a great deal of critical attention. She replied that she hadn't yet had the chance to see it. They spent the next twenty minutes sharing casual conversation. Had it been an ordinary dinner date, Kelsey would have considered it a very pleasant one. But there was nothing ordinary about the confusing relationship that seemed to be developing between her and Cole, and "pleasant" was much too bland and uncomplicated a term to describe the time they spent together.

Their conversation came to an abrupt halt when a man who'd been passing the table stopped with an almost humorous double take to look incredulously from Cole to the baby sleeping beside him. "Cole! What in the world...?"

Glancing up, Cole unsuccessfully attempted to conceal a grimace before sighing, glancing at Kelsey and then back at the man beside the table. "Kelsey, allow me to introduce my uncle. My mother's brother, Edward Grayson."

Chapter Seven

Kelsey sat awkwardly through the introduction, aware of the mistaken conclusions Cole's uncle must be drawing from seeing her with Cole and the baby. If only Jared didn't look quite so much like his brother, she thought in despair. Her formerly impeccable reputation was taking a beating.

"It's very nice to meet you," she lied, smiling at the man who stared at her in open stupefaction. Cole had introduced her only as "my friend, Kelsey Campbell, and her nephew, Jared." She wondered if he intended to elaborate on his own relationship to Jared.

Apparently Cole had no such intention. Edward murmured something polite in response to Kelsey's words and then stammered that he really had to be going. He was dreadfully late for a function at his club.

"I'll talk to you tomorrow, Cole," he added before walking away, accompanying the words with a meaningful lift of an eyebrow.

"Well, hell." Cole downed the last half of a glass of wine in one gulp as soon as his uncle was gone.

Kelsey looked down at her hands.

"Are you ready to go?" Cole asked abruptly.

"Yes." She was more than ready to go, she could have added. There was nothing she wanted more at the moment than to be totally alone. Unfortunately, it would be a while yet before she'd manage that luxury.

She said little else until she and Cole were in her living room and Jared was in his crib. Then she locked her unsteady hands behind her and turned to Cole, who, having shed his jacket and loosened his tie in apparent preparation of a long confrontation, loomed silently nearby, watching her. "This is all getting very complicated," she said with a sigh. "I was afraid it would."

"Our seeing each other?" he asked for clarification.

She nodded. "It's a very awkward situation."

"Only if you allow it to become a problem," he replied dismissively.

She shouldn't be surprised any longer by his innate arrogance, she thought. Yet it still amazed her. "Cole, it's already a problem. That has nothing to do with whether I've allowed it to become one."

"Why?" he asked bluntly.

"Why?" She lifted her hands in exasperation. "How can you ask that? What is your mother going to say when her brother tells her that you were having dinner with her ex-husband's sister-in-law and his newest son?"

Cole didn't even blink. "Edward doesn't know you're Paul's sister-in-law. Or that Jared is his son."

"That's true," she conceded irritably. "Right now he probably just thinks I'm your hidden mistress who has borne you an illegitimate child. Do you think your mother will like that any better?"

"I'm a bit too old to be overly concerned with pleasing my mother," Cole returned flatly. "I'll tell her the truth, if she asks, but our relationship concerns no one but us."

"Cole, we *have* no relationship," Kelsey said heatedly.

He didn't seem particularly discouraged. "Don't we?"

"Even if we did," she continued, "it would never work out. Your family will be furious to learn that you're seeing me."

"Then they'll have to get used to it," he answered coolly. "They're going to have to find out about Paul, anyway, particularly if I retain any contact with Jared."

"Are you planning to do so?" Kelsey asked curiously.

"I haven't decided," he answered evasively. "I'm aware, of course, that there are obligations connected with the bonds of blood."

Kelsey rolled her eyes in disgust at the stuffy statement. "I thought we'd settled that from the beginning. No one, least of all Jared, will appreciate you spending time with him out of a sense of 'obligation.'"

"I only meant that I intend to honor my responsibilities," he returned defensively.

Tired and cross, Kelsey half turned away from him, her arms crossing at her waist. "Frankly, Cole, you've become such a slave to responsibilities that you're hardly human."

Her arm caught in an iron grip, she found herself facing him again almost before she knew what had happened.

"I'll show you how human I can be," Cole growled just before his lips covered hers.

Fueled by anger, the sparks that had ignited when they'd kissed on the dock flared into a passionate conflagration that engulfed them both. Kelsey shied from the heat for only a moment before throwing herself willingly into it. Going up on tiptoe, she threw her arms around Cole's neck as he bent down to her. He lifted her higher, devouring her mouth with his own.

"Damn it, Kelsey, what are you doing to me?" he muttered without releasing her, his mouth moving against hers. "Why do I want you this much?"

How was she supposed to answer that when she didn't understand her own feelings? She and Cole were all wrong for each other. It couldn't have been a worse time for them to get involved. And yet he was holding her—and every nerve ending in her body shivered in response. It had been so easy before to avoid becoming involved with anyone, using her total dedication to her work as a security buffer. But with Cole she hadn't even bothered to try that excuse. She had simply found herself involved before she'd even realized what was happening.

So what was she supposed to do now?

He didn't give her a chance to answer, even had she known how to express her own confusion. Instead, he took her mouth again, deepening the kiss until their tongues tangled eagerly.

Cole's hand slipped downward, drawing her closer. She felt his growing arousal with a quiver of excitement. Her eyes closed, her pulse pounded heavily. She wanted the kiss to last forever.

"Kelsey, I—Oh. Excuse me."

Kelsey jerked out of Cole's arms with a gasp, her hands going to her burning cheeks. They hadn't locked the door when they'd returned from dinner, so it hadn't been necessary for Lauren to use her key or ring the bell. "Lauren. I—I didn't hear you come in."

Lauren, too, was suspiciously pink. "Obviously." She looked away, turning toward the crib where her son slept. "I'll just get Jared's things and—"

"I'll help you," Kelsey offered immediately, stepping safely out of range of Cole's touch. "Cole was just leaving. Weren't you, Cole?"

He scowled at her.

She planted her fists on her hips and stared him down. "Weren't you, Cole?"

"Yeah," he grunted, conceding. "I guess I was."

With a look at Kelsey that conveyed a silent promise of retribution, he reached for his jacket. He spoke only briefly to Lauren before leaving, without looking back at Kelsey. That last glance had said enough, apparently.

Her arms loaded with diapers and blankets, Lauren immediately rounded on her sister. "Just what is going on between you and Cole Saxon?" she demanded.

Kelsey started to downplay the incident, but instead found herself answering all too honestly. "I think I'm about to have an affair with him."

Lauren's jaw dropped, her eyes going round with consternation. "Kelsey, the man is stiff-necked, stubborn and rigidly unforgiving. He comes from a family of snobby, self-styled aristocrats and, from everything Paul says, Cole's just like them. What could you possibly find to even like about him?"

Kelsey took the question seriously. "The way his face softens when he smiles," she murmured. "The pleasure he received from sending a sick boy to Graceland. His excitement at helping another sick boy catch a big fish. The vulnerability he tries so hard to hide behind the stern facade he's developed over the years. Should I go on? There are other things."

Her sister exhaled in disgust. "No. That's plenty. You're falling in love with him, aren't you?"

A feeling very much like panic grabbed Kelsey by the throat. "No, of course not! I hardly know the man."

"You know him well enough to consider going to bed with him."

"That's—that's only sex, not love."

Lauren scowled. "Is this my straitlaced, conservative sister talking?"

"I'm twenty-four years old, Lauren. Don't you think it's time I experience a bit of life?"

"I have a feeling that this man will only give you experience with heartache."

Because she knew her sister was genuinely concerned, Kelsey reached out a hand to touch Lauren's shoulder reassuringly. "Look, I know what I'm doing. Don't worry about me, all right?"

"How can I help it? You're my baby sister. I love you."

"I love you, too. And I promise I'll remember everything you said about Cole. Just…give him a chance, okay?"

"The way he's giving Paul a chance?" Lauren shot back with a trace of bitterness. And then she shook her head and turned away. "Never mind. As you said, you're old enough to know what you want. I just hope you're not making a huge mistake."

"So do I," Kelsey whispered before helping Lauren prepare to take her son home.

An hour later Kelsey headed for bed. Tired, aching, confused, she stared into her vanity mirror as she brushed her hair. Despite her care to use sunblock, her nose and cheeks glowed pink from the morning hours on the boat. The glow in her eyes, however, was caused by exposure to Cole. Her uncharacteristic expression made the reflection in the mirror look strangely unfamiliar. Had he changed her so much already? she wondered, that earlier frisson of fear returning in force. She'd so confidently assured Lauren that she knew what she was doing.

What a lie that had been.

She had no idea what she was getting into with Cole Saxon. She only knew that she seemed unable to pull back now, and it had nothing to do with her earlier determination to intercede on Paul's behalf.

She crawled into bed with a pessimistic certainty that sleep would be a very long time coming that night.

* * *

Cole was half-buried beneath a mountain of paperwork in his office Monday morning when his secretary buzzed him to announce that his mother was waiting to see him. With a mental groan, he told Alice to send her in. He knew, of course, why she was there.

Standing, he watched Belinda Grayson Saxon sweep into the office with characteristic elegance. She was a tall woman, attractive in an understated way. Though she looked her age—early fifties—she made the most of her assets. Her figure, swathed in a designer suit, was trim, her hair perfectly coiffed, makeup skillfully applied. Had there been any softness in her smooth face, she might even have been considered beautiful.

"Hello, Mother. What brings you here this morning?" As if he had to ask.

"Cole." She drew off her gloves as she spoke. Only Belinda Grayson would wear white gloves on a Monday morning in August, Cole thought irreverently.

She sank into a deep leather chair close to his desk, her back straight, feet together, hands crossed on the leather purse in her lap. She hadn't offered a kiss or touch of affectionate greeting. As he returned to his seat, Cole wondered exactly when his mother had last kissed him. Christmas, maybe? His birthday?

Unexpectedly, he found himself remembering the way Lauren had nuzzled Jared's throat before leaving him with Kelsey. The gesture had been warm, loving, utterly natural. Had Belinda ever nuzzled her son? If she had, it had been earlier than Cole's memory extended. And yet, despite her lack of demonstrativeness, Cole knew that Belinda loved him as much as she was capable of loving, just as he loved her. She was his mother.

Which didn't mean he looked forward to the next few minutes with any less dread.

Belinda didn't bother with polite niceties, but cut straight to the purpose of her visit. "Edward said he saw you dining at Andre's Saturday evening with a woman and an infant. He said the child looked very much like you. I would appreciate an explanation, Cole."

Cole leaned back in his seat, his pose deceptively casual. "Edward works fast, I can say that for him. Of course, I fully expected him to come running to you. It isn't as if I'm his favorite relative, is it?"

Belinda's gray eyes flared, her mouth tightening in the only sign of temper she allowed herself. "Unlike you, apparently, Edward still cares about the family's reputation. Did you really expect him to believe that the child was your companion's nephew?"

"And what *did* he believe?"

"He believed, as I suspect, that the child was your bastard. Honestly, Cole, how could you be so irresponsible? And what do you intend to do about the situation?"

Cole's eyes narrowed. "Jared is not a bastard, Mother, and he is not my son, regardless of your suspicions. I told Edward the truth. The child is the nephew of the woman I was with Saturday night."

Obviously startled, Belinda looked at him searchingly. "This is the truth?" she asked.

"Have you ever known me to lie to you?" he returned.

She hesitated only a moment. "No," she admitted. "I haven't. You've always had too much arrogant pride to lie, even when it would have been to your advantage."

He couldn't quite suppress a faint smile. He inclined his head in concession to her comment.

Her expression wryly resigned, Belinda relaxed just perceptibly. "Then Edward was mistaken. I should have known, I suppose. He knows nothing about babies, probably saw a resemblance that wasn't there at all. You have to admit, however, that the situation was an awkward one.

Why on earth did the woman bring her infant nephew on a date with you?''

"She was baby-sitting for her sister." And then, after a brief mental debate, he decided he may as well get the whole story out now. After all, he fully intended to see Kelsey again and would probably be spending some time with his half brother. He had decided sometime during the past two days that the boy would need a man's influence in his life after losing his father. Who better than his older and wiser brother to teach him to respect his responsibilities and to honor the family name Paul had chosen to scorn?

"Edward wasn't mistaken about the resemblance. Apparently, the boy looks very much like me. Even Bob thought he was mine when he first saw him."

"Bob Herrington? Why did your attorney see the child?"

"That's a long story. I'm trying to tell you, Mother, that the baby is a Saxon."

"A—"

"Paul's son," he added, as gently as possible.

Belinda went utterly still, her face paling. "Perhaps you'd like to explain," she said after a moment, no emotion in her voice. "Are you saying this child is your... your half brother?"

"Yes. Paul married a woman several years his junior and Jared is their son."

"And the woman with whom you were dining?"

"Paul's sister-in-law."

"I find this very hard to comprehend, Cole. Why were you with her? What did she want from you?"

"Kelsey doesn't want anything from me." And this time, he fully believed that himself. He had finally decided that Kelsey Campbell was exactly what she appeared to be—softhearted, somewhat naive, scrupulously honest. She would have liked very much to convince Cole to see his father, but she wanted nothing for herself. Perhaps that was one of the reasons he was so utterly captivated by her. Her selflessness was such a refreshing change from the majority of people he'd encountered.

Where the hell had she been yesterday? he asked himself for the hundredth time. He'd tried all day to call her, reaching only her answering machine. It had been all he could do to keep himself from going out looking for her. He'd refrained only because he'd believed she needed time to come to terms with the affair that was rapidly becoming inevitable. An affair that would have already begun, had it been left to him.

"Cole?" Belinda prodded when his distracted silence stretched too long. "What is going on?"

Taking a deep breath, Cole explained from the beginning—Paul's illness, Kelsey's reason for contacting Cole, Cole's continued refusal to confront Paul in his hospital bed, Lauren's rejection of Cole's offer of financial assistance.

"The woman doesn't need financial assistance," Belinda said then, the first time she'd spoken since Cole had begun the explanation. "Paul has been quite successful with his software designs."

Startled, Cole straightened in his chair. "You knew about that?"

"Yes. I also knew that he'd married. I did not know about the child or about Paul's illness."

"But how—"

"The families keep track of their own, Cole," she cut in coolly. "We had to be sure that he did nothing to further humiliate us—at least not without our knowledge."

Cole felt winded. "You mean you've known where he's been and what he's done since he left? The entire family knew?"

"Of course," Belinda answered irritably. "And, yes, his parents knew, as well as mine. My father has kept me informed."

"And what about me?" Cole demanded heatedly, shoving himself out of his chair. "Why wasn't I told? Why did I find it necessary to hire an investigator to research Paul's activities for the past twenty years?"

"You never asked."

He whirled to stare at her. "I never asked," he uttered blankly. "You didn't think I'd want to know?"

Belinda didn't quite meet his eyes. "It really didn't concern you."

"The man is my father."

Her chin lifted regally. "He gave up that privilege when he walked away from you—from us. It was two years later before he even attempted to contact you again."

Cole shook his head. "No. He only contacted me for the first time when I finished college. I refused to see him then, just as I have the other times he's reached me since." And then, reading his mother's expression, he asked slowly, "He did try to contact me earlier?"

"A few times," she admitted.

"And you didn't tell me. Did you consider that none of my concern, as well, Mother?"

"Everything we did was for your own good," Belinda asserted firmly. "Your grandfathers agreed that it would be better if you weren't exposed to his influence during your formative years. We couldn't be sure what he would tell you, what delusions had driven him to walk out on us, whether he would try to turn you against us. It was better this way. Obviously, you agree, since you have repeatedly refused contact with him."

"I thought he'd ignored me for twenty years!"

She rose, facing him squarely. "Would it have made a difference if you'd known he had not, entirely?"

"I don't know," he muttered, shoving a hand through his hair. "But, damn it, I should have had the chance to decide for myself."

"Cole, if your father had truly cared about your welfare, he would have stayed to help raise you. Who sat with you when you had the measles and chicken pox? Who spent a night in a hospital waiting room when you were thrown from that horse when you were thirteen? Who sat in the bleachers during your baseball games? Who worried during the long nights when you were out as a teenager doing God-knows-what in that powerful sports car you wanted so badly? Who paid for your college education?"

"All right, I get your point," Cole answered wearily, rubbing at his temple where a dull ache had started. "I only wish you had trusted me enough to tell me the truth, Mother. It concerned me. I should have been told."

"Perhaps you should have," she agreed, making a very rare concession. "Perhaps we made a mistake trying to shield you. We only wanted what was best for you."

We. The families. Not I, your mother. Cole sighed, knowing that some things would never change. Was it too late for *him* to change, or was he destined to be nothing more than a clone of generations past?

And did he even have a chance with Kelsey unless he learned to change?

Belinda took a deep breath and slipped her purse under her arm. "You still haven't told me why you were having dinner with Paul's sister-in-law and... her nephew."

Cole noted with a reluctant tug of sympathy that it was hard for Belinda to refer to the child. Had she wanted other children with Paul? He'd never known exactly why he'd been an only child. Had Belinda loved Paul? He would probably never know.

"I was dining with Kelsey because I enjoy her company, Mother. She's attractive and bright and interesting. I think you'd like her," he added, though he wasn't at all sure he meant the words.

Belinda prickled immediately. "I doubt that I shall ever meet her. I don't want you to see these people again, Cole. You have no responsibilities to your father or his child."

"I disagree," he replied, trying to hide his anger behind a bland tone. "The child is a Saxon. As such, he deserves to know about his family—and they to know about him."

"That's absurd."

"Paul is dying, Mother," Cole said bluntly. "His son will need the guidance of the family. He will be raised as a Saxon."

Her lip curling in barely repressed fury, Belinda glared at him. "What makes you think the Saxons will want him?"

"I suppose that's up to them," he returned evenly. "But he is my half brother. And, as you have so clearly pointed out, I have been raised to honor my responsibilities to family."

"And this woman? Are you truly foolish enough to have an affair with the sister of your father's ridiculously young wife?"

"Paul's wife seems quite nice, Mother, whatever you may think of her. And I want you to leave Kelsey alone, as well. What's between the two of us has nothing to do with Paul."

"You're a fool if you think you can keep your affair with her separate from her connection to your father. It's a ridiculous situation, Cole."

"Perhaps. But this decision is mine, Mother. To use your own words, it really doesn't concern you."

Though he spoke gently, his tone effectively silenced her. Belinda departed with only a muttered warning that he would very likely regret ignoring her advice.

Cole was left to hope that she was wrong. Sighing wearily, he buzzed his secretary with a request for her to find him something to take for a headache. And then he reached for the phone, determined to talk to Kelsey.

Chapter Eight

Kelsey was sitting at her desk, trying to find a way to stretch two thousand dollars to cover three thousand dollars' worth of expenses. The state of the Children's Dream Foundation bank account reminded her painfully of her own, which had been severely depleted by the sizable cost of getting her poor old Dodge out of the shop. The buzz from the telephone at her elbow was a welcome distraction from her dollar balancing. She lifted the receiver to her ear, wincing when it clanked against the oversize silver earring she'd worn with a vaguely southwestern-styled dress. "Kelsey Campbell."

"How about telling me where you were yesterday?"

Torn between annoyance at the demand and pleasure at hearing his voice, Kelsey laid her pencil down. "Hello, Cole."

"I tried to call you all day."

"I was busy."

"All day?"

"All day." She had no intention of elaborating. Cole may as well know from the beginning that she would not be intimidated by him.

He was silent for several long, taut moments, then grudgingly conceded. "So how's it going?"

Kelsey relaxed. "Okay, I guess."

"Problems?"

"Nothing out of the ordinary. I'm speaking at a fund-raiser tomorrow evening and I expect it to be a successful one."

"What about tonight? Are you keeping the kid?"

She noted that he still tended to avoid using Jared's name and wondered why. "No. Paul and I have convinced Lauren that she needs a quiet, restful evening at home with her son. She's wearing herself out. She spent most of the day yesterday at the hospital. A woman from her church kept Jared, since I was tied up in fund-raising planning meetings."

And then she stopped in self-disgust, realizing that she'd just told Cole exactly where she'd been the day before.

The smug satisfaction underlying his voice let her know he'd made the same connection. "So will you have dinner with me? Just the two of us this time?"

Just the two of them. Kelsey pressed her hand against the butterflies beating madly in her stomach. "I had intended to run by the hospital this evening. I hate for Paul to spend the entire evening alone."

Again, there was silence at the other end. And then, "All right. I'll take you by the hospital on the way to the restaurant."

Hopefully, she asked, "You mean . . . ?"

"I'll wait in the lobby while you visit him."

Disappointed, she knew better than to argue with him. "If that's the way you want it."

"I'll see you at seven, then."

"Fine."

"Kelsey?"

She'd already started to hang up. She drew the receiver back to her ear. "Yes?"

"I missed you yesterday."

And then the buzz of a dial tone prevented her from telling him that she'd missed him, too. And that she'd spent half the night wondering just how deeply she'd fallen for him and whether Lauren had been right. Was Cole going to break her heart?

Only if she gave it to him, she reminded herself, turning resolutely back to her paperwork.

Aware of Cole following closely behind her, Kelsey entered her apartment later that evening and laid her purse on a table near the door. She cleared her throat, noting how loud it sounded in the silence of the apartment. Funny how much difference Jared's absence seemed to make. She hadn't felt quite so alone with Cole when her nephew had been sleeping in his crib.

"Can I get you anything?" she offered, without looking around.

"No. I had plenty at dinner."

"Oh. Me, too."

Actually, she'd been much more comfortable at dinner, surrounded by other people in the restaurant. Though refusing to discuss her brief visit with his father, Cole had exerted himself to be charming during the meal, and, again, he had succeeded quite well.

Kelsey twisted her hands behind her back. "Wouldn't you like to sit down?"

He stepped closer, instead. "Kelsey. Surely you're not nervous at being alone with me?"

"I'm not?" she asked, and then shook her head. "No, of course I'm not. Why would you think that?"

He touched her cheek and gave her that oh-damn-there-go-the-knees smile. She stiffened her legs and looked warily up at him. "Are you sure I can't get you anything?" she tried again, her voice annoyingly breathless.

He didn't even bother to answer. Instead, his hand slipped behind her head and he lowered his mouth to hers.

They wouldn't be interrupted this time, Kelsey thought. Her sister wouldn't be coming by to stop her from making a foolish mistake. If she were going to draw back, she'd better do so now, while she could still think rationally. While she could still remember all the reasons she and Cole Saxon should not become involved.

"Cole," she murmured, pressing her hands to his chest.

He lifted his head slowly, his arms still around her. "Yes?"

She stared up at him, her lower lip caught between her teeth. *Remember the problems between you,* her mind urged. *Remember that you've known him less than two weeks.*

You want him, her heart argued.

She didn't even try to put her body's urgings into words.

He held her gaze with his own smoldering one. "I want you, Kelsey." The words were raw, unsteady. He made no effort to hide his hunger for her.

Being wanted so badly, so openly, was as much a seduction as romantic dinners and long, skillful kisses, Kelsey realized in despair. How could she possibly resist him when he looked at her this way?

Why was she even trying?

"This is crazy," she whispered. "We're all wrong together. And there's Paul—"

His fingers covered her mouth, more gently than she would have expected from him. "No. This is just you and me. Do you want me?"

She trembled at the blunt question, suddenly overcome by a wave of shyness. "Cole..."

His lips curved upward. Oh, what his smile did to her! He pulled her closer. "Kelsey?"

She sighed. "Yes. Yes, I want you. But—"

His mouth muffled the rest.

Surrendering, Kelsey slid her arms around his neck and melted into the kiss.

She'd expected fire, urgency. She got, instead, warmth, tenderness. Would this man ever stop surprising her?

She should have known, she thought dazedly, opening her mouth to Cole's subtle urging. She couldn't have resisted him, even if she'd tried.

He explored her mouth as if they had an eternity to discover each other. Realizing that he wasn't going to rush her, she slowly relaxed, her fingers unclenching to tentatively stroke his nape, sliding into the softness of his hair.

He was so strong, so very male. She felt the power beneath her palms as she slid one hand down his back. And he was so big. She was stretched as high as she could go to reach his mouth, and still he had to bend his head to close the remaining distance. Her brief flare of courage faltered.

Bringing one hand around to press against his chest, Kelsey pulled back as much as his embrace allowed. "Cole?"

He lifted his head to smile down at her. "Yes?"

She swallowed and moistened her lips. "There's something I think you should know."

His eyes on her glistening mouth, he stroked his thumb across her lower lip. "If you're worried about protection, I'll take care of it."

Oh, mercy. "No, that . . . well, yes, that's important, of course, but I . . ." She was making a real mess of this. She stopped and squeezed her eyes shut in self-disgust.

"What is it, Kelsey?" he urged encouragingly.

"I've—uh—never done this before. Exactly. I mean, not all . . . damn it, Cole, I'm a virgin."

He went still, his expression curiously suspended. "Are you?"

Though she searched, she could find no particular emotion in his passion-darkened green eyes. She'd expected surprise, dissatisfaction, maybe even disbelief. She could find none of those. But then, Cole was very good at hiding his feelings, she reminded herself. "Yes, I am. I just thought you should know, before we ... you know."

His hand cupped her cheek. "This is a pretty big step," he said evenly. "Are you sure you're ready to take it? Now? With me?"

She paused only a moment before nodding. "I'm sure. But I'm a little nervous. What if I ... stumble?"

"Then I'll catch you," he answered quietly, his voice deep, husky.

He must have known just what she'd needed to hear. She smiled tremulously and pulled back, catching his hand in hers. "The bedroom's this way," she murmured.

She didn't have to urge him to follow her.

Kelsey flushed when Cole crossed the darkened bedroom to snap on the delicate little bedside lamp. He looked around with a lifted eyebrow, then glanced back at her.

"I guess I'm a sucker for romance," she murmured, imagining how frivolously feminine her lace and ruffles must look to him.

"I'll remember that." He reached out a hand. "Come here."

She took the four or five steps that separated them and placed her hand in his, wondering what she should do now. Should she unbutton his shirt? No, he was still wearing his jacket and tie. Maybe she should first—

"Kelsey." Again, he cupped her cheek, this time with both hands.

She looked up at him.

"I'm not a gentle man," he murmured. "You know that."

She covered his hands with her own, sliding painlessly, totally into love with him. "But for me—you will be," she whispered, showing her trust in her eyes.

She felt the tremor in his hands and was awed by it. "Oh, Kelsey. I hope so," he muttered.

Still holding her face between his hands, he kissed her. Slowly. Deeply. Gently.

And suddenly she didn't have to think, didn't have to worry about what she was supposed to do. She slid the jacket from his shoulders and reached eagerly for his tie, wanting very much to feel his skin beneath her fingertips. Cole cooperated, his smile urging her on as she unbuttoned his crisp white shirt, remembering at the last moment to unfasten the cuffs. And then his chest was bare, and her breath caught hard in her throat.

"Cole. You're so beautiful," she said, hardly conscious of speaking aloud. Tentatively, she stroked from the pulsing hollow of his throat down his powerful chest to his lean, flat stomach. The light mat of dark hair arrowing from his nipples to his navel tickled her fingertips.

The sound he made was somewhere between a strangled laugh and a groan. "I may not be sane by morning."

The tip of her tongue caught between her teeth, Kelsey smiled up at him. She discovered that she liked shaking him up. She liked it a lot. Her fingers slid slowly just inside the waistband of his slacks.

His humor faded abruptly. He lifted her into his arms and crushed her mouth beneath his. He wasn't gentle, but she found she really didn't want him to be. Shyness, nerves, hesitation were gone. She wanted this, wanted Cole, wanted him to be as lost in passion as she was. When he twisted to lay her on the bed, she knew he was thinking of nothing but her.

Slowly he eased her out of her silk print dress, his lips touching soft, pulsing places as he exposed them. She was lost in his caresses, so deeply that she didn't want to cover herself when he unsnapped the front clasp of her wispy bra and brushed the lacy garment aside. "Ah, Kelsey," he said, his hand going to her small breasts.

Too small? she worried.

"Perfect," he breathed, lowering his mouth to one hardening nipple.

She arched into him, gasping at the sensations exploding inside her as a result of his warm, moist suckling. Her eyes closed, her fingers clenched in his hair. He divided his attention between her straining breasts, and just when she thought she could feel no more intensely, he slid his hand down her stomach and inside the waistband of her tiny satin panties.

"Cole!"

He pressed a butterfly kiss to her throat. "Easy, babe. Relax."

Her fingers clutched at his shoulders as she shifted restlessly beneath him. "I don't know if I can."

Murmuring reassurances, he kissed her lips slowly, thoroughly. His fingers stroked her, lightly at first and then more deeply, until she arched instinctively into his hand, silently asking for more. He lifted his head and smiled down at her. Finding it surprisingly hard to focus, she looked up at him.

His glossy hair was tousled from her hands, his eyes dark, gleaming. His stern features were softened by his smile. His pulse pounded visibly in his corded throat. She found it difficult to believe this was the same man who'd once seemed so cold and unapproachable, hiding behind his perfectly groomed hair, dauntingly expensive suits and sleek limousine. Just as she knew this warmer, more vulnerable side of him was real, she understood that Cole was also the man she'd first met—cynical, suspicious, hardened by too much money and too much power from a very early age. And, God help her, she loved him anyway.

Pushing that uncomfortable realization away, she reached for him, dragging his head down to hers. She covered his mouth with her own, desperately trying to lose herself again in passion. She didn't want to think, didn't want to spoil this moment with worry about the future. "Love me, Cole," she murmured, hoping he wouldn't read the double meaning in the words.

He held back for a moment, as if sensing her inner conflict, but she ran her hands over him, urging him on. "Please, Cole," she murmured, kissing his jaw, his throat, his collarbone, everywhere she could reach.

He groaned and swept her panties away, his hand returning immediately to the damp brown curls between her legs. This time Kelsey didn't flinch, but lifted eagerly into his touch, reaching for the waistband of his slacks. He drew away only long enough to rid himself of his clothing and protect her from pregnancy and then he returned to her willing arms and proceeded to slowly, thoroughly drive her out of her mind.

Her breath was raw, ragged, her skin damp, flushed, her breasts heaving by the time he slipped inside her. He'd prepared her so well that, if there was pain, it was fleeting, unimportant. Deliciously filled with him, she wrapped her arms and legs around him and held tightly, surrendering herself to his guidance. And the places he took her proved her trust justified.

"Cole! Oh, Cole." She clung to him as the explosions of climax rocked through her, knowing he would hold her safely.

"Kelsey." He buried his face in her throat and shuddered with her, his body arching, freezing and finally relaxing to lie warmly, contentedly on hers. He was heavy, but she didn't care. Her eyes still closed, she snuggled deeper into his shoulder, her arms locked around him as if she'd never have to let him go.

He had to move. He knew he had to, but still lingered, his body cushioned by a softer, rounder one, his face still hidden in the sweetly scented hollow of her throat. If it were up to him, he'd stay right where he was for the rest of the night. But he knew he was too heavy for her.

With a long sigh he rolled, pulling her closer when she murmured a protest and attempted to hold him. He cradled her against his side, where she burrowed contentedly, one hand curling on his chest, just over his heart. Cole closed his eyes and savored her warmth.

It was a long time later before Kelsey seemed to find the energy to speak. "Cole?"

Her voice was sleepy, husky. The sexy sound of it had him stirring restlessly. "Hmm?"

"Stay the night?"

His eyes opened, though he stared at the ceiling, not quite trusting himself to look at Kelsey. "Tomorrow's Tuesday. We both have to work."

"Yes. You'd have to leave early. But will you stay?"

He rested his cheek against her hair. "I'll stay."

He felt her smile against his chest. "Good."

Cole wondered at his own actions. He'd never been one to linger after sex. He rarely slept with any woman, preferring the solitary comfort of his own bed, the privacy of waking alone for his shower and newspaper over coffee. But it was different with Kelsey. He couldn't think about what had passed between them as just sex, nor did he want to leave her bed and return to his own, alone. In fact, the way he was feeling right now, he wasn't sure he'd ever want to let her out of his arms.

What was he getting himself into, with her? he wondered on a ripple of unease.

Just to prove to himself that he could do it, he opened his arms and slipped out from beneath her, pushing himself upright. And then he made the mistake of looking at Kelsey. And almost groaned.

She looked so damned beautiful, so infinitely desirable with her short, silky hair tousled, her dark eyes big and questioning. Her skin was still flushed with the remnants of the passion they had shared. It was all he could do not to reach out for her again.

He cleared his throat. "I'll be right back."

Glancing from him to the bathroom in sudden understanding, she smiled and nodded. "I'll be waiting."

The thought of her arms welcoming him back into her bed made him hurry. And when he returned, she snuggled against him as comfortably, as unselfconsciously as if they'd been sleeping together for years. Mentally flinching from the thought that he might never want to sleep without her again, Cole distracted himself by rolling her beneath him, covering her mouth with his.

Her eager response was everything he could have wished for. And suddenly he knew he would never be quite the same as he'd been before knowing Kelsey. For now, however, he couldn't seem to be particularly concerned. He had more interesting things to think about. More delightful things to do...

Kelsey often made hospital stops on her way to work, heading straight for the children's wards to visit the patients she'd met through her work. She usually carried an armload of donated children's books and comics or coloring books and crayons. She spent Tuesday morning making such visits, saving the hospital where Paul was until last so she could check on him while she was there.

She found Lauren at the nurses' station outside Paul's room. Jared was being cared for by a sitter. After greeting the nurse behind the desk, Kelsey turned to her sister. "Good morning. How's Paul?" she asked.

Lauren smiled, and for the first time in almost three weeks she looked happy. "He's stronger today," she announced. "The doctor said there was definite improvement during the night. If he keeps this up, there should be no reason not to operate on Monday."

Kelsey drew Lauren away from the desk into a tiny, deserted waiting room nearby. "Lauren, that's wonderful news! You must be so relieved."

Trying to be cautious, Lauren nodded. "It was only a slight improvement, of course, and the operation is still dangerous. But it's the best news I've heard since he was admitted. Three weeks ago today," she added, as though she felt it had been longer. It seemed longer to Kelsey, too.

"I just know it's going to work out," Kelsey assured her fervently. "Paul's a fighter, Lauren, and he has so much to live for."

Lauren nodded tearfully. "That's what he keeps saying. Oh, Kelsey."

The sisters hugged tightly for several long minutes. And then drew back, smiling their optimism. "You look wonderful today," Kelsey said approvingly. "You must have gotten some rest last night."

"I really needed the evening at home with Jared," Lauren agreed. "How about you? Did you enjoy your night off from baby-sitting? Paul said you came by to see him, and that you told him you were going out for dinner afterward. Did you go with Tina?" she asked, naming one of Kelsey's friends.

"No, I . . . had dinner with Cole."

Lauren's smile faded. "Oh."

Kelsey winced at Lauren's obvious disapproval. "I asked you to give him a chance."

"And I thought you understood why I can't."

"He's really not the way you think, Lauren. He's hard, yes, but he's had to be. Despite his wealth, or maybe because of it, his life hasn't been easy."

"What do you want, violins?" Lauren crossed her arms over her breasts defensively. "Paul hasn't exactly had an easy time of it, either, remember? His entire family turned their backs on him when he realized that he had to break away from a failed marriage and a career he hated. He had to start over with nothing, but he made it. On his own, without the Saxon money or influence. He had to walk away from the son he loved because he couldn't fight the Grayson power. He tried for years to see Cole and wasn't allowed to even speak to him. Now he's sick, maybe dying, and his son won't even give him one last chance to talk to him. And I'm supposed to feel sorry for Cole, the fair-haired darling of the Grayson and Saxon empires?''

"Maybe Cole thinks Paul didn't try hard enough to see him. He could have gone to court. Surely the courts would have ordered visitation rights."

Lauren nodded grimly. "Paul regrets not trying harder, but he didn't think he had a chance against them. He knew they'd all gang up to testify to what a terrible father he'd been, accuse him of abandoning his wife and child. He didn't think he could win and he didn't want to hurt Cole by putting him in the middle of an ugly custody battle. All he wants now is a chance to tell Cole his side of the story rather than what he's heard from the families all his life. It's not so much to ask, Kelsey."

"No," Kelsey agreed with a sigh. "It's not so much to ask. But it's more than Cole can give, apparently."

"If he can't even give that much to his own father during an emergency, then what makes you think he'll be there for you if you need him? Don't get involved with a man like that, Kelsey. You deserve better."

Kelsey looked away, chewing her lower lip.

Lauren groaned. "It's too late, isn't it? You've already been to bed with him."

Flushing, Kelsey looked quickly around, relieved to see that no one was within hearing. She'd wondered if she looked any different today, if Cole had changed her on the outside as well as the inside. Maybe he had. Maybe everyone could look at her today and know that she would never be the same as she'd been before she'd met Cole. "Honestly, Lauren."

"I'm sorry, but I don't want to see you hurt. My life was nearly ruined by a man who got off on power, who thought other people exist only to cater to him. I don't want to see the same thing happen to you."

"Cole's not like that!" Kelsey protested immediately. "He can be very sweet, Lauren. Kind and gentle."

"Yeah. I thought the same thing about Tom, until after we were married and I learned the truth. It took me four years of sheer hell to get away from him."

"Cole's not like Tom," Kelsey repeated somewhat desperately, wishing she could make Lauren understand. She knew in her heart that Lauren was mistaken, but she had to admit that some of her accusations were too uncomfortably close to reality.

Yes, Cole was hard and inflexible and arrogant. It was as much a part of him as the gentleness he'd shown when he'd made love to her. But he would never use his strength to hurt her. As for being there for her if she needed him—well, that remained to be seen. Their relationship was still so new, so tentative. They had so much still to learn about each other. If only everything could be simpler. If they were an average couple with no awkward ties between them, no family loyalties pulling them in different directions...

She held out a hand to her sister pleadingly. "Please, Lauren, trust me to know what I'm doing."

Lauren hesitated, then sighed and quickly squeezed Kelsey's hand. "I guess you have to find out for yourself. God knows I wouldn't listen when anyone tried to warn me about Tom. I only hope you aren't hurt the way I was."

Kelsey changed the subject, saying that she wanted to stop in to see Paul and then had to get to work. Lauren said no more about Cole, though her doubts were still clearly visible in her eyes. Kelsey hated worrying her sister when she had so many more things on her mind. But she couldn't promise to stay away from Cole. It was much too late for that.

She knew Lauren was wrong about Cole, she reminded herself many times as the morning crept by, her thoughts wandering all too frequently from her job.

If only Lauren's words hadn't left a niggling of doubt behind, despite Kelsey's brave attempts at denial.

By midafternoon, Kelsey had a pounding headache and a desperate need to hear Cole's voice. They hadn't discussed their plans for the evening, since he'd left hurriedly that morning so that neither of them would be late for work. She wavered for a moment over whether to call him, then abruptly picked up the phone and dialed the number of his office.

"Cole Saxon's office. Alice speaking."

Kelsey grimaced. "May I speak to Cole, please? Tell him—oh, just tell him it's Kelsey."

The secretary's voice cooled. It was obvious that she remembered Kelsey, and that she wasn't aware that her employer had been seeing the woman who'd been so persistent in her efforts to meet with him only two weeks earlier. "I'm sorry, Mr. Saxon is in a meeting. May I take a message?"

"Just tell him Kelsey called, okay? And give him my number." Kelsey reeled off the digits of her work number, hoping the woman was bothering to write them down. Surely Cole would call her if Alice gave him the message, she reasoned. After all, they were lovers now, and it was perfectly acceptable for her to call him. Right? So why did she feel so intimidated by his ultraefficient secretary, as if she had to apologize for having the nerve to bother him?

Scowling, she picked up the receiver again. Tomorrow was the birthday of a little girl with cystic fibrosis who had, through an arrangement with the foundation, traveled to Chicago a few months earlier to meet Bozo the Clown and watch the filming of his television program. Kelsey had grown particularly fond of the impish six-year-old and was delighted that the child seemed to be doing well for her seventh birthday. She ordered a balloon bouquet to be sent to the child's home. She gave her own address for the billing. She would pay for this gift herself, as she did so many others whenever she could.

She'd just hung up when the phone buzzed under her hand. She answered it immediately, telling herself it probably wasn't Cole, not yet.

But it was. "Hi, Kelsey. I'm on my way into another meeting, but Alice said you'd called. Is anything wrong?"

Disappointed that he didn't have time to chat, Kelsey quickly assured him that nothing was wrong. "I just wanted to remind you that I'm speaking at a fund-raiser tonight. I wasn't sure you'd remember, since we didn't mention it this morning."

His sigh carried through the lines. "Yeah, I'd forgotten. I was hoping to see you tonight."

"I'm sorry. It will probably be late when I get home. Would you like to come to dinner tomorrow night? I make a mean lasagna."

"That sounds good—no, damn it, I can't. I've got a boring reception to attend. Why don't you go with me?" he asked impulsively. "It won't be nearly as boring if you're with me."

Regretfully, she turned him down. "Oh, Cole, I can't. I'm keeping Jared tomorrow night."

"Is that really necessary? It's not as if you haven't done more than your share of baby-sitting for your sister."

"I've kept him because I wanted to, not because I'm trying to meet a quota," she retorted rather curtly, not liking his tone. "And I didn't keep him last night, nor will I tonight because of this fund-raiser. I've already promised Lauren I'd watch him tomorrow night."

"So we'll hire a sitter."

"No. I gave my word."

"Fine. Then I guess I'll see you later in the week, whenever you have time to work me into your schedule."

He was obviously annoyed. "Don't be that way, Cole," she said quietly. "You know this isn't an easy time for me or for Lauren."

He was silent for a moment, then conceded. "I know. I'm sorry. I just want to be with you."

"I want to be with you, too."

"I'm glad you called, Kelsey. But I really have to go. They're waiting for me."

"All right. Oh, one more thing, Cole."

"Yes?"

She could tell he was trying to hide his impatience to get to his meeting. Though she wasn't sure he'd appreciate what she had to say, she took a deep breath and blurted out the news. "Your father showed some improvement last night. The doctors are cautiously optimistic about his condition. They're planning to operate on Monday."

"Oh. Well, I guess your sister must be relieved."

"Yes." She didn't know why she'd hoped he'd sound more pleased, nor why she was disappointed that he didn't.

"I've really got to go, Kelsey. I'll call you, okay?"

"Sure. 'Bye, Cole."

He hung up without saying goodbye. Kelsey replaced her own receiver slowly, then pressed her fingertips to her increasingly pounding head, hoping she'd fight off the headache—and her sudden depression—in time to be sparkling and witty for the fund-raiser that evening.

Something told her it wasn't going to be easy.

Chapter Nine

"All right, that'll wrap it up. Murphy, I want those cost projections as soon as you can get them. No excuses."

"Yes, sir. First thing in the morning. No later."

Cole nodded without looking at the man, or any of the others quietly and quickly leaving the conference room. He knew they weren't wasting time getting away from him. He hadn't exactly been in a cheery mood during the extended meeting. Not that he ever was, exactly, but he'd been particularly short-tempered this morning. Fairly or not, he blamed that on Kelsey. He'd spent a miserable, lonely, near sleepless night because of her, missing her, worrying that she was becoming too important to him. No woman had ever interfered with his concentration at work before. He didn't like it at all that this woman did.

"Should I kneel at your feet to request your indulgence in signing these contracts?"

The dry, faintly chiding voice brought Cole's head up abruptly. He narrowed his eyes at the older man facing him in challenge. "Knock it off, Bob."

The attorney tossed a sheaf of papers on the table in front of Cole and sank into one of the recently abandoned chairs nearby. "I got here just in time to hear the end of that meeting. A real sweetheart today, aren't you?"

Cole growled something unintelligible and pulled a gold pen out of the breast pocket of his jacket. "What am I signing? And what are you doing delivering papers for signatures? Don't you have clerks for that sort of thing?"

"Yep. Thought I'd see if you could break away for lunch."

He'd been scanning the papers Herrington hadn't deemed it necessary to identify. At the casual invitation, Cole looked up suspiciously. "Why?"

Bob lifted an eyebrow in exaggerated innocence. "Is it so unusual I'd want to have lunch with you? It's not as if we don't eat together fairly regularly."

"True. Which means I know you well enough to tell when you're conning me. What is it you really want, Herrington?"

Bob sighed and shook his head. "The boy wounds me," he murmured.

"Bob..." Cole made sure the warning was very plain in the softly drawled syllable.

Dropping the pretense, Bob grimaced. "Your mother called me yesterday. Your grandfather—Grayson—called this morning. Both of them want to know whether you've given any money to your father's brat—their words—or his sister-in-law, with whom, they believe, you're having a torrid affair."

His jaw tensing, Cole very carefully laid down his pen. "And just why did they think you'd know anything about it if I had given them money?"

"Your mother seems to think I'm involved in some way. Said you'd mentioned me in connection with the child. I assume you mentioned that we were dining together the night Ms. Campbell confronted you."

"Damn."

"Belinda's concerned about you, Cole. She said she believes you've been taken in by a pretty face and a hard-luck story. I pointed out, of course, that you're not so gullible. She said normally she would agree but you've been acting out of character for the past week or so."

Cole slammed his fist against the heavy walnut conference table, his flashpoint temper igniting. "Damn them! The least they could have done was come to me. I hate it when people go behind my back in matters concerning me!"

Bob prudently remained silent, his fingers tented in front of him as he sat back in the chair, waiting for the first heat of Cole's anger to abate.

Cole took a deep breath to help him regain at least partial control. "What about my other grandfather? Have the Saxons gotten involved, as well?"

"No. Belinda and Harold have chosen not to tell your paternal grandparents about Paul's son. They seem to think it would only hurt them."

"Bull. They're afraid they'd want to see him. Worried that Paul may somehow work himself back into their good graces. That wouldn't sit well with the Grayson pride. They want Paul to suffer for the rest of his life for what he did."

Herrington seemed fascinated by Cole's imprudent words. "Does this mean you're beginning to understand why Paul left?"

Scowling, Cole shook his head forcefully. "No, of course not. If he wasn't happy with the way the family worked, he should have had the guts to stand up to them. Instead he ran away like a scared, sulky kid. You can bet I'll let them know how *I* feel about their interference."

"Yes, I'm sure you will," Bob replied equably. "You've always been a strong man, Cole, even before you should have been a man. Not everyone has that strength. Paul and I went to school together, you know. It was always difficult for him to stand up for himself, to deliberately hurt people."

"Easier to run away," Cole muttered.

"Perhaps. Or maybe walking away from the Grayson and Saxon empires took more courage than he'd ever had to call upon before. And maybe you can't understand because you've never wanted anything desperately enough to give up everything else to have it. The way Paul must have wanted his freedom."

Cole cocked his head and glared suspiciously at the man he'd called a friend for so many years. "You sound like you approve of what he did."

"Leaving you? No. I have kids of my own. No force on earth or in hell could have made me walk away from them when they were young and needed me. Even now that they're grown and self-reliant, for that matter. But then, my circumstances were different from Paul's. No one can say what he'd do in another man's place, Cole. Not even you."

"He left me." And this time even Cole heard the pain in his voice, the bewildered, aching resentment of a boy betrayed by the father he'd loved and admired. He flinched from the too-telling glimpse of self-revelation and picked up the pen again, scrawling his name at the bottom of the unread contracts, his trust in Bob obviously unshaken. And then he stood and shoved the pen back in its pocket. "You said something about lunch," he said abruptly. "I've got an hour. Where do you want to eat?"

Unperturbed by Cole's curtness, Bob stood and slid the contracts into his thin leather briefcase. "You choose."

"Fine." Cole headed for the door, followed closely by Bob. He nodded in approval when his secretary met them in the hallway, obviously looking for him, her hands full of telephone messages. "Alice, tell Fred to meet me downstairs. We're going to lunch."

"Yes, sir. Um . . . these messages . . . ?"

"Just handle everything until I get back."

"Yes, sir."

"Thanks, Alice."

The secretary hurried away to alert the chauffeur that their employer was on his way down. Cole punched the elevator call button, speaking without looking over his shoulder. "Bob?"

"Yes, Cole?"

"I don't want to talk about this anymore today, okay?"

"Whatever you say, Cole." The attorney's voice was suspiciously bland.

"The shrimp's excellent today," Bob commented lazily, making an effort to carry on a mostly one-sided conversation over lunch.

Hardly tasting his own meal, Cole chewed grimly, only nodding at Bob's words, as he had for the twenty minutes or so since they'd sat down to eat. Dull anger at his mother's actions seethed inside him. And he still found himself fighting thoughts of Kelsey, unbidden memories of their night together.

Had she missed him last night, as he'd missed her? Had she lain awake, remembering? Was she thinking of him even now?

"So, are you?"

Blinking, Cole frowned across the table at Bob, who seemed to be concentrating on his lunch. "Am I what?"

"Are you having a torrid affair with Kelsey Campbell?"

Cole choked and reached for his iced tea. "Damn it, I said I didn't want to talk about this anymore today," he complained, after taking a long swallow.

"I wasn't talking about your father," Herrington pointed out mildly, looking faintly amused at Cole's reaction to his question. "I asked about you and Kelsey. You seemed quite taken with her the night she found us at Brandreth's. And according to your mother, you've been seeing her since."

"I've seen her a few times," Cole admitted without looking up from his plate.

"And?"

"And—it's none of your business."

"I liked her, Cole."

Disarmed, Cole sighed. "Yeah. I do, too."

"She seems dedicated to the organization she works for."

Cole smiled wryly. "Oh, yeah. She's even gotten me involved a couple of times." He told Bob about the fishing trip the past Saturday, finding that his pleasure in Ronnie's excitement still lingered. He was keeping his word about having the fish mounted. He'd checked on it only that morning, reminding the taxidermist that speed was critical. Cole wanted the boy to enjoy his trophy for as long as possible—and he was willing to pay to see that he did.

At first Bob seemed astonished by Cole's role in fulfilling the boy's wish, and then he was greatly pleased. "Must have been something to see his face," he murmured.

Picturing Ronnie's smile, Cole nodded. "Yeah. It was. It made me understand why Kelsey keeps doing what she does."

"She sounds like a very special young woman."

Cole remembered that he'd called her that, himself, just before he'd kissed her the first time. "Yeah. She is."

"She still after you to visit Paul?"

Cole's faint smile vanished. "She accepts my right to decide for myself. She hasn't nagged me about it."

"Still, it must be awkward for the two of you. She seemed quite fond of Paul."

"She is. And she's very close to her sister."

"But it's not a problem between you?"

Exhaling deeply, Cole pushed his plate away. "It's a problem," he admitted. "As you said, it's a very awkward situation."

"Would it be so hard for you to see him, just once? For your sake, as well as Kelsey's?"

Cole leaned his elbows on the table and stared at his hands. "Damn it, Bob, you don't think I've asked myself that a dozen times? I waited in the hospital lobby while Kelsey visited him Monday night and I tried to make myself go up—but I couldn't. I broke into a cold sweat just thinking about it. I kept telling myself I'd only have to stay a minute, let the guy say whatever has been on his mind, then I could leave with a clear conscience. Paul would be satisfied—or so he's said, Kelsey would be pleased, maybe her sister would quit looking at me like I'm some sort of heartless monster. But I couldn't do it."

"Because you still can't face the pain. You've buried it so deep over the years that you're afraid to dig it up, afraid of what you'll feel if you do."

"You think it isn't clawing its way out anyway?" Cole asked bitterly. "Just when I think I've got a handle on it, something else happens. Did you know that Paul had tried to contact me when I was a kid, that my mother and grandparents conspired to keep me away from him? I'm thirty-four years old and I found that out for the first time Monday, when Mother let it slip."

"So now you feel you've been betrayed again. Not only by your father, but by your mother and grandparents."

"I don't know what I think anymore," Cole answered wearily. "Damn it, things were okay until Kelsey came looking for me, bringing this all out in the open again."

"Were you really happy a month ago, six months ago? Or were you just going through the motions, working sixteen-hour days and wasting time with an occasional woman who meant nothing to you? Is that the way you want to spend the rest of your life, Cole?"

No. Now that he'd met Kelsey, he didn't think he could ever go back to a choice between an empty bed or even emptier sex. So what the hell was he supposed to do? It looked like the only way he and Kelsey had a chance was for him to face up to his father. Funny, Cole had scorned Paul for his cowardice. Yet he'd been doing the same thing. Running away from something too painful to confront.

Slowly his eyes lifted to the kind gray ones watching him steadily from across the table. "I don't...I don't know what to do, Bob," he said quietly, his jaw clenched with the difficulty of the admission.

The older man nodded his understanding. "It's the first time in your life you've felt that way, isn't it, Cole? I think it's probably past time you allow yourself to see that you're only human, that you've got the same weaknesses as the rest of us poor mortals. But I've known you since you were just a kid, son, and I know you're a good man. A strong man. You'll make the right decision."

"I wish I could be as certain of that."

"Give yourself a chance." Bob glanced at his watch. "I'd better be going. I'll take a cab back to the office from here."

"Don't be ridiculous. Fred and I will drop you off." Cole reached for his wallet. "Lunch is on me. Sorry I wasn't better company today."

"You're forgiven."

"Bob." Cole cleared his throat and briefly met his friend's eyes before looking away. "Thanks."

"Anytime, Cole. Tell Kelsey hello for me, will you? And bring her over for dinner some night. I think Hannah will like her."

"Hannah will love her. She's been after me to find a nice girl ever since it was obvious that your girls weren't interested in going out with their dad's friend."

"Hmmph. My girls are too good for you and you know it."

"Oh? I suppose the biker Janice has been dating is more your idea of son-in-law material?"

Grinning at Bob's immediate and anticipated tirade, Cole followed him out of the restaurant, part of his mind still on the conversation that had made him question his own feelings about the past, as well as his plans for the present and future.

Kelsey missed Cole. She'd known him for only two weeks, had spent less than forty-eight hours away from him, and already she missed him.

She was in real trouble this time.

"That frown could only mean you're contemplating our budget."

Startled, Kelsey looked up to find Dylan leaning against the doorjamb of her office, watching her with his gentle smile. "You're early," she accused, glancing at her watch. "Nearly twenty minutes early. That's certainly not like you."

He chuckled and pushed himself away from the door, well aware of his usual tendency to be late for everything. "I found myself with some free time on my hands and decided I may as well spend it here. Besides, I have some news for you."

"What news?"

"Polly Patterson was in this morning for a physical."

Going still, Kelsey held her breath. Kelsey had met Polly when the child was five and facing very slim odds of living to see six. Despite all the dire predictions, Polly had recently celebrated her eighth birthday. Kelsey had sent a gift. "Well?" she prodded impatiently, when Dylan paused for dramatic effect.

"She looked great. Every test clear."

Kelsey stood slowly. "No sign of cancer?"

His grin deepened, his dark eyes glowing with satisfaction. "Not a one. One full year free of cancer. We'll watch her closely for the next few years, of course, but right now it looks like she's got a long, healthy life ahead of her."

Her own eyes filling with delighted tears, Kelsey rounded the desk and threw herself at him, hugging as much of his lanky frame as she could reach. "Oh, Dylan, that's wonderful! Thanks for telling me. I knew she's been fine, of course, but I've been worried about the results of her physical."

"Me, too," he admitted with a sigh, his hands locking comfortably behind her back. "That was one battle I didn't think we had a chance of winning. I never expected full recovery."

"But you fought for her, anyway. Just as you always do." She rose on tiptoe to give him an affectionate kiss on the cheek. "Proving again," she added, "that heroes don't necessarily ride white stallions or carry guns."

He flushed and started to say something along the lines of "aw, shucks, ma'am," but was forestalled by a cool male voice from behind him.

"Am I interrupting something?"

Kelsey knew that voice immediately. Her nerve endings quivering to attention, she drew away from Dylan and automatically smoothed her dress. "Hello, Cole."

Dylan turned, as well, his eyes lighting up when he saw the man who'd already contributed generously to their organization and could well prove a frequent source of funding in the future. "Nice to see you again, Saxon."

Oblivious, as he so often was, to the tension in the air around him, he smiled at Cole and then Kelsey, obviously pleased with the visit. She realized in mild exasperation that it hadn't even occurred to him that Cole hadn't been pleased at finding her in Dylan's arms. Sometimes Dylan could be so dense, she thought, before turning her irritation to Cole. Did he have to stand there looking so...so damned belligerent? "This is a surprise, Cole. I wasn't expecting you."

"No."

Now what was that supposed to mean? Frustrated, she tried to read his expression. She may as well have tried to read a statue. "Dylan just gave me some very good news about one of his patients, a little girl we provided a wish for several years ago. It looks as though she's completely recovered, against all odds."

Cole's frown lightened fractionally. "That is good news," he conceded, obviously trying to decide whether it justified physical contact in celebration.

The sound of a door opening in the reception area behind Cole made Dylan step forward. "That will be Billie. Our Wednesday afternoon clerical volunteer," he added for Cole's benefit. "Excuse me, I have a few instructions to give her before we leave."

Cole stepped into Kelsey's office to give Dylan room to pass through the doorway. Dylan closed the door behind him as he left, leaving Kelsey to wonder if he'd been as oblivious to undercurrents as she'd mentally accused him of being.

"You're leaving?" Cole asked.

"In a few minutes. Dylan and I are speaking to a women's volunteer organization this afternoon. They're taking us on as a project and we're supposed to give them some rudimentary training in working with our foundation."

She wanted very badly to kiss him. Thinking longingly of the kisses—and so much more—they had shared Monday night, she cleared her throat and tried to concentrate on anything else. "I thought you were going to be very busy today."

"I am. I'm supposed to be in a meeting in less than half an hour."

"Then what are you doing here?"

"I found myself in need of something."

"What?" she asked, confused by the sudden change in his voice.

It took him only three steps to reach her. Only a moment to draw her into his arms. "This," he murmured.

"This" was a kiss that nearly short-circuited her body's life-support systems. Her pulse went wild, her breathing irregular, her knees threatened to buckle. She was clinging to his forearms when he finally raised his head, and she wasn't at all sure that she'd remain upright if she released him. She thought it safest not to try.

"You..." She had to clear her throat again to speak clearly. "You came all the way across town for a kiss?"

He was smiling now, for the first time since he'd surprised her with Dylan. Even the smile was dangerous—very male, very predatory, very much satisfied with her reaction to his kiss.

She was in a whole lot of trouble, she thought again, but this time with a fatalistic awareness that it was already too late to pull back. It had probably been too late for her since their eyes had met in the lobby of his office building only two weeks earlier.

"Since you went to all that trouble..." she murmured, not bothering to finish the sentence. Instead, she slipped her arms around his neck and tugged his mouth back down to hers.

He seemed to be thoroughly pleased with her cooperation.

Kelsey couldn't have said how much time passed before the door opened and Dylan entered, not at all flustered at walking in on a sizzling embrace. "Time we headed out, isn't it, Kelsey?" he asked cheerfully.

Wanting very much to strangle him—and rather amused that Cole looked as though he shared the impulse—Kelsey slowly drew back and moistened her well-kissed lips. She'd have to repair her makeup in the car, she thought. She smiled at Cole. "I'll see you tonight?" And then immediately remembered, "No, you have plans for tonight. I'd forgotten."

"I'll call you tomorrow," he promised, looking at her a minute longer as though he were reluctant to leave. And then he flicked a glance at Dylan before looking back at her. "Behave yourself," he ordered lightly, touching her cheek with the fingertips of his right hand.

"You, too."

He was gone a minute later. Kelsey took a deep, unsteady breath and turned to Dylan, who was watching her with a grin. "Well?" she asked, resigned to his teasing.

"Aren't you going beyond the call of duty in recruiting contributors, Kelsey?" he responded with exaggerated innocence.

She didn't find that particularly funny, especially since Cole had once implied something similar, though she'd quickly disabused him of that impression. "We'd better be going. We'll be late."

"He seems quite nice, Kelsey," Dylan said, dropping the teasing as he watched her gather her purse and thin briefcase.

"He can be," she agreed wryly. "If it suits him."

"Sounds like you have some reservations."

"By the carload," she agreed, looking over her shoulder at him as she headed for the door. "But they don't seem to be stopping me from getting involved with him."

"I understand that love isn't always logical and orderly," he said gently. "That's why I've always avoided that particular condition, myself."

"Probably a good idea," she mused aloud. "Much safer all around." Dylan patted her shoulder in silent agreement.

He hadn't liked finding her in another man's arms. In fact, he had hated it.

Glaring at the stack of papers on his desk, Cole tried to concentrate on work, though his thoughts seemed determined to stray. Always in one direction. Kelsey's direction.

If he hadn't already known he was getting more deeply involved with her than he'd ever been before, the surge of sheer fury he'd felt at seeing her kiss another man would have told him. He couldn't remember ever being jealous before, not cold, deadly, primitively jealous. No woman had ever mattered enough for that particular waste of energy.

Until Kelsey.

Two weeks, he thought in mild amazement, staring at the calendar on one corner of his desk. He'd known her two weeks. He'd had entire affairs that hadn't lasted that long. And yet every minute he spent with Kelsey took him deeper under her spell.

It was definitely time to do something about it. Either pull back now, or make sure she knew he intended to be the only man whose kisses she sought for some time to come.

Since pulling back no longer seemed to be an option, it looked like he'd better get busy staking his claim.

But first he had something else to do. Something that had been bothering him for several days.

Chapter Ten

Cole didn't go straight home from work that evening. Nor did he attend the mayor's reception for some ambassador from an eastern European country, though he knew his mother and maternal grandparents would be there and were expecting him to join them. Instead, he found himself standing on the step of the Saxon family manor, one finger on the doorbell as he wondered what the hell he was going to say once he was inside.

"Mr. Saxon!" The thin, nearly bald butler was obviously surprised after opening the door. "We weren't expecting you this evening."

"Yes, I know. Are my grandparents in, Billings?"

"Yes, sir. They're in the family room. I'll tell them you're here."

"No need. I'll announce myself."

The long-time retainer nodded respectfully. "Yes, sir."

As he strode down the magnificent hallway toward the family room, Cole briefly wondered how Kelsey would respond to the old-world formality of his grandparents' life-style. He suspected she would find it greatly amusing, doubted that she'd be easily intimidated—by wealth, or anything else, for that matter.

His grandmother looked up first when he entered the room. She immediately closed the trendy bestseller she'd been reading. "Why, Cole! What a nice surprise."

His attention drawn away from the twenty-four-hour cable news channel he was addicted to, Phillip Saxon stood, discreetly assisting himself with the arms of his chair. Rapidly approaching his eighties, Saxon refused to concede that his health was failing, still standing as tall and straight as he had thirty years earlier, though the impressive physique once maintained by strenuous exercise was now thin and occasionally unsteady. "What are you doing here, boy? Thought you were going to that blasted dull reception the mayor's throwing tonight."

"I was supposed to," Cole agreed. "But I skipped it."

"Can't say I blame you," his grandfather said with a smile. "That sort of thing always bored the hell out of me. Especially when I was as young as you are. So what are you doing visiting these old folks when you've got a free night? Why aren't you doing the town with a pretty lady?"

"Phillip," Eudora Wallingford Saxon chided with a long-suffering roll of her faded blue eyes. "Honestly. Leave the boy alone. Sit down, Cole, and tell us why you're here. Would you like a cup of tea?"

"Hell, no, he doesn't want tea. Scotch, that's Cole's drink, isn't it, boy? Help yourself."

"No, nothing right now, thank you." Cole waited until his grandfather had settled back into his chair before taking a seat on an uncomfortable sofa facing them both. "I need to talk to you. Both of you."

Reading something in his voice, Eudora set her book aside, her eyes locked on her grandson's face. "What is it, Cole? What's wrong?"

Cole ran a finger beneath his collar and plunged in. "It's about Paul."

Eudora flinched, casting a quick, nervous glance at her husband. Phillip's face hardened into the stern mask that had quelled many an opposing attorney in the courtrooms in years past. "What about him?" he demanded harshly. "Has he been bothering you again?"

"He's...very ill, Grandfather. Possibly dying. I thought you should know."

He didn't miss Eudora's quick intake of breath, though her expression remained impassive. He looked to his grandfather. The older man's silver brows had drawn together in a frown. "What's wrong with him?"

"It's his heart. He's having surgery early next week, but I understand there's a chance he may not survive it."

"So what does he want from us? He doesn't need money."

Cole wasn't surprised, this time, to discover that Paul's circumstances were not unknown. After all, he'd been the only one kept in the dark over the years. Swallowing his anger, he kept his voice even. "He doesn't want anything from you that I know of. He's asked to see me."

"He called you?" Eudora inquired, leaning slightly forward.

Cole shook his head. "His...his sister-in-law approached me. I assume you know he married eighteen months ago?"

Phillip nodded grimly. "A woman nearly half his age."

"Yes. I've met her. She seems nice."

"A gold digger. Why else would she marry a man twenty-five years her senior?"

"According to her sister, she married him because she loves him."

Phillip snorted his skepticism. Eudora remained silent.

Again, Cole tugged at his tie. "Were you aware that Paul and his wife have a son?"

The older couple went utterly still. Cole had his answer. They hadn't known. It seemed the families' sources weren't quite as reliable as they'd believed.

"His name is Jared. He's just over three months old. I've seen him. He looks like a Saxon. Like me, I'm told."

"Paul...has a baby?" Eudora asked finally, in little more than a whisper.

Cole nodded.

"That's the most foolish thing I've ever heard," Phillip blustered. "A man his age. It's obscene." And then, "You say the boy looks like a Saxon?"

"He has the eyes. And the nose."

"This woman—Paul's wife. She's a good mother?" Eudora asked.

"Yes, I believe so. She's been spending a great deal of time at the hospital with Paul, but Kelsey—her sister—has been taking care of the boy. They're both devoted to him."

"You're claiming him as your brother?" Phillip asked bluntly.

Cole took a deep breath and nodded. "Yes. He'll need a man's guidance if...well, if something goes wrong."

Phillip nodded. "He should know what it means to be a Saxon. You'll bring the boy to us."

Cole hadn't expected that. He looked questioningly at his grandfather, aware that his grandmother was doing the same. "What do you mean? You want to see him?"

"Of course I want to see him," the older man snapped. "He's my grandson. Not his fault his father's an irresponsible fool."

Eudora made a muffled sound that might have been a protest.

Cole looked steadily at Phillip. "You won't take him away from Lauren. She's a good mother. She won't give him up."

"I didn't say I was going to try to take him away from her," Phillip retorted with asperity. "Hell, what kind of monster do you think I am, boy? I just want to make sure he's raised properly, that he has the opportunities he deserves as a scion of this family. Grayson won't like it, I imagine, but that can't be avoided."

"Cole, are you going to see him? Your father, I mean."

"I haven't decided, Grandmother," Cole answered hesitantly. "I've been thinking about it."

"You owe him nothing."

Cole nodded at his grandfather's hard words. "I know. But he is my father."

"He's our son," Phillip retorted, and Cole thought he heard just a trace of his own old pain. "That didn't stop him from walking away from us when he left his wife and boy. We haven't heard a word from him since. You know what that did to his mother?"

So many scars. So much pain. Did Paul bear them, as well? Cole found himself wondering. Did he ever regret all he'd lost when he'd walked away twenty-six years earlier? Did he wish he'd handled it differently, made changes without making such a sharp break? Or would it have been possible? Would the families have turned him away, regardless? Refused to accept Paul's decisions unless they coincided with their own wishes?

Had Paul truly felt that he'd had no other choice but to walk away?

So many questions. And only one man knew the answers. A man who may be dying, who may take those answers with him before Cole had a chance to hear them.

"You'll bring the boy to us," Phillip repeated, still occupied with thoughts of the newest Saxon heir.

"I'll think about it," Cole promised. "And I'll discuss it with his mother."

"You'll keep us informed? About Paul's condition?" Eudora asked quietly, her frail, spotted hands clasped in her lap.

Cole nodded. "I'd better be going. I'll talk to you tomorrow." He leaned over to kiss his grandmother's cheek.

And then he turned to his grandfather. And the question left his mouth before he'd even realized he was going to ask it. "Grandfather, what would you have done if I'd wanted to be a policeman rather than CEO of Grayson Shipping?"

Saxon was obviously startled. "A policeman? What on earth are you talking about, Cole?"

"It was just a question, Grandfather. I know I was given a choice between working for Grayson or going into the Saxon law firm. But what if I had wanted something else?"

"Don't be ridiculous, Cole. You were always too aware of your family responsibilities to fill your head with such nonsense. You had an obligation and you've handled it admirably. We're proud of you, boy."

"Would you have been proud of me if I'd chosen to wear a cop's uniform, instead?"

Phillip met his eyes without blinking. "Fortunately, that never became an issue."

It was, of course, all the answer Cole needed.

He felt strangely tired as he climbed behind the wheel of his car. And he knew there was only one place he could rest comfortably.

Jared was noisily unhappy, and Kelsey wasn't far from crying, herself. Holding him on her shoulder, she paced the living room, patting his diapered bottom and crooning. "I know your gums hurt and you want your mommy, Jared. She'll be home soon. So be good for Aunt Kelsey, okay?"

Jared screamed louder, his tiny fists pounding her shoulder, his body rigid in her arms.

Kelsey swallowed a sob and attempted a shaky lullaby. Not that her nephew seemed the least impressed with her singing.

The doorbell rang, cutting through a particularly lusty bawl. Since Lauren usually let herself in, Kelsey knew it wasn't her sister. She could only hope it wasn't an irate neighbor.

Balancing the baby in one arm, she used the other to pull open the door, too flustered to bother with asking for identification. Her eyes widened. "Cole!" He seemed to be making quite a hobby out of taking her by surprise. "I thought you had a reception to attend tonight."

"I skipped it." He'd raised his voice to be heard above Jared's cries. "I heard him all the way up the stairs. What's wrong with him?"

"I guess it's teething pain," Kelsey answered wearily, stepping back to allow Cole to enter. "I've tried the gel Lauren left, but it doesn't seem to be helping. He won't eat, and I've tried rocking and singing and...everything else, but nothing helps." She regretted the break in her voice that must surely have let him know exactly how close she was to tears.

"And you're exhausted." Cole shrugged out of his jacket and draped it over the back of a chair in a move that was becoming oddly familiar to her. And then he held out his arms. "Give him to me."

Jared screamed. Kelsey stared at Cole. "I...uh..."

Cole reached out and removed the baby from her arms. If he felt awkward he certainly didn't allow it to show. "Now, go do something for yourself. Take a break."

She hesitated, not at all sure he knew what he was doing. Jared hadn't even paused for breath during the transfer. "Can I get you anything?"

"No. I'm fine. Why don't you take a warm bath or something? You look beat."

She thought wryly that she probably looked as though she'd been dragged through a bramble bush. She automatically lifted a hand to her hair, wincing when she felt it standing on end. "Are you sure you—"

"I can handle it," he cut in firmly. "Now go."

With a shrug, she turned and headed gratefully for her bedroom.

Okay, she thought, he asked for it.

* * *

A warm bath sounded like the best idea she'd heard in ages. She turned on the faucets and liberally added the expensive bubble-bath powder she occasionally bought as a special treat for herself. She closed her eyes and inhaled deeply as the floral scent filled the steamy room. What luxury!

Stripping out of her shorts and T-shirt, she tossed them at the hamper, her underwear following immediately. And then she pushed the Play button on the small tape recorder she kept in the bathroom and sank to her neck in hot, soothing bubbles as Rachmaninoff's *Rhapsody* began to play quietly behind her. "Oh, yes," she moaned blissfully, closing her eyes.

Thanks to the music and the two closed doors between her and the living room, she couldn't even hear Jared crying now. Though she felt vaguely guilty at leaving Cole to deal with him alone, she knew she'd been very close to breaking. How could he have known how desperately she'd needed him tonight?

She leaned her head against a contoured plastic bath pillow designed for that purpose and allowed tension to leave her body on a long, deep sigh. And for the next ten minutes she didn't move, didn't open her eyes, didn't even think. Just soaked and rested and lost herself in the music flowing continuously from the tape player.

The tub gradually began to cool. She added more hot water, knowing she should get out but reluctant to give up the quiet peace. Poor Cole, she thought with a rueful smile. She hadn't even said hello. Hadn't kissed him or told him how very glad she'd been to see him. He was probably wishing right now that he'd gone to the boring reception, after all.

The bathroom door opened slowly. "Feeling better?" Cole asked, stepping in without bothering to ask permission, carrying two filled wineglasses.

Aware that the bubbles provided only scant protection, Kelsey cleared her throat and reminded herself that he'd seen her in less. "Yes. What did you do with Jared?"

"He's asleep. Out cold. I put him in the crib. I've left the bedroom door open so we can hear him if he cries again." He crossed the small room to perch on the edge of the tub, holding one of the wineglasses out to her.

She took it and lifted it to her lips. "Thanks," she murmured before taking the first sip.

He nodded and tasted his own wine cautiously. "Not bad," he admitted after a moment. "For last Monday's vintage," he added with a smile.

She laughed softly and looked up at him, "Cole. Thank you," she said again, and this time she wasn't referring to the wine.

Cradling his glass in his left hand, he reached out with his right to wipe a cluster of bubbles from her cheek. "Are you ready to talk now? What's wrong? What happened between the time I saw you at your office and now?"

"How did you know?" she asked blankly, staring up at him.

His smile was so tender it made her throat ache. "C'mon, honey, it takes more than a crying baby to put you in the shape you were in when I got here. Tell me what's wrong."

She was caught off guard by the casual endearment. She tried not to let him see that it had shaken her. "You're right. I received some bad news just before leaving the office today. After the good news about Polly, I guess I wasn't prepared for tragedy. Jared's tantrum just made it worse."

"What happened?"

"We lost one of our kids. He wanted very badly to meet his favorite television star. I had gotten an okay from the actor and was setting up the arrangements for early next week. Jeffrey seemed to be stable, but he turned critical last night and was gone by this afternoon."

Cole groaned. "I'm sorry, Kelsey."

"It's just so frustrating that he never got to meet his hero. If I'd known earlier—but he wouldn't tell us what he wanted. He was a sweet, unassuming child who made sure we knew what all the other kids in the ward wanted but would never ask for anything for himself. I visited him one morning last week and found him watching a tape of his favorite TV detective show. He told me then that he'd always wanted to meet the star. I went right to work on it, and the man turned out to be charming and very cooperative. If only we'd had more time..."

Cole stroked her cheek. "You did your best."

She sighed. "Yes." And then she reached up with soapy fingers and covered his hand against her cheek. "That wasn't the only thing that happened. Ronnie MacKenzie was hospitalized. He probably won't be going home again."

Cole's eyes darkened in automatic protest. "There's nothing they can do?"

"They're trying, of course. He begins a new chemotherapy treatment tomorrow."

"Is money a problem?"

"If you're asking if he's getting the best treatment available, you needn't worry. He is. There's only so much that can be done, Cole. Sometimes a patient survives this type of cancer. Usually they don't."

Cole looked away and cleared his throat violently. "Maybe you can handle this job. I don't know if I can."

It touched her that he was so tenderhearted with the kids. "You don't have to get personally involved, Cole. I won't ask you to participate again if it's too painful for you. I'd understand."

He sighed and looked back at her. "Yeah, you would, wouldn't you? You're so accustomed to going it alone."

"Not alone. Dylan and I have an entire army of volunteers who help us keep this going. And there are organizations like ours all over the country. I'm hardly the Lone Ranger, Cole."

He gave her a smile, trying to lighten her mood. "Just an ordinary hero-type, huh?" He'd obviously overheard her earlier words to Dylan, about heroes who didn't ride white stallions or carry guns.

As Dylan had, she flushed in embarrassment. "Hardly."

"What hospital is Ronnie in? I'd like to visit him."

She looked at him from beneath her lashes. "He and your father are in the same hospital."

He avoided her eyes and waited for her to say something else. He probably expected her to point out that he was willing to visit a child he'd met only once but had refused to see his own sick father. She wouldn't say that, of course. She'd promised him the decision would be his and she had no intention of nagging him to change his mind. She could only hope he'd do so on his own.

When it was obvious that Kelsey wasn't going to speak, Cole trailed his fingertips from her throat to the water that came just to the top of her half-submerged breasts. He swished his fingers in the water, causing the remaining bubbles to spread. "Kelsey. Are you aware that you're beginning to resemble a prune?"

She'd almost forgotten that she was lying naked in front of him, and that her bubbles were dissolving even as he spoke. She swallowed the last of her wine and handed him the glass. "If you'll move back, I'll get out before I complete the transformation."

He moved away, but not very far. When she stepped out of the tub and reached self-consciously for her towel, he was there, wrapping it around her, the wineglasses deposited by the sink and as quickly forgotten. Before she could say anything, he lifted her against his chest and kissed her deeply. "It seems like forever since we were alone together," he muttered against her lips, and then kissed her again.

She knew exactly how he felt. Already her body was remembering, straining toward him in longing for the fulfillment she'd found with him during their night together. The intensity of her feelings unnerved her. She was getting in too deep, she tried to tell herself. She wanted him too fiercely. Loved him too much.

As if there was anything she could do about it now.

Cole drew back slowly, with obvious reluctance. Worried about what he'd read in her eyes, she looked away. "I'd better get something on. Lauren will be here soon."

"I'll go check on the kid," he said, his voice husky. He picked up the wineglasses on his way out, leaving Kelsey to cling weakly to the countertop until her knees had regained sufficient strength to carry her into the bedroom.

She pulled on mint-green terry-cloth slacks and a matching peach-and-mint crewneck top, then ran a brush through her short hair. She'd washed away the faded makeup she'd worn earlier; she didn't bother to replace it, opting for a quick dab of peach gloss on her slightly kiss-swollen lips. She was only a few minutes behind Cole when she left the bedroom.

She found him sitting in an armchair, Jared on his knees. Jared stared in fascination at Cole, who had been talking quietly when Kelsey entered the room.

"What were you telling him?" she asked, smiling at the domestic picture the two brothers made. Hardly a conventional relationship, she thought, but she was beginning to believe it would work. Cole seemed to be developing a bond with the child that could prove a lasting one; for both their sakes, Kelsey hoped it would.

"I was just reminding him that I owe him a Porsche. That was the bribe I'd offered earlier if he'd take a nap and give me a few minutes alone with you."

"Well, it worked. Your brother is obviously the materialistic type."

Cole shook his head, looking rather dazed. "My brother. That sounds so strange."

"He *is* your brother," she pointed out gently. "Your half brother, anyway."

"Yes. He's a Saxon."

Kelsey wasn't sure she liked the way he said that. She suspected that Lauren would like it even less, had she heard him.

Jared made some of those interesting baby noises that aren't quite babbling and not quite fussing. In response, Cole looked back down at him, only to be the recipient of a full-blown grin.

Kelsey giggled when Cole couldn't help grinning in return, emphasizing the disarming resemblance between them.

"You're a very weird kid," he scolded the baby gently. "Half an hour ago you were driving your poor aunt crazy with a temper tantrum, and now you're grinning like a Cheshire cat."

Kelsey sat on the arm of the chair, reaching down to tickle Jared's fat cheek with one finger. "Please. No references to that story just now."

Cole looked at her with a grin. "Afraid he'll turn into a pig?"

Kelsey lifted an eyebrow in surprised admiration. "You've read *Alice's Adventures in Wonderland?*"

His smile only deepened. "Hasn't everyone?"

"You're a very complex man, Cole Saxon," she told him, only half teasing. "You're always surprising me."

"Just keeping you on your toes," he answered lightly.

She leaned over to kiss him, surprising both of them. "You certainly do that," she murmured.

The kiss lingered.

Both of them drew back sharply when the front door opened and Lauren walked in. She stopped abruptly when she saw Cole in the chair, her son in his lap, Kelsey at his arm. "Well. Isn't this cozy," she remarked coolly.

Kelsey immediately rose to her feet. "Cole's been helping me entertain Jared," she said, feeling ridiculously like a teenager caught necking with her boyfriend. "I think his gums are bothering him," she added. "He was quite cross earlier."

Lauren reached out to take the baby from Cole, holding him close. "Poor darling," she murmured.

Cole stood and pushed his hands into his pockets, and Kelsey wondered at how withdrawn he suddenly looked. Was this the way he appeared to everyone but her and the few others fortunate enough to really know him? How young had he been when he'd learned to mask his emotions so effectively? Had he begun when his father had left him, or even earlier?

He made an effort to ease the tension by speaking to Lauren, distantly polite. "How was Paul tonight?"

"Your *father*," Lauren replied, emphasizing the relationship, "is listed in serious, but stable condition. The operation is scheduled for Monday morning."

"I spoke to my grandparents earlier this evening," Cole told her. "The Saxons. They'd like to see their grandchild. I told them I'd discuss it with you."

Lauren immediately held her son more tightly. "Forget it."

Kelsey bit her lip to hold back a protest at Lauren's tone. This was between Lauren and Cole, she reminded herself, stepping back.

Cole's attention was focused solely on Lauren. "Why?"

"Because they'd probably try to take over Jared's life, the same way they tried to run Paul's. I don't want Jared ruined with too much money and an overinflated perception of the Saxon heritage."

Cole straightened slowly. Most people probably would have quailed at the look he gave Lauren, Kelsey thought, watching him. To her credit, Lauren faced him squarely, not backing down. Kelsey knew her sister would walk bravely through the flames of hell if she thought it necessary to protect her son.

"Your son should be proud of his heritage," Cole said, his words clipped. "The Saxon name is an old and honorable one. And he should have a chance to know his grandparents. You have no right to keep him from them."

"I have every right. He's my son." Lauren gave Cole a look that spoke volumes. "Jared doesn't need the Saxon wealth or power. He will grow up happy and loved for himself and his own worth, not as a symbol of a powerful old family. He will be free to choose his own path in life, a career he wants, a wife he loves, not a socially-advantageous match arranged from childhood."

She lifted her chin even higher before continuing. "Do you really think I'd want him to grow up to be like you? A man so hard, so entrenched in tradition and family expectations that you won't even spend a few minutes with your own father at what may very well be his deathbed?"

"Damn it, I'm tried of being treated like the villain here!" Cole told her with barely suppressed fury. "I wasn't the one who walked out twenty-six years ago! Now I'm supposed to pretend it didn't happen? Tell me, how would you feel if he did the same thing to you and your boy that he did to my mother and me?"

Obviously startled by Cole's unexpected vehemence, Lauren studied him in silence for several long, tense moments. Her voice was strained when she finally spoke. "He had his reasons, Cole. If you'd only let him tell you—"

"Look, I know what he's going to say, all right? He hated his job, he didn't love my mother, he didn't think he could win in a fight for custody or visitation rights. Maybe he did what he felt he had to do. During the past few days I've learned some things that were kept from me before. Now I need time to think about them, to decide how I feel about what happened."

Lauren nodded coolly. "While you're deciding how you feel, you might keep in mind that you may not have very long to brood. There are no guarantees that Paul will make it through the surgery. He can't survive at all without it.''

"I'm aware of that. And I'm sorry. I wish things were different.''

"That does a lot of good, doesn't it?'' Lauren asked bitterly. She turned to Kelsey. "Are Jared's things ready?''

"Packed in the diaper bag,'' Kelsey answered. "Do you need help getting to the car with him?''

"No. Jared and I will manage just fine.'' It was very clear that she wasn't just referring to the walk to her car.

Cole stood silently to one side as Lauren left. Lauren didn't speak to him again, though she thanked Kelsey for watching Jared and promised to talk to her the next day. And then she left, and Kelsey and Cole were alone, the tension between them thick enough to touch.

Chapter Eleven

Kelsey closed the door behind Lauren and locked it. She turned to find Cole watching her with a hard, shuttered expression.

"Well?" he asked finally. "Don't you want to take up where your sister left off? Tell me what a selfish jerk I am?"

"No," she answered gently, her heart aching for him, for Lauren, for all of them.

He crossed his arms, tucking his hands into the crooks of his elbows in an oddly defensive gesture. "Why not? It's what you think of me, isn't it?"

She stepped closer. "No. I'm not saying Lauren doesn't have reason to feel the way she does. But she doesn't know you the way I do. All she's seen is the facade you show everyone else. She hasn't yet learned that there's a warm, generous man inside who is capable of both gentleness and deep caring."

Cole looked startled. And shaken. "Kelsey."

"It would be very easy to love that man," she continued bravely, her eyes locked with his. "*If* he were capable of offering love in return. If he ever learns that he can be vulnerable, can admit to fear and pain. If he learns that sometimes people make mistakes and they pay dearly for them, but they can be forgiven because they're only human.

"I think Paul made a very big mistake twenty-six years ago, Cole. I think walking away from his son was the wrong thing to do, and I know you've suffered because of his weakness. But I also believe that you'll be making a mistake if you refuse to meet him halfway now, if you wait too long to decide it's something you need to do to get on with your life. I think you'll pay as dearly as Paul has if he dies before you have a chance to see him again."

Cole caught his breath and turned away. But before he did, Kelsey saw the truth in his eyes. Stunned, she took another step forward, laying her hand on his arm. "Cole?"

"Look, I don't want to see him, all right? There's nothing left to say. I've hated him for twenty-six years for what he did to me."

"And you're afraid of losing that hatred, aren't you?" she asked slowly, putting her new suspicion in words. "You're clinging to it now just as you have since you were seven, because it's easier to hate him than to love him and lose him. Now you're afraid he's dying and you don't want to be hurt again."

His arm was rigid beneath her hand. "What is this, amateur psychology? You don't know what you're talking about."

"Cole—"

In a sudden surge of fury, he shook her hand off and whirled away from her. "Damn it, would you just leave me *alone!*"

She fell back as if he'd slapped her. The pain was that great. "Cole, I—"

"It's always so easy for you, isn't it?" he went on, as if he couldn't stop the words. His eyes had a curiously blind look to them. "You come in like a fairy godmother, waving your magic wand and granting wishes, and then you bask in the gratitude and adulation. You're not the one who has to deal with the suffering or the pain or the empty rooms full of bittersweet memories after the child is gone. You don't know what it's like to be the one left behind."

"You think not?" she threw back, her own temper igniting. "My mother is dead, Cole. No matter how badly I may want to see her again, I can't, because she's gone and nothing I can do will bring her back. My father's off somewhere on a job that will always be more important, more interesting to him than his children. He sends me a card on my birthday and at Christmas and visits when he passes through town. You think it doesn't hurt to be in the same room with him and know he's counting the minutes until he can be off on another big job?"

Her breath caught in a sob, but she ignored the tears coursing down her cheeks, her anger as deep as her pain. "And do you really think I don't care when those kids die? Do you really think I don't bleed every time? That I won't think of Jeffrey every time I walk by his hospital ward and remember how sweetly he smiled at me when I... when I promised him that I'd help him meet his hero?"

His face pale, Cole ground out a curse between his clenched teeth. He took an awkward step toward her, his hand going out to her. The jerky, uncharacteristically graceless movement bumped him into a small table beside him. Kelsey moved instinctively as a little ceramic cat she'd had for years rocked and then fell, but she was too late to catch it, as was Cole. The cat broke into pieces at his feet.

Appalled, Cole looked at the shards and then slowly up at her. The haunted expression in his eyes twisted her heart. Both of them knew that twenty-six years of icy control had shattered as jaggedly as the scattered bits of pottery. And both wondered if Cole would ever be able to patch it back together.

He tried. Drawing himself up straight, he cleared his throat and attempted to mask his emotions. "Kelsey, I'm sorry. I shouldn't have said those things. I didn't mean them."

She couldn't bear to see him withdraw from her. She'd rather have his anger than this brittle distance. Without stopping to think, she threw herself against him, her arms going around his waist. "It doesn't matter, Cole. I know why you said them. Please don't pull away from me. Hold me."

She heard the desperation in her own voice. Something told her that if she let him leave now, if he succeeded in rebuilding that shell between them, she'd never have another chance to get inside it. She prayed it wasn't already too late.

It seemed like forever before he touched her, lightly at first, tentatively, his fingers just brushing her back. And then he made a sound that could have been a curse or a groan, and his arms closed around her so tightly she could hardly breathe. She didn't complain. She was holding him just as fervently. "Oh, Cole."

One large hand tangled in her hair, pulling her face to his with little gentleness. "Kelsey," he muttered thickly, his breath hot against her emotion-chilled skin. "I need you. God, how I need you."

His mouth covered hers before she could tell him that he had only to reach out to find her there for him.

He'd had no time to regain the control he'd lost in their emotional confrontation. Its absence was strongly evident now as he ravaged her mouth, his hands moving over her with heated demand. She could tell that he was trembling. She trembled, too, even as she responded with a fire of her own.

He swept her into his arms without releasing her mouth. Clutching at his powerful shoulders, she was intensely aware of the difference in their sizes. He was so big, so solid, so very male. She'd never been so conscious of her own small stature, her own weakness in comparison to his strength. And yet there was no fear, no intimidation in her mental comparisons. Only a profound satisfaction, a quiet rejoicing in her femininity. And the deep contentment that came with the knowledge that this big, strong, powerful man wanted her so badly that he trembled when he held her.

It was just as well there were no buttons or zippers on her pullover top or elastic-waist slacks. In his rush of impatience, Cole would have probably dispensed with them permanently. As it was, he had her out of her clothes almost before she was aware of it. He stripped without ceremony and tumbled with her to the bed, his mouth moving on hers once more.

She didn't know what furies drove him then, why he seemed so desperately intent on driving her slowly, inexorably insane. She had no time to try to analyze his actions, but could only cling to him as an anchor in the sensual storm he created. Unable to form a complete thought, she arched and writhed wildly beneath him, gasping, incoherent sounds torn from her throat by his stunning caresses. She tried to tell him to slow down, to allow her to savor, to memorize each new sensation. She wanted to urge him to hurry, to grant the release her overloaded nerve endings were pleading for. She could only say his name, over and over, the sounds little more than ragged moans.

His mouth was on her breast, his hand moving between her legs when the powerful tremors rocked her, beginning without warning and making her arch and cry out, her fingers clenching in the sheet beneath her. He gave her little time to recover before he was pushing her toward another pinnacle, his mouth moving hungrily down her abdomen to replace his fingers. She buried her fingers in his hair with a half-formed intention to pull him away, but somehow found herself holding him there instead. And moments later she was arching again, shuddering heavily, her breath catching in heaving gasps.

Only then did Cole pull himself upward, his mouth seeking hers as he fitted himself between her trembling thighs. He thrust deeply into her at the same moment his tongue plunged into her mouth.

His movements became more frantic, his need more desperate. She stroked him fiercely, murmuring his name, wanting only to soothe the pain she sensed in him, though she didn't completely understand its origin. And when he stiffened and groaned her name, she buried her face in his throat, holding him so tightly her arms ached, holding him until the spasms had passed and he lay bonelessly across her, his face hidden against her hair, his ragged, gasping breaths sounding almost like sobs.

She loved him. She loved him so desperately. She could almost feel his pain as her own. Tears dripped slowly down her cheeks as she stared at the darkened ceiling, still holding him.

Two weeks, and her life had changed forever. She suspected that his had, as well, though she couldn't have begun to speculate on whether she would be a permanent part of his future.

As if in protest of even the possibility of losing him, her arms tightened around him and her tears began to fall faster. She hid her face in the juncture of his neck and shoulder, determined to regain her composure by the time he recovered his own.

Kelsey could almost feel Cole's control returning and, with it, his chagrin at its temporary loss. She wasn't surprised that his expression was shuttered when he finally lifted his head from her throat, though memories of the passing storm lingered in his eyes. She raised a hand to stroke his cheek, refusing to allow him to pull too far away. "Where are you going?" she asked, her voice still husky.

"It's late. You're tired. I should—"

"—stay right where you are," she finished for him, smiling. "Unless, of course, you'd rather go?"

Cole hesitated, and she knew he was struggling with his own internal debate. She held her breath. When he nodded, she released it silently. "I'll stay," he said a bit gruffly. "If you want me to."

"I want you to."

He sighed and shifted heavily to lie back down beside her. "Then c'mere," he ordered, pulling her into his arms.

She didn't resist. She snuggled against him, one knee bent to rest on his leg, her hand lying on his chest, just over his strongly beating heart.

They lay quietly for a time. And then, sensing that Cole was lying awake, staring at the ceiling and lost in his own thoughts, Kelsey started to talk. She didn't plan her words, had nothing of particular import to say, but she wanted to distract him from whatever had his arms so rigid around her, his brow so deeply furrowed. And she succeeded.

He began to relax when she told him she'd once wanted to be Miss America, but had changed her mind when she'd decided she was too short and had nothing to do for the talent competition. He smiled when she told him about the time she'd forgotten her lines in a school play and had burst into song instead. She'd gotten terrible reviews, she added morosely. He even chuckled when she talked about her first boyfriend, a shy, studious type with flaming red hair and a fascinating talent for wiggling his prominent ears.

"My first date was arranged by my grandparents—the Graysons," Cole said somewhat hesitantly.

When Kelsey immediately urged him to tell her about it, he did. Carefully at first, choosing words designed to mask his real emotions. At her prompting, he soon dropped his guard and talked almost as frankly as she did, telling her how nervous he'd been, how convinced that any mistakes he made on that first all-important date would be broadcast among every old, influential family in Savannah. At fifteen, that first date with a suitable young lady had seemed the very threshold to "future success."

"What horrible pressure to put on a boy!" Kelsey protested indignantly.

"The pressure was all in my own mind, of course," he assured her. "No one actually said anything."

Didn't they? Kelsey wondered skeptically, but bit her tongue. "Did you kiss her good-night?" she asked instead, her tone teasing.

"On a first date with a 'good girl' whose family had been connected to mine since James Oglethorpe founded Savannah? Of course not."

"You had a lousy time, didn't you?"

"You could say that."

Crossing her hands on his chest, Kelsey rested her chin on them and looked up at him with a smile. "You should have waited and had your first date with me. I'd have shown you a good time, sailor."

He tweaked her nose, his easy grin delighting her. "You were five when I went out on my first date," he reminded her.

"Details," she dismissed airily, earning herself a quick kiss.

She trailed a fingertip through the hair on his chest. "Have you ever been in love, Cole?"

"No." He hadn't even stopped to think about it.

"Why not?"

He shrugged beneath her. "Never the right person at the right time, I suppose."

"But you've had—mistresses?" She almost cringed at the old-fashioned word, but could think of no other term for it.

He shifted restlessly. "Kelsey."

"You have, haven't you? Women you were involved with for a while, both of you knowing it wouldn't last."

"I haven't been a monk, if that's what you mean."

"I know that. I just have the impression that your past relationships have been rather cold. Did you choose your women because they were beautiful and knew the score? Did you give them things—diamonds and furs and money?"

Again, he squirmed, and she knew she'd been right on the mark with her guesses. She winced, wishing now that she'd never brought the subject up. The thought of those sophisticated, experienced, beautiful women who'd preceded her in his arms proved daunting.

"Kelsey." His voice was rough with protest of her bluntness. "What do you want me to say?"

"I don't know," she admitted. "Maybe I was just trying to find out if you think of me as just another temporary diversion."

He caught her chin in his hand and lifted her face so that she had to look at him. "You," he said firmly, "are not like any woman I've ever known. Whatever I feel for you, it's nothing like what I may have had in the past. You could never be just a convenient companion who waits quietly in the wings until I have time for you, content with a few baubles to play with in my absence. You aren't the type who'd allow yourself to be treated that way, and I couldn't ignore you if I tried. Does that answer your question?"

His words convinced her that he didn't still think of her as just another woman who wanted something from him, preferably his money. That had worried her a little. Yet he still hadn't been particularly clear about what *he* wanted from *her*. Maybe because he wasn't sure of that, himself.

She loved him. She had no doubt of that, she thought as she lay snugly in his arms. But she could no more have predicted a future for them than she could read his mind now. So many obstacles lay ahead of them. And, though Kelsey had made a career of overcoming obstacles, she wasn't at all sure she would be able to do so for herself.

At the moment the most pressing problem between them was his ambivalence about Paul, who was such an important part of Kelsey's life. But she was fully aware that Paul was only a symbol of the real conflict still facing her and Cole. His family—both maternal and paternal—still waited out there somewhere, their demands and expectations hovering over Cole even as he rested in her bed, her hand on his heart. And Kelsey could not have said whether his feelings for her had any chance of surviving thirty-four years of conditioning and training.

She knew the families wouldn't approve of him seeing her. Knew their relationship was an awkward one, to say the least. Her brother-in-law was his mother's ex-husband, for Pete's sake. She winced, thinking it sounded a lot like a really bad television soap opera scenario. She hadn't expected to fall in love with Paul's son when she'd set out in search of him. But she had, and now she found herself afraid to look beyond this night in his arms.

She shifted suddenly and threw her arms around his neck, her face buried in his throat. "Hold me, Cole," she murmured. "Just hold me."

As if driven by his own private demons, Cole promptly drew her closer.

Cole lay awake long after Kelsey fell asleep in his arms. He kept remembering something she'd said earlier. She'd implied that she was falling in love with him—or thought she was. The very idea had stunned him. Still stunned him.

Was it possible that Kelsey could love him? Really love him? If so, why?

He was under no delusions that he was an easy man to love. Other women had wanted him in the past, a few had even said they loved him. He'd always known better. It had been his money they'd loved, his connections to the wealthy and powerful, his social acceptance. They'd never bothered to get to know the real Cole Saxon, never even suspected there was more to him than the facade he projected. And yet Kelsey had looked into him almost from the beginning and found something she seemed to find worthwhile. Something she might even grow to love. What?

He'd never known anyone like her. Never met anyone more generous, more caring, more selfless. And according to her, there were many people like her, people who gave without asking, people who volunteered before they were asked. Why had he never encountered them? Or had it been that he'd simply been too self-absorbed to look for them, or to recognize them when he'd met them in the past?

Even Lauren, though she detested him, seemed like a good person, devoted to her husband and child. She didn't seem to resent the ill health of her older husband, which was making her life far from ideal. He wondered how many beautiful young women in her position would have stood so staunchly by Paul's side. Paul must have done something to earn that sort of love from his wife.

He thought about Paul's parents, who'd obviously been concerned with their son's illness, but, in their pride, too stiff-necked to admit it. Willing to let him die without any further contact between them rather than accept that he may have had reasons for his conduct twenty-six years ago.

Hadn't Cole been just like them?

He thought of his mother, who'd never given out hugs and kisses like other mothers, who'd considered it her duty to raise her son with an all-consuming respect for tradition and responsibility. A woman very much like her hard-nosed, power-driven father, a man Cole had been in danger of emulating before Kelsey had entered his life.

That wasn't the man Cole wanted to be. The man Kelsey could love.

He hadn't realized his arm had tightened convulsively around Kelsey until she stirred and lifted her head. "Cole?" she asked huskily, peering at him through the shadows. "Is something wrong?"

He knew at last what he had to do. "I can't make any promises," he said aloud, as if Kelsey should know exactly what he'd been thinking while she slept.

She cocked her head curiously. "About us, you mean?" she asked, her tone hesitant. "I haven't asked you to—"

He realized that she'd misunderstood. "No, not about us. About Paul. I'll go see him . . . tomorrow, if you like. But I won't make any promises. I'll let him have his say and then we'll take it from there. One step at a time."

"Cole, you're sure you want to do this? You're not just doing it for me, are you?"

"You have something to do with my decision," he confessed. "I don't like this hanging over us. But I'm also going to see him for my own sake. It's something I should have done years ago. I need to learn the truth about what happened to make him leave."

"I think you're doing the right thing, Cole. Not just because Paul wants to see you, but because you'll always regret it if you don't. I don't want you to have to live with regrets."

"Tomorrow, then. And you'll go with me."

"To the hospital? Of course, if you want me to."

"No. I meant you'll be there while I talk to him. You started this, Kelsey. You can damn well see it through."

"But, Cole—"

"Kelsey." He touched her cheek. "I need you."

He'd known it was all he had to say. She capitulated immediately. "All right. I'll be there."

"So giving," he murmured, moving his hand to stroke her throat. He only wished there was something he could give her in return. He suspected she wouldn't care at all for a diamond necklace or a fur, particularly after her earlier comments about his former lovers.

But it seemed there was something she wanted, after all. Her lips sought his in a silent demand for his full attention.

She ran her hands over him with building greed, seeking out the excitement they'd found together before.

He rolled and had her on her back almost before she knew it. If this was all she wanted from him for now, he would give it willingly, he thought, his mind already beginning to spin from the intoxication of her kisses. For once, his own needs and desires were of very minor importance to him as he concentrated wholly on giving Kelsey pleasure.

It was barely five-thirty when the telephone rang. Jolted awake, Kelsey and Cole both reached for the receiver at the same time, their hands colliding. Waking enough to remember where he was, Cole fell back and let Kelsey pick up the phone.

He squinted against the sudden light when she turned on the bedside lamp. It was obvious from her expression that the call was bad news.

"When?" she asked. "Oh, Lauren, I'm so sorry."

Cole's chest tightened. *Damn,* he thought.

"Where's Jared...? Should I take her anything for him...? All right, I'll be there soon."

She hung up and turned immediately to Cole. "It's Paul," she said.

"Is he dead?" The question came out more bluntly than he'd intended.

She shook her head. "He went into cardiac arrest an hour ago. They're fighting to keep him alive. Lauren said his condition is extremely critical."

Cole was already throwing off the covers as Kelsey stood and reached for her robe. "Where's Jared?" he asked.

"Lauren's neighbor has him. She said for us not to worry about him, that he'll be well cared for today."

He found his briefs and slacks on the floor beside the bed. "I'm going to the hospital with you."

"Thank you. I was hoping you would."

She hurried to get ready, leaving Cole to dress grimly, cursing his lousy timing. Why had he been so stubborn? he demanded of himself furiously. So damned arrogant. Why hadn't he gone to see Paul the first time Kelsey had asked him to? And now it looked as if he'd waited too long. He'd been so busy being a Grayson-Saxon that he'd missed a chance to simply be human.

"Kelsey?" he called out, shoving his feet into his shoes, aware of the need for haste.

"I'm ready," she answered, appearing in the bathroom doorway, dressed in jeans and a pullover top, a hairbrush in her hand. "Let's go."

Lauren looked terrible. Her hair was tangled, her skin pale, her eyes red and puffy. Kelsey's heart twisted in shared pain. She wondered whether Lauren would ever be the same if Paul didn't survive.

"Oh, Lauren. I'm so sorry." She took her sister in her arms.

Lauren's breath caught on a sob, though she was too tired and worried to cry. "There's been no change since I called you," she said, her voice raspy. "Thanks for getting here so quickly. I needed you."

Only then did she realize Kelsey wasn't alone. Spotting Cole over Kelsey's shoulder, Lauren straightened slowly. She looked hard at Kelsey. "You called him?"

"It wasn't necessary," Kelsey answered candidly. "Cole was with me when you called."

"Oh." Lauren crossed her arms at her waist and looked at the floor.

"Lauren." Cole stepped forward when Kelsey would have spoken. "I'm sorry."

Holding herself stiffly, Lauren nodded. "He'd be pleased to know you're here," she said quietly. "Whatever your reason."

"I'm here for Kelsey," he replied just as softly. "And for you, if you need me. And I'm here because he's my father—and I want him to come through this."

Arms still crossed tightly, Lauren looked searchingly up at him. So did Kelsey. Cole looked rumpled and tired, as they all did, his morning beard giving him a rough, dangerous appearance that was contrary to his usual clean-shaven, neatly groomed immaculateness. He also looked gravely sincere, his wonderful green eyes warmer than most people would ever see them, holding enough sadness to make Kelsey have to fight back tears. "I'd like to stay, Lauren," he said, "but only if it's all right with you. If my presence makes this any worse for you, I'll leave."

Because she was so much like Kelsey in so many ways—or maybe because she simply needed all the emotional support she could get—Lauren held out her hands to him, obviously touched by his sincerity. "Don't go," she said simply. "Thank you for being here, Cole."

He took her hands in his, squeezed them, then released her. "Can I get you a cup of coffee or anything?" he asked, his voice unusually husky.

"That sounds good. I take it with cream, no sugar."

He looked pleased that she'd accepted the offer. He turned to Kelsey. "I'll get you some, too."

"Thanks, Cole. Just sugar in mine, please."

He touched her cheek as he passed her in search of a coffee machine. Kelsey realized that she was becoming addicted to those fleeting touches.

She turned to her sister. "Thank you. It would have hurt him if you'd sent him away."

"You asked me to give him a chance," Lauren reminded her. "As I remember, you had your concerns about Paul at first, too—because he was so much older than I. And yet you still gave him the chance you asked me to give Cole."

She pushed a weary hand through her hair. "Besides," she added, "it's what Paul would want me to do. He wants so badly to patch things up with Cole. I only hope he has a chance to try."

"Cole was going to visit him later today. He'd already told me, hours before you called."

Lauren looked gratified. "I'm glad. And I hope he still has the opportunity."

"He will," Kelsey assured her, wishing she could sound more confident.

Lauren attempted a smile, though it was a faint one. "Always trying to grant wishes, aren't you, honey?"

"It's a habit, I suppose."

Cole returned with the coffee a few minutes later. He cleared his throat as he handed Lauren her foam cup. "I hope you don't mind," he began, "but I called my grandparents. Paul's parents. They're on their way. They want to be here if—"

He didn't finish the sentence.

Lauren frowned. "Why do they want to be here? They haven't seen Paul in years."

"Maybe they have regrets, too," Cole suggested. "They've paid dearly for driving their only son away, Lauren. Now they're old and they have what may prove to be their last chance to be available for him. Don't deny them that, please."

Lauren nodded and turned away to sip her coffee and to worry in silence.

Cole sat beside Kelsey on one of the low couches provided in the otherwise-deserted waiting room. After a moment, he clasped her free hand in his own. They drank their coffee without speaking, lost in their own thoughts.

Chapter Twelve

It was Cole who first spotted the elder Saxons as they hesitantly entered the CICU waiting room. He squeezed Kelsey's hand before releasing it to stand and greet his grandparents. He noted that they'd taken time to dress as usual, Phillip in a dark suit and neatly knotted tie, Eudora in a designer suit, her hair and makeup immaculate. He was uncomfortably aware of his own unshaven dishevelment. His grandparents wouldn't have seen him looking this grubby since he was a kid—and rarely then.

"What's happening?" Phillip demanded without preamble.

"We're not sure," Cole answered. "The staff isn't exactly being forthcoming with updates."

Phillip scowled. "I'll see what I can do about that," he promised grimly.

"Before you alienate the nurses, why don't you meet your daughter-in-law?" Cole turned his head to look at Lauren, who was standing stiffly to one side. "Lauren."

She approached with visible reluctance.

Cole rested a supportive hand on her shoulder. "Lauren, these are my grandparents, Eudora and Phillip Saxon."

Three stiff nods followed the introduction. Cole realized that his grandmother was examining the composed young woman with what might have been surprised approval. Had they really been expecting a brassy gold digger? he wondered wryly. And then he reached out a hand for Kelsey.

"This is Lauren's sister, Kelsey Campbell," he said, when her hand slipped into his. Noting its coolness, he squeezed again for reassurance. Her fingers entwined with his.

Sharp-eyed Phillip didn't miss the silent exchange. Looking from those clasped hands to Cole, he then turned his attention to Kelsey, scrutinizing her minutely before glancing back at Lauren. "Where is your boy?" he asked gruffly.

"My son is staying with a neighbor."

Cole was pleased that Lauren didn't sound overtly belligerent. Perhaps she saw his grandparents as he was now beginning to see them—two people who were growing very old, clinging somewhat desperately to their dignity and former status. Two people whose pride and stubbornness had denied them twenty-six years with their only son.

"We understand the baby looks very much like Cole," Eudora said, her thin, spotted hands tightly clasped around her small handbag.

"Both Cole and Jared look very much like their father," Lauren agreed.

Cole wasn't surprised when bighearted Kelsey smiled sweetly at the older woman. "I have a recent snapshot of him in my purse. Would you like to see it?"

"I'd like that very much," Eudora answered gratefully.

Moments later, their heads were bent together over the packet of snapshots Kelsey had taken of her nephew only a few days before. Eudora exclaimed at the photos in pleasure. "Oh, Phillip, look. He's the image of Cole—and of Paul."

Phillip took the photograph somewhat stiffly. Though his expression didn't change, Cole knew the older man well enough to sense that he was moved by the image of the smiling infant. Still holding the snapshot, Phillip shot a look at Lauren. "You'll bring the boy to visit when you're able," he ordered. And then, less autocratically, "My wife and I would like very much to see him."

Lauren hesitated, aware of four sets of eyes focused on her. And then she nodded. "I'll bring him to see you."

The tension eased. Phillip handed the photograph back to his wife and turned abruptly toward the nurses' station. "I'm going to find out what the hell's going on back there. The family has a right to know."

Cole placed his hand back on Lauren's shoulder. "Thank you," he murmured, too softly for anyone else to hear.

She managed a weak smile. "It's time to stop hurting people, isn't it?"

"Long past time," he assured her.

He looked to where Kelsey still sat beside his grandmother. She looked up at the same moment, and their gazes met. Held. He wondered if she could read his gratitude in his eyes. Wondered if she could see how much she meant to him.

She smiled, and his heart turned over. Before he could do anything to embarrass both of them, he turned abruptly. "I'll try to keep Grandfather from getting us kicked out of here."

Despite Phillip's arrogant efforts, it was another forty-five minutes before Paul's doctor entered the visiting area to talk to Lauren. He found himself surrounded by family he'd never met, seemingly surprised at being introduced to Paul's parents and son, though he didn't comment that they'd waited so long to appear. Instead, he assured them that Paul had stabilized and was out of imminent danger—for now.

"How does this affect the surgery that was scheduled for Monday?" Lauren asked, relieved, as they all were, yet still terribly worried.

"We're going to have to risk it," the doctor replied quietly. "We simply can't wait any longer, Mrs. Saxon."

"And if he's not strong enough for the procedure?"

"We really have no other choice," he repeated, though not without sympathy.

Lauren took a deep, unsteady breath. Kelsey slipped an arm around her sister's waist in support. Cole stood closely at her other side, his grandparents nearby. "When can I see him?" Lauren asked.

"Someone will let you know. We'll want to keep the visits short during the next forty-eight hours, the stress at a minimum. Don't do or say anything to upset him."

"That won't happen," Lauren assured him, glancing at her husband's estranged family as she spoke.

The doctor lingered only a few minutes more in a low-voiced consultation with Lauren. Cole drew Kelsey aside.

"I hate to do this, but I have to get to the office," he muttered. "If it had been strictly necessary, I would have stayed, but I've got people coming from the West Coast for a meeting that starts in an hour. Since Paul's all right, I'd probably better go on."

"I understand," she assured him, taking his hands in her own. "I'll stay with Lauren for a while and then I have a few things I have to do today, as well."

"You'll call if you need me? I'll be at the office most of the day. I'll give Alice directions to put you through to me no matter what I'm doing."

"I'll call if anything important happens." Looking up at him, she reached up to cup his unshaven cheek. "You look so tired," she murmured. "I wish you had time to rest."

It touched him deeply that she was concerned for him at such a time. He lowered his head to kiss her. "I can rest later," he assured her, and then kissed her again.

She was blushing brightly when he pulled away, and she was obviously aware of his grandparents' eyes on her. Deciding that Lauren and Kelsey could use some time alone, he pulled his car keys from his pocket and handed them to Kelsey. "Here, you'll need transportation. Grandfather, will you give me a lift to my office?"

Phillip frowned. "You're going to your office looking like that?"

"I can shower and change in the executive suite. I keep an extra suit there for emergencies."

"I'll give you a ride," Phillip agreed, "but try not to let anyone see you on your way in. What would people think?"

Cole winked at Kelsey, who was struggling with a smile. "I'll use the back door," he promised.

He gave his grandparents only a few minutes to say their goodbyes to Lauren and Kelsey and then he reminded them that he had to go. He allowed himself one last long look at Kelsey before he reluctantly left her. Their eyes held until he forced himself to turn and walk away. He carried the warmth of that shared glance with him, knowing that no one else had ever made him feel so special with only a look.

"Does Harold Grayson know you're sleeping with your stepmother's younger sister?" Cole's grandfather demanded the minute his ever-present and paid-to-be-patient chauffeur had closed the door of the elegantly aging limo behind him.

"Phillip!"

Ignoring his grandmother's shocked exclamation, Cole only settled more deeply into his plush seat and nodded grimly. "He knows I'm seeing Kelsey."

"And . . . ?"

"What do you think?"

"I think he's probably vehemently opposed to it."

"You're right. He is."

"Surely you aren't surprised."

"No. But then he hasn't met Kelsey," Cole answered. "He hasn't even given her a chance. All he knows is that she's connected to Paul."

"Surely you can see his point. She's totally unsuitable for you."

"Phillip, really," Eudora protested again. "This is Cole's business."

"The connection between the Saxons and the Graysons, both socially and professionally, has existed for years," Phillip pointed out coolly. "Paul's desertion severely shook the foundations of that mutually beneficial relationship, but we recovered. For Cole to slap his mother and grandfather in the face by continuing his affair with this woman would be more than Harold could swallow."

"I am not slapping anyone in the face by having an affair with Kelsey," Cole snapped, hating the tone the older man was using in reference to her. "Stop making our relationship—and her—sound so sordid. I care about her."

"She seems like a very sweet young woman, Cole," Eudora assured him, not bothering to mask her approval.

"Young is right. She's years younger than you are. Must you emulate your father in every way?" Phillip sputtered.

"She's twenty-four—ten years younger than I am," Cole replied evenly. "We're considerably closer in age than Paul and Lauren, though age seems to have very little to do with compatibility. You're several years older than Grandmother, aren't you?"

"Your grandmother and I knew each other from childhood. The match was eminently suitable, to us and to our families. There was nothing about our relationship to cause the sort of distasteful gossip this affair will receive."

"I don't care about gossip."

Phillip drew himself straighter. "You no longer care about the family's reputation? It wouldn't bother you to be compared to your father, who hasn't been received by our friends in twenty-six-years?"

"Paul chose to walk away from those 'friends,'" Cole pointed out. "I have no intention of walking away from anything unless it suits me to do so."

"And if it comes down to a choice between that girl and your relationship with your mother's family?"

Cole eyed the older man steadily. "It won't."

"I wouldn't lay odds on that if I were you," Phillip returned just as flatly.

The limousine drew to the curb in front of Cole's office building. Cole reached for the door handle before the Saxons' driver could put the vehicle in Park. "Thank you for coming to the hospital when I called, and for being courteous to Lauren," he said, looking at his grandmother, though the words were directed to both. "I think your being there helped her. She needs all the support she can get right now. As for Kelsey," he added, turning his attention to Phillip, "whatever is between us is no one's business but our own. You will not belittle her or upset her. Is that clear?"

"You will not talk to me in that manner, Cole," his grandfather warned.

"I'm no longer a child, Grandfather. And I won't be given orders concerning my personal life. You may as well accept that now."

"We won't interfere, Cole," Eudora assured him quickly, shooting her husband a look of warning. "We have no intention of alienating you. Nor will we lose our chance to see our new grandson. Will we, Phillip?"

Phillip nodded grudgingly. "As you say, you're a grown man. If you choose to ruin your future with the Graysons, that's up to you. You'd just damned well better hope she's worth it."

Exhaling in exasperation, Cole climbed out of the limo and barely resisted the impulse to slam the door behind him. How was it, he wondered irritably, that his grandfather could still make him feel like a recalcitrant adolescent when

Cole had only to walk into a boardroom to command absolute deference and respect?

It didn't help his mood in the least that his mother was waiting for him in his office.

She took one look at his appearance and curled her lip. "Well. It seems that you had an interesting night. More interesting, I suppose, than the Mayor's reception."

"What are you doing here this early, Mother?" he asked wearily.

"I was worried about you," she replied with dignity. "We were expecting you to join us last night. When you didn't, we tried to call you several times to ask why. I wanted to stop by this morning to see for myself that you were all right. I assume you spent the night with that woman?"

"I was with Kelsey," he confirmed flatly. Damn it, he thought, he was getting fed up with everyone talking about her as though she were some sort of inferior life-form. How could they not realize how very special she was? Loving, thoughtful, unselfish, tenderhearted. Why didn't they understand that he was damned lucky even to have met her?

He reminded himself that his mother hadn't yet met Kelsey. Maybe it was natural for her to be concerned, considering the circumstances. He really didn't have time to get into it just now. "Mother, I have a very important meeting starting in just over half an hour. I need to shower, change and shave first."

She flicked her eyes over his rumpled clothing. "Obviously. I'm appalled that you allowed your employees to see you looking like this."

"I was very discreet. And I don't think morale would be permanently damaged if anyone saw the boss in need of a shave, do you?"

She only shrugged.

"Look, I'll call you this evening, okay?"

"I have plans for the evening. I'm dining at the club with Edward and Beverly. Perhaps you'd like to join us?"

He ran his hand through his hair and sighed. He fully intended to spend the evening with Kelsey. She'd probably have Jared, who wouldn't be at all welcome with Belinda or her brother.

Belinda nodded when his silence gave his answer. "I see."

"Mother—"

"My garden club is meeting for brunch. I really must be going. Perhaps you'll give me a call when it's convenient for you to do so."

She left him wincing at the memory that he'd said something very much like that to Kelsey only a day or two earlier. Had he sounded as irritatingly priggish? Why had he never noticed before that the Graysons and Saxons shared an annoying talent for sounding so damned superior?

"Kelsey, you really don't have to hang around here any longer. I know you have many things you need to be doing." Lauren gave Kelsey a hug as she spoke.

Kelsey looked worriedly at her sister. "You should rest. When are you going home?"

"I will as soon as I've seen Paul again. I promise."

Glancing at her watch, Kelsey nodded. "They said you could go back in at eleven. It's nearly that now."

"I know. So why don't you go on? I'm sure you'd like to stop by your place and change. Get something to eat, too."

"Save your mothering for Jared," Kelsey murmured affectionately. "I can take care of myself."

"So you keep telling me." Lauren pushed a strand of hair from her face. "Kelsey, I may have been wrong about Cole. He was very thoughtful this morning. I hadn't expected that from him."

"I told you he could be sweet. It's just that it's not easy for him to show his feelings. God knows he's had enough training in hiding them," Kelsey murmured, thinking of Cole's intimidating grandfather. And he'd led her to believe that his other grandfather was even more daunting! She found that hard to believe, but just thinking of meeting Harold Grayson—or, she thought with a gulp, Cole's mother—made her hands begin to tremble.

"He really seems to care for you, Kelsey. The two of you haven't known each other very long, of course, but judging from the way he looked at you, I think he's definitely getting involved. And," she added, "you were giving him some pretty warm looks, yourself."

"I'm crazy about him," Kelsey admitted ruefully. "Or maybe I'm just crazy. It's such an awkward situation. And it's glaringly obvious that his family's not going to approve. Maybe you didn't see the way his grandfather looked at me, but I certainly did. He doesn't like it that Cole's seeing me."

"I got that impression, too," Lauren admitted. "The Saxons weren't quite as bad as I expected them to be, especially Eudora, but the old man is every bit as rigid and demanding as Paul said he was. Still," she added thoughtfully, "I don't think Cole's the type to allow them to tell him he can't do something if he really wants to. And I think he really wants to keep seeing you."

"I won't be the cause of another rift in Cole's family," Kelsey whispered miserably, looking away. "He's had enough family conflict. He doesn't need more."

"And if he chooses to go against their wishes, anyway?"

Sighing, Kelsey pushed at her bangs. "He's known me for a few weeks, Lauren. They've had him thirty-four years. I won't put him in a position of having to make that choice. I'll stop seeing him first."

"You think it'll be that easy?" Lauren asked skeptically.

"Easy?" Kelsey repeated, her voice hollow. Already her heart ached at the very possibility of having to stop seeing Cole, even if it were for his own good. "No, Lauren, it won't be easy. But I'll do whatever I have to do to keep from having him hurt again."

And then, seeing the anxiety in her sister's eyes, Kelsey managed a smile, not wanting Lauren to worry about her when she had so many other problems. "Let's not worry about something that may not even be an issue, all right? As we've said, Cole and I have only known each other a few weeks. Hardly enough time to make a lifelong commitment. For now, let's just concentrate on getting Paul well and back home with you and Jared, shall we?"

Though her eyes still mirrored concern, Lauren nodded. "You may be the one to decide it's not worth it," she pointed out lightly. "Two weeks really isn't very long. You hardly know the man, after all."

Kelsey smiled and nodded, though she knew two weeks had been more than enough time for her to fall in love with Cole. Her feelings were the permanent, once-in-a-lifetime, heartbreak-waiting-to-happen variety. Which meant the most important thing in the world to her now was making sure Cole was happy. And if his happiness could only be ensured by her telling him goodbye, she'd do it.

She'd gotten very good at doing whatever she had to do to make others happy during the past few years. It had been a long time since she'd found it necessary to worry about herself. To long for a secret wish of her own. A wish that may very well prove to be hopelessly unattainable.

"I had a feeling he'd be here tonight," Cole said, smiling at the baby in Kelsey's arms when she opened the door to her apartment.

Though he hadn't called, Kelsey wasn't surprised by Cole's arrival. She stood back to allow him to enter. "Are you hungry? I stopped for a bucket of chicken earlier, since there wasn't anything much here to cook."

He kissed her as he walked past her, the gesture as natural as a long-established habit. So why did it make her heart pound so furiously?

"Chicken sounds good. Thanks." Setting a large paper bag on a chair, Cole reached for Jared. "C'mere, kid. I've got a present for you."

Jared went willingly into the now-familiar arms.

Kelsey put her hands on her hips and cocked her head in curiosity. "What present?"

"Hold on. Let Jared open it," Cole chided.

She crossed her arms with an impatient sigh. "Sure. A four-month-old baby's going to open a package."

"With a little help from his big brother," Cole conceded. Holding Jared in one arm, he dug in the bag with the other and pulled out a miniature baseball glove. As small as it was, it would be a good three years before Jared would be able to keep it on his hand.

"He's a little young, isn't he?" Kelsey asked indulgently.

Cole only grinned and pulled out a larger glove, obviously also new. "This one's mine," he announced, looking at Jared. "I figure I've got a couple of years to practice up on my fielding before we can get in a game of catch. Whaddaya' think, Jared?"

Jared laughed and reached for Cole's nose.

"I think he approves," Cole decided, looking up at Kelsey.

She clung to her own smile with an effort. Every time she almost convinced herself she could let Cole go if she had to, he did something impossibly sweet, like this. How was she supposed to resist him?

Quite simply, she couldn't.

She cleared her throat and headed for the kitchen, avoiding his eyes. "I'll get dinner ready. I need to heat the potatoes and gravy. D'you want a cola or wine with yours?"

"Cola's fine. I'll save your wine for a special occasion," he answered with mock gravity.

Any other time she would have thrown a sassy retort back at him. Now she simply concentrated on getting into the kitchen before she gave in to the urge to throw herself in his arms and hold him as if she'd never have to let go.

Since Paul needed his rest, Lauren didn't stay long at the hospital that evening. Kelsey and Cole had hardly finished eating before she arrived to pick up Jared. She turned down an offer of leftover chicken, explaining that she'd eaten at the hospital with her minister. Her manner toward Cole was notably warmer than it had been before.

"I don't think she hates me quite as badly as she did," Cole said optimistically when he and Kelsey were alone.

"She doesn't hate you at all. She never did."

"I hope you're right. You and Lauren are so close, and I'd like her to accept me."

Kelsey wanted Cole's family to like her, too, but she was terribly afraid that was never going to happen. Biting her lip, she thought of saying so, but then she noticed the dark smudges under his eyes. He looked so tired. After very little sleep the night before, followed by a draining morning at the hospital and what had obviously been a demanding day at the office, he needed to relax. She didn't have the heart to bring up anything that might upset him. Not tonight.

Walking to the chair where he sprawled, she stopped behind him and began to rub his neck. His head fell forward in immediate response, a low moan rumbling from his chest. "Ah, sweetheart, that feels so good. How did you know my neck was killing me?"

Kelsey's heart tripped at the endearment, though he seemed to have used it almost unconsciously. She tried to speak normally so he wouldn't know how the word had affected her. "Maybe the way you've been rubbing it tipped me off."

He chuckled. "Seven hours of boring meetings will stiffen the old ligaments every time. God, I thought the day would never end. I couldn't wait to get home to you."

Home. The word had a nice sound to it, of course, but he could hardly call her apartment home. Which made her realize and say, "I don't even know where you live!"

Cole turned his head to slant a look up at her. "You don't?"

"No. We've never been to your place, remember?"

"We'll have to remedy that soon. I bought one of the row houses on Jones a couple of years ago. I've had it furnished with period pieces. I think you'll like it."

Her fingers faltered in their rubbing as it was once more forcibly brought home to her just how different Cole's circumstances were from her own. Of course he would live at one of the most coveted historic addresses in Savannah. He was probably a valued member of the Historic Savannah Foundation, founded in the 1950s to restore the grandeur of the old downtown district when it had fallen victim to severe neglect. Kelsey couldn't even imagine the money he had invested in his home.

Even if it weren't for the strain of their family problems, she and Cole were such an improbable couple. He was wealthy, powerful, socially prominent; she struggled to pay her bills, spent most of her time with disadvantaged children and their families and did her shopping at discount stores. She had never fancied playing the role of Cinderella.

It wasn't going to work, she thought again, her throat as tight as the muscles in Cole's neck.

And then he lifted his head and shoved himself out of the chair. "I almost forgot," he said, when she looked up at him in question at his abrupt movement. "Jared wasn't the only one who got a present today. I brought something for you, too."

She frowned. "You brought me a gift?"

"Yeah." He turned and reached for the bag from which he'd pulled the baseball gloves that even now sat neatly in the crib. Kelsey had assumed the bag was empty now. It seemed she'd been wrong.

Not diamonds, Cole. Please don't make me feel like just another of your women, she thought, her hands clenching behind her back.

She hadn't expected a book. It was a hardback, the newest Quinn Gallagher novel she'd been saving to buy for herself, but still far less in value than the expensive diamonds she'd half expected in such dread. Her eyes filled with tears before she could stop them.

He'd done it again, damn him. "Oh, Cole. Thank you."

His cheeks rather flushed, he cleared his throat. He didn't quite shuffle his feet, but she thought he wasn't far from it. "It's only a book, Kelsey," he said. "I wanted to get you something, but you'd made your opinion of diamonds and furs fairly clear."

She smiled tremulously at his wry tone. "I'd much rather have this," she assured him, eagerly opening the cover. Only to find another delightful surprise. Just inside the cover, in a neat, precise script were the words: "Kelsey—I hope you enjoy the adventure you find in these pages. Quinn Gallagher."

"Cole, it's autographed! This is wonderful! How in the world did you...?"

"I told you I knew him," he reminded her, obviously pleased with her delight. "He owed me a favor, so I gave him a call a couple of days ago."

Hugging the book to her chest, she asked curiously, "He owed you a favor?"

He nodded. "Yeah. I met him several years ago. He was a Miami vice cop, I was just getting started in my grandfather's shipping business. He was on loan for a few weeks to the Savannah police department to break a drug ring. One of my employees was a suspect. I worked with Quinn to find the proof he needed."

She looked at him with new respect. She wouldn't have expected her so-proper, sometimes-stuffy Cole to have been active in a police investigation that might well have proven dangerous. "Wow. That was very brave of you."

He flushed. "I'm not exactly a hero. My part was mostly shuffling papers. And it was, after all, my duty as a citizen and businessman to cooperate with the police operation."

"Of course it was," she agreed gravely. "You probably hated every minute of it."

"Well, no," he admitted. "I rather enjoyed it, actually."

Because he'd once wanted to be a policeman, though he'd always known he wouldn't be. Her throat going tight again, Kelsey rose on tiptoe to kiss him. "Thank you, Cole."

His arms went around her immediately, though he seemed compelled to point out again, "It's only a book, Kelsey."

"Yes, I know. And I love it." *And you. I love you, Cole. So very much.*

She didn't tell him, of course. She'd retained that much caution. But she didn't even think of protesting when he took the book from her hands and set it aside, then swooped her into his arms and headed for the bedroom.

Chapter Thirteen

Stopping by Cole's office the next afternoon was purely impulsive on Kelsey's part. She'd been on her way home from Lauren's house with Jared when she'd suddenly found the steering wheel turning in the direction of Savannah's business district. Even as she entered the elevator and pushed the button that would take her to Cole's office, she wondered if she was doing the right thing.

"What do you think, Jared?" she asked the baby she held in the crook of her left arm. "Should we forget about this and head home?"

His shiny little head bobbing as he looked around with wide, fascinated eyes, Jared gave Kelsey a quick grin before his attention was captured by the numbers flashing above the door.

"You're a lot of help," she muttered, unable to resist giving him a hug. She thought he looked particularly adorable in his one-piece navy sailor suit with red-and-white nautical trim on the oversize collar. The jaunty red knot under his chubby chin was a bit damp from his dribbling, but he still looked quite dashing. Perfectly suitable for an office visit, Kelsey decided, aware that her own bright red sweater and floral print skirt was one of her more becoming casual outfits. Which, of course, didn't make it any easier for her to enter Cole's reception area and face his dragon-lady secretary.

"Good afternoon, Alice," she said breezily, as if she'd been a welcome visitor in Cole's office for years. "Is Cole in?"

Visibly startled, which Kelsey found secretly amusing, Alice looked from Kelsey to the baby on her hip. "Well...um...yes, he is, er—"

"Kelsey Campbell," Kelsey reminded her, her smile a friendly one. "Is Cole very busy? If so, there's no need to disturb him. This is just a social call."

Alice was obviously disarmed by Kelsey's manner—and evidently had a decided weakness for babies. She was smiling at Jared when she shook her head. "I've been instructed to always put you through when you call, Ms. Campbell. I'm sure Mr. Saxon will want to see you."

Trying to hide her pleasure at Cole's instructions to his secretary, Kelsey straightened Jared's tie while Alice announced her. It was only a moment later when Alice assured Kelsey that she'd been invited into Cole's office.

Cole was just rounding the desk to meet her when Kelsey opened his door. She was relieved to see that he was smiling, apparently pleased by her visit. "This is a surprise," he said, looking from her to Jared. He closed the door behind them for privacy. "What's going on?"

"We have something to show you," Kelsey answered with mock gravity. "A major landmark in young Master Saxon's development."

Cole looked at her quizzically. "What are you talking about?"

In answer, she pressed a finger against Jared's lower lip, opening his mouth to reveal a tiny white nub in one slobbery gum. "Isn't it awesome?" she asked Cole with a smile.

His answering smile was the one that always charmed her, the full, easy grin that exposed the long slashes of dimple in his right cheek. "He has a tooth," he announced unnecessarily.

"Yep. This is probably the reason for the tantrums recently. It must have been bothering him. Most babies don't get their first teeth for several more months yet. My nephew is extremely advanced for his age."

Cole reached for Jared, handling him with rapidly developing skill. "Good for you, kid," he told him approvingly. "Now you're almost ready to get rid of those wimpy bottles and chow down on a thick, juicy steak."

"Oh, great. You're going to give him clogged arteries before he's walking," Kelsey complained, though she felt like laughing, for no particular reason except that Cole made her happy.

He only gave her a lofty look. "A little red meat never hurt anyone. Especially a Saxon. We're tough, aren't we, kid?"

Jared gurgled and made a wild grab for Cole's striped tie. Cole didn't seem perturbed when the exquisite strip of silk was crushed in a chubby fist. "Why aren't you working today?" he asked, his attention turning to Kelsey. "You don't usually take Fridays off."

"I worked this morning, but I told everyone I was out for the afternoon. I talked Lauren into making an appointment with the beauty salon for a couple of hours of pampering. She's getting a perm, having a manicure—the works. And then I told her to find herself a new dress so she'd look gorgeous for Paul when he comes out of surgery Monday. She really needed some time off."

His expression thoughtful, Cole lifted his free hand to stroke Kelsey's cheek. "Your sister is very lucky to have you."

She felt herself flushing beneath his touch. "I hope we aren't disturbing you," she said, quickly changing the subject. "I just stopped by on an impulse."

"You haven't interrupted anything important," he assured her. "I was only going over some reports."

"I know you need to get back to it, so we'll only stay a few minutes."

"Don't hurry away." Still holding Jared, Cole sat on a sofa against one wall. He balanced the baby on his knee and motioned Kelsey to sit beside them.

She complied readily enough. "I stopped by to see Ronnie MacKenzie late this morning," she commented. "It seems I wasn't his first visitor today. You must have gone by immediately after you stopped by your house to change."

"Yeah, I stopped at the hospital on the way to the office," Cole admitted rather sheepishly. "I just wanted to see how he was doing. I met his mother."

"Linda's a sweetheart. Was Al there?"

"No. He was on a job."

"Poor Al. Supporting four children, one with a serious illness, is financially devastating. Linda has a part-time job as a waitress, but I think they're really struggling."

"Maybe I could help."

She rested her hand on his arm. "That's sweet of you, but Al is very proud. I don't think he'd allow you to do more than you've done. If I see any major problem occurring, I'll let you know, okay?"

"Do that." Cole jiggled Jared for a moment, making the baby gurgle delightedly, then spoke again. "The boy in the room with Ronnie—the one with diabetes. Did you know he really wants a personal computer? The nurse said the boy's a real prodigy with math and that he'd like to try some programming."

"I only met that boy for the first time this morning. He hasn't been signed up for the wish list yet. But now that you've told me about it, I'll check into it—make sure he qualifies medically and financially and—"

"Never mind. I've already ordered the PC," Cole interrupted gruffly, avoiding her eyes. "I thought I'd better tell you so we wouldn't duplicate efforts. And I want you to help me arrange to give it to him anonymously."

She couldn't help smiling, though with a measure of exasperation. "Cole, you can't personally grant the wish of every sick child in Savannah. No one, least of all me, expects you to do so."

"Ah, hell, a low-end PC's not going to break me," he muttered, his cheeks suspiciously, endearingly pink.

She wondered if he'd ever made such generous, thoughtful gestures before. It was glaringly apparent that he enjoyed making them now, that he found it rewarding to give without being asked for a change. "I warn you," she said, trying to speak lightly. "Getting involved with these kids is addictive. If you can't handle the losses, you'd better pull back now."

"I can handle it. Not that I intend to do this sort of thing full-time," he added quickly. "It was just a coincidence that I found out about the kid wanting the computer. I probably won't come into contact with many others."

Kelsey privately believed that Cole was already being drawn into her own calling. She had no intention of discouraging him; she believed that he needed a worthwhile cause almost as badly as her organization needed him as a regular contributor. There was nothing like a child's artless, undemanding smile to break through a shell erected against years of pretentiousness and avarice.

She was trying to think of something to say when the office door burst open and a tall, gray-haired, daunting-looking man entered, still talking over his shoulder to Alice. "Of course there's no need to announce us," he asserted forcefully. "I run this show, remember?"

Both the man and the somewhat younger woman following him stopped abruptly at the sight of Cole and Kelsey side by side on the sofa, Kelsey's hand lying intimately on Cole's arm, Jared sitting on his knee and babbling.

Kelsey gulped silently. She really should have just picked up Jared and gone home, she thought despairingly. These impulses of hers always tended to get her into trouble.

Cole stifled an inappropriate urge to curse fluently. Aware that Kelsey had gone stiff beside him, he nodded without allowing his displeasure to show in either his manner or his voice. "Hello, Mother. Granddad."

He knew why they were there, of course. They'd probably already heard that the Saxons had been at the hospital the day before, at Cole's instigation. They were really going to love finding him like this, he thought wryly.

Belinda Grayson Saxon stared in horror at the baby Cole still held. "Oh my God," she murmured weakly. "Don't tell me that's—"

"Paul's son, Jared," Cole supplied when her voice failed. Ignoring Kelsey's furtive attempt to take the baby from him, he stood, shifting Jared to one arm. "My brother."

"Don't be ridiculous," Harold Grayson blustered. "Cole, this infant—"

"Is my brother, Granddad," Cole interrupted flatly. "I know it's hard to accept, but it's a biological fact. Your disapproval doesn't change it."

"Biologically, I suppose you're right. The boy is obviously a Saxon, so I assume there's no reason to question the parentage."

Though he was still looking at his grandfather, Cole sensed Kelsey's indignant movement beside him. "The baby is Paul's," he confirmed tonelessly.

"Still, there is no need for you to become involved with the child," Grayson continued. "You are not responsible for your father's foolishness."

"I think Jared and I had better go," Kelsey said quietly, reaching again for her nephew.

Again, Cole eluded her. "I'm sorry, I should have introduced you. Kelsey Campbell, this is my mother, Belinda Grayson Saxon, and her father, Harold Grayson. Kelsey is Jared's aunt," he added, though they already knew exactly who she was.

Both Grayson and Belinda winced at the awkwardness of the situation, even as Kelsey pasted on a determined smile and nodded. "It's—um—very nice to meet you," she said, her voice strained.

Knowing how uncomfortable his family was making her, Cole wished he could put an arm around her for moral support, but decided that would only embarrass her more. Instead, he contented himself with a quick smile of encouragement for her, which he knew had not gone unnoticed by his mother or grandfather.

"Why did you bring this child here?" Grayson demanded, giving Kelsey a look he usually reserved for importunate social climbers. "What do you want from Cole?"

"Kelsey is here on a social visit, Granddad," Cole answered for her, a note of warning in his voice. "I was pleased to see her."

"I can speak for myself, Cole," Kelsey said smoothly, taking a step forward so that she wasn't half-hidden behind him. "I don't want anything from Cole, Mr. Grayson. He and I have become friends during the past few weeks and I simply dropped in to say hello while I was in the neighborhood."

"Friends?" Grayson repeated suspiciously, looking from Kelsey's somewhat flushed face to Cole's impassive one.

Cole's eyes narrowed at his grandfather's tone. God, had he ever sounded so coldly arrogant? he wondered suddenly. Sending mental apologies to anyone he'd ever snubbed so discourteously, he gave in to the impulse to rest his free arm on Kelsey's tense shoulders, drawing her closer to his side. The top of her head came barely to his shoulder, and his sudden surge of protectiveness was as surprising as it was unprecedented. He looked in challenge from his grandfather to his disapproving mother. "Was there anything else the two of you wanted?"

"We want to talk to you, Cole," Grayson answered. He glanced resentfully at Kelsey. "Alone."

"I was just leaving," Kelsey said, her chin lifted in admirable pride. One more time she reached for the baby, and this time Cole passed him over. She thanked him with her eyes. He could see she was impatient to go. He didn't blame her. He would have liked to leave with her.

"I'll call you later," he promised, his voice low, meant only for her.

She nodded.

He wanted very much to kiss her. He contented himself with touching her cheek in what by now was a pleasant habit. "Drive carefully."

Kelsey murmured a polite goodbye to his family and left with as much haste as she could gracefully manage. Cole watched the door close behind her, then took a deep breath and turned to face the Grayson wrath. "All right," he said flatly. "Let's get it over with."

"Surely you aren't getting involved with that young woman," Belinda began, twin spots of color burning in her otherwise pale cheeks. "Surely you can see how totally unsuitable such a relationship would be. My God, Cole, don't you care that you'd make us a laughingstock among our acquaintances? An affair with your father's young sister-in-law! And you carrying your father's infant around as casually as if the child were your own. I don't know how I'd face my friends."

"I realize the situation is awkward, Mother," Cole answered, keeping his temper tightly reined. "And, yes, it bothers me, though not because of anything our 'acquaintances' may say. But you may as well get used to it, because that baby is my brother and I'm not turning my back on him. He needs me, especially if Paul doesn't make it. I'm not asking you to accept him—there's no reason for you to be involved with him or his parents. Just know that he'll be a part of my life."

"I suppose there's nothing we can do to prevent you from seeing the boy," Harold conceded grudgingly. "Particularly now that you've gotten the Saxons determined to see him. If he's going to be raised as a Saxon, it'll be up to you to see to it, whether Paul lives or not. As for this other thing, you understand, of course, that it has to stop."

Cole's throat tightened. He tugged at his tie. "What other thing?" he asked very carefully, though he suspected he already knew.

"Your affair with that girl. Damn it, Cole, she's just like her sister. She's on the lookout for a rich husband, and one Saxon will do as well as the next. Are you really going to allow yourself to be as foolish as your father?"

Cole wasn't sure he'd ever been quite this angry. As clearly as a recording, Bob's words rang through his head. *You've never wanted anything desperately enough to give up everything else to have it.* Did his grandfather really intend to put it to a choice—his position in the family business or his deepening relationship with Kelsey?

Was this what Paul had faced twenty-six years earlier? Do what they say or get out?

"Kelsey," he said icily, "is not on the lookout for a rich husband. Our relationship developed despite our better judgment and has nothing to do with Paul or with you. And nothing—*nothing*—you can do or say will make me stop seeing her before I'm damned well ready. Is that clear?"

The two tall, powerful men faced each other squarely, eye to eye, will to will. Belinda held her breath. Cole was well aware that no compromise was possible. Grayson would accept Cole's right to make his own decisions, or an ugly family conflict would ensue. Unlike Paul, Cole had no intention of walking away from what he considered his, by both birth and achievement. Not without a fight.

No one seemed particularly surprised when Grayson was the one to back down. "Are you planning to marry the girl?" he asked sullenly.

Cole didn't allow his stance to relax, though he felt the tension easing inside him. "Marriage hasn't been discussed. We've only known each other for a few weeks."

"Is it a possibility?" Belinda asked tentatively, watching him as if her son had suddenly been transformed into a commanding, intimidating stranger. Cole thought it was entirely possible that Belinda had never even considered the possibility that her father would eventually be defeated in a battle of wills. She'd always regarded Harold as all-powerful, unbeatable. Until recently—perhaps even until now—Cole had thought of the older man in much the same way.

"She's very important to me, Mother," he told her, trying now to make his voice more gentle. "I'd like you to give her a chance. I know it won't be easy for you, but it will make it easier for all of us if you learn to accept her. She had nothing to do with whatever happened in the past. She wasn't even born when Paul left us."

"You're going to forgive him, aren't you? You're going to allow him back into your life." Belinda looked tired, and suddenly old.

"Paul is very much a part of Kelsey's life," Cole answered carefully. "Like you, I have to put the past behind me to get on with my future. I'll probably have to learn to associate with him for her sake. That doesn't mean I'll ever forget the pain he caused us. And it doesn't mean I'll stop loving you. Any of you," he added, looking quickly at his grandfather. "You're my family. You're the ones who have been there for me all my life, whenever I needed you. We're not a comfortable group—we're all a bit too accustomed to having our own way. But we're family. I've only recently begun to realize how important that word is."

"If this woman is really so important to you, then I'll try to accept her," Belinda said with admirable dignity. "I could refuse, of course, but then I would lose you. And I will not lose my son. I won't be left alone again," she finished quietly, turning toward the door to the office, her slender, elegantly clad body held straight and proud.

My God, Cole thought in stunned silence. *She'd loved Paul. She'd really loved him. Didn't she ever tell him?* It saddened him to realize that she probably never had, that Paul had very likely never known. No wonder they'd had no chance of making their marriage work.

Belinda looked back at him just before stepping out the door. "The boy looks exactly like you did when you were a baby," she said, her smile sad. "I've always regretted that I never had another child. For your sake and mine." She took a deep breath. "Bring Kelsey to dinner one night next week. Let me know when to expect you."

She walked out without looking back again.

Harold seemed to want to say something. Whatever it was, he bit it back. With a gruff mutter about seeing his daughter home, he left, too. "I will talk with you later," he said just before closing the door behind him. He made his meaning perfectly clear. Neither of them would enjoy the conversation when it occurred.

Alone at last, Cole closed his eyes and released his lingering tension in a long, drawn-out exhalation.

Of course it was one of those days when Cole was inundated with work, a day when he was least inclined to deal with it. He had to remind himself of his responsibilities several times during the afternoon to overcome the urge just to put everything on hold and go in search of Kelsey.

It was nearly seven before he could get away from the office. He headed straight for Kelsey's apartment, never even considering going to his own house first. Ever since she'd left that afternoon, he'd had a heavy feeling that they had to talk or he was going to lose her. He'd seen the distress in her eyes after the unwarranted attacks from his grandfather. He wouldn't have blamed her if she'd decided she wouldn't risk being treated that way again. But he'd be damned if he'd let his family scare Kelsey away.

A dull ache had begun in his chest just at the thought of losing her, of never again waking up with her in his arms. She'd made herself a part of his life in a way no woman had before. He wasn't going to let her go without a fight.

He'd been prepared to soothe her ruffled feelings. To overcome her hesitation at getting involved with his overbearing families. He hadn't been prepared to knock on her door until he was finally forced to accept that she wasn't home.

Where was she? She hadn't said anything about being gone this evening. He realized he'd gotten accustomed to her letting him know her plans. Damn, he should have called earlier, but he hadn't wanted to get into a serious discussion on the telephone.

Had she left because she knew he'd shown up? he asked himself grimly as he climbed back into his car. Was this her way of letting him know she blamed him for the way she'd been treated? Would she give him a chance to assure her he wouldn't allow anyone ever to talk to her that way again?

He'd spent the day in anticipation of being with her again. He'd wanted to talk to her about several things. His mother's tentative offer of a truce. His own belief that time would bring the remaining members of his family to accept his relationship with Kelsey. But most of all, he'd wanted to hold her, touch her, bask in the warmth of her caring brown eyes.

His fist tightened on the steering wheel as he stared seethingly at her darkened apartment.

He sat in his car for another twenty minutes, waiting for her to come home. Finally realizing how foolish it was for him to continue sitting there when she could be out for hours yet, he started the engine and backed out of the parking space, annoyed, hungry, tired, frustrated. But the predominant emotion he could identify at that moment felt suspiciously like despair.

Kelsey was tired. Physically, emotionally, spiritually. It took a massive effort just to walk into her bedroom and change from the clothes she'd worn to work that morning into comfortable pajamas. Only then did she look at the clock. After midnight. It was even later than she'd thought.

The blinking red light on her answering machine caught her attention, though it certainly didn't surprise her. She'd known Cole would call. He'd probably been at her door, expecting to find her at home. It wasn't hard to imagine the displeasure he must have felt at finding her gone.

She thought of ignoring the message. She really wasn't up to listening to it tonight. Besides, she thought, dragging a hand through her hair, it was too late to call him back, anyway.

And still she found herself pressing the rewind button. Maybe because she only wanted to hear his voice.

The first caller was a volunteer worker listing some contributions received at a fund-raiser held in another part of the state and donated to the Children's Dream Foundation. Kelsey tried to be pleased by the call. And yet she was impatient for the message to end.

The message was followed by a couple of beeps indicating hang ups. Cole? she wondered. Had he not bothered to leave a message, after all?

But then she heard his voice. Her eyes closed as she allowed its rich tones to flow over her. "It's ten o'clock," he said without identifying himself. "If you're there, pick up the phone, damn it."

He paused only a moment before adding, "Whatever time you get home, call me. God knows I won't be asleep." He gave her his home number before hanging up.

She wouldn't call him, of course, she told herself, turning off the machine and crawling miserably into bed. It was much too late. Both of them needed rest after the little sleep they'd managed the night before.

God knows I won't be asleep. She groaned as the words replayed in her mind. Was Cole lying awake, waiting for her call? Worrying about her, perhaps? She couldn't bear the thought of that. Damn it, why did she have to be so soft-hearted?

Muttering at her weakness, she climbed out of the bed, replayed his message and memorized his number. And then she picked up the phone. If she woke him out of a sound sleep it was no one's fault but his own, she decided peevishly.

He picked up the phone after one ring. "It's about time." He didn't even give her a chance to identify herself. And he quite clearly had not been asleep. "Where the hell have you been?"

"Out. You should be in bed, Cole. You need to rest."

"You're right. I *should* be in bed. Your bed."

"Cole—"

"You didn't tell me you had plans for the evening. Where were you?"

She tried to take offense at his tone. "That's really none of your business."

"Kelsey—"

The low growl rumbled warningly. It sounded as though Cole had just about reached the end of what little patience he possessed. She spoke heatedly. "Look, I just needed to be alone for a while, okay? I knew you'd insist on talking if you could find me, and I wanted some time to think. I can't think rationally when you're with me."

She no longer even cared how much she was telling him with that particular admission. Surely he had to know already how he affected her when they were together. Look at how easily he'd disarmed her the night before, first with the baseball gloves and then with the book for her. All it took was a smile, a touch, a sweet, unexpected gesture and she'd do or say whatever he wanted. She couldn't risk that tonight, not when she'd needed so badly to put their relationship into perspective.

"You've been thinking about us?" he asked perceptively.

"Yes." The answer was stark.

"And?" Again, she heard the warning in his voice. But then, she'd known he wouldn't make it easy for her.

"I think ... It's not ... Oh, Cole, surely you see how impossible it is. We should end it now, before one—or both—of us is badly hurt." As if it weren't already too late for her.

Cole swore colorfully. "I'm coming over," he said grimly. "We can't talk about this on the telephone."

"No!" She talked fast, knowing it wouldn't be easy to stop him. "Cole, I'm tired. So tired. You must be, as well. Please, I can't do this tonight."

"Damn it," he grumbled, but she could tell, to her immense relief, that she'd gotten through to him. "Kelsey, if it's my family you're worried about, you shouldn't be. I know they can be obnoxious, but they'll come around."

"And if they don't? I'm not going to be the reason for a second painful split in your family, Cole. I could never be happy if that happened because of me."

"It won't, Kelsey. My mother has already agreed to give us a chance. She'd like us to have dinner with her one night next week."

Kelsey panicked at the very thought. "It's—it's not just your family." Though mostly, of course, it was. "We're so different, Cole, in so many ways."

"And so alike in others. Kelsey, I . . ."

Whatever he'd meant to say, he obviously decided it was the wrong time. The words faded into another muttered curse.

She closed her eyes and rubbed at the bridge of her nose, fighting a building headache.

As if he sensed her pain, he spoke more gently. "As you said, we're both tired. Go to bed, Kelsey. We'll talk tomorrow."

His tone brought tears, though she forced them back. "All right. Good night, Cole."

"Good night, sweetheart. Sleep well."

Fresh tears cascaded down her cheeks as she hung up the phone. She didn't even have to be with him, it seemed, for his unexpected tenderness to shatter her willpower. It had been all she could do not to beg him to come over, anyway, despite her efforts to be logical and practical.

Chapter Fourteen

Cole found Kelsey at the hospital the next day. He'd called first, gotten her answering machine and hung up without leaving a message. On a hunch, he'd stopped by the hospital on his way to her apartment. Kelsey and Lauren were sitting in the waiting room, Jared asleep in an infant carrier on the floor at Lauren's feet.

Kelsey's eyes widened when she looked up and saw him standing in the doorway. He chose to believe that her first reaction, before she had time to mask her emotions, was pleasure. He kept his gaze on her as he entered the waiting room, though his first words were to her sister. "How's Paul this morning?"

"Still stable," Lauren replied, looking from Cole to Kelsey and back again.

"That's good news, isn't it?"

"It only means that he hasn't lost any ground since yesterday," she explained.

Cole nodded, really looking at Lauren for the first time. She looked significantly better than she had the day before. Her hair was styled, her makeup neatly applied, the blue dress she wore quite flattering. Though he preferred Kelsey's gaminely wholesome charms, he had to admit that Lauren was a beautiful woman. He could understand why his father had been attracted to her. "You look very nice today," he told her.

She smiled with pleasure. "Thank you."

He turned to Kelsey, who looked great in her own brightly colored short-sleeved sweater and poplin slacks. "You don't look bad, yourself."

He knew he'd caught her off guard with his teasing, that she'd been expecting an immediate return to the discussion they'd begun on the telephone the night before. He had no intention of doing so. Not yet, anyway.

"Thank you," she murmured.

"Do you still want to visit Paul?" Lauren asked, catching Cole off guard as he stood smiling at Kelsey's adorable confusion.

"You mean today?" He shoved his hands in the pockets of his slacks. "Do you really think he's up to seeing me yet?"

"I think it would mean a great deal to him," she answered confidently. "I told him you were here yesterday, along with his parents. He was surprised, of course, but grateful. He wants to see you."

"You told him I was going to see him?"

She nodded. "You haven't changed your mind, have you?" she asked, with just a hint of challenge.

He frowned. "No. I haven't changed my mind. But, damn it, Lauren, what if something goes wrong? What if he gets upset and has an attack? Do you really want to risk that?"

"I suppose you'll just have to make sure he doesn't get upset, won't you?" she asked softly.

He knew the tone. It was one he'd found very effective when dealing with difficult subordinates. He couldn't say he liked having it turned on him—but he *had* said he'd visit Paul. He couldn't honorably back out now, despite his craven urge to do so.

"All right," he said a bit more curtly than he'd intended. "I'll see him. When?"

"The next visiting period is in fifteen minutes. I'll go in and tell him you're here. If he's up to seeing you, that would be as good a time as any."

Cole nodded, then shot a look at Kelsey. "You said you'd go in with me."

She moistened her lips. "I know. The offer still stands, if you need me."

He reached out a hand to her. "I need you."

Kelsey looked from that hand to his face, her gaze locking with his. He saw the emotions flit through her eyes. They both knew that her next move was a momentous one, that taking his hand would be an admission of feelings she wasn't going to be able to deny later. His hand held steady.

Her hand trembled when she touched it to his. Only as his fingers closed firmly around hers did Cole allow himself to breathe again.

He wasn't looking forward to the visit with his father. But with Kelsey beside him, he could face it.

Couldn't she see that he needed her too badly to let anything come between them?

Cole's hazy memories of his father were of a man in his late twenties. Though he knew Paul had aged in twenty-six years, he still wasn't prepared for the reality of a man grayed by time and made gaunt by illness, his skin pasty, his cheeks hollow. Paul was hooked to tubes and monitors. The sickly smell of illness and medication hung in the air. Cole's first impulse was to turn and bolt for the fresh air waiting on the outside.

Kelsey's hand tightened in his, as if she'd somehow read his thoughts.

Cole approached the bed reluctantly, finding himself being thoroughly studied by a set of green eyes that glinted with unexpected intensity. Cole had the impression that Paul was a man who wouldn't easily accept the physical limitations of illness. He could understand; Cole couldn't imagine being bedridden for very long, himself.

"Cole." The voice was raspy, but strong.

He didn't know what to call him. Twenty-six years ago, he'd called him Daddy. "Hello, sir," he said instead, falling back on the formality he'd been trained in for so long.

Paul winced at the address, but let it pass. "Knowing Kelsey, I'm sure she's nagged you into coming. She's like a bull terrier with a bone when she sets her mind on something."

"I make my own decisions," Cole answered, watching the man on the bed and trying to analyze his feelings about him. At the moment, he couldn't say that he felt anything at all. "I understand you wanted to see me."

"Yes." Paul gestured weakly at the monitors and machines surrounding him. "I guess you've figured out that the outlook isn't good for me. This surgery they've scheduled for Monday—well, I've been told I might not come through it."

"Yes, I know." Again, Kelsey's hand twitched in his, as if in silent protest of his bluntness. Had she expected him to stand here and mouth soothing lies? She should know him better by now.

Paul nodded, obviously satisfied with Cole's answer. "I know you don't owe me anything, Cole. God knows you've got grounds for hating me. But I don't want to go through this surgery without knowing for certain that Lauren and the baby will be taken care of. I'm asking you to keep an eye on them if anything should happen to me. Financially, they're in pretty good shape. And Lauren's fully capable of raising our son alone. But I'd like to know you'd be there for them if they need you."

"I've already offered," Cole assured him. "Anything they need, they have only to ask."

Paul nodded. "I appreciate it. Lauren said you've got my parents interested in the boy."

"They want to see him, of course. He *is* their grandson."

"And I'm their son," Paul returned steadily. "They haven't wanted to see me for years."

Cole shook his head. "I don't think that's exactly true. I think they've wanted very badly to see you. The Saxon pride got in the way."

Paul's left eyebrow rose in an expression Cole recognized as his own. Seeing the resemblances between himself and the man in the bed shook him. "You don't seem to be lacking in the Saxon pride, yourself," Paul accused mildly. "I've been trying to get you to see me since you graduated from college, to no avail."

Cole winced. "I thought you'd waited all those years to try. I wasn't told about your earlier attempts. I suppose pride—Saxon or my own—played a large part in my actions."

Paul shook his head against the pillow, his expression sad. "I'm not blaming you, Cole. I've never blamed you. God knows you were the innocent victim in all this. I handled things very badly twenty-six years ago. I know that—I've always known. My only excuse is that I had reached a point where I honestly thought I had no other choices. I was wrong, of course. There are always better options than running away. I've suffered the price of my mistake ever since."

"I understand that you were unhappy," Cole conceded. He glanced at the beeping monitors. "Perhaps you'd rather talk about it at another time. You need to be building strength now. If you want to see me again after the surgery, I'll be here."

Kelsey looked up at him with gratitude shining in her eyes. Though his offer hadn't been for her benefit alone, Cole was glad now that he'd made it. He wanted her to know that she'd changed him, that he wasn't the same hard, inflexible man she'd first met.

But, again, Paul shook his head. "I can't talk long," he admitted, "but there are some things I want you to know now. In case...well, in case there aren't any other chances."

Resignedly, Cole inclined his head and waited.

Paul lay quietly for a moment, as if gathering his thoughts and his strength. And then he looked gravely at his son. "Your mother and I were married when I was twenty-one and she was nineteen. I don't remember asking her to marry me—it was taken for granted that we would wed from the time we were children. She was a strong, intelligent, attractive young woman, and I thought we'd grow to love each other. After all, we had so much in common, knew each other so well. I thought we'd be happy. I was wrong."

"You're so certain Mother didn't love you?" Cole couldn't help asking.

"If she did," Paul answered carefully, "she was never able to show it, through words or affection. I needed more than that, Cole. The first year was—difficult. And then you were born. I tried for the next six years to make it work.

"I was good at my job, but I was growing to hate it more with each passing day. It wasn't what I wanted to do, you see. My actions, my schedules—hell, my very thoughts were dictated by Harold Grayson. Belinda was perfectly willing to have her father running our lives, couldn't conceive of ever standing up to him. Or wanting to. Finally, when you were six, I asked for a divorce."

Lost in unhappy memories, he stared blindly upward, his voice oddly distant. Cole listened without interruption, knowing he was probably crushing Kelsey's fingers in his own, unable to release her.

"Your mother," Paul said, "categorically refused the divorce. Her parents were outraged that I'd hurt her with the request. Mine were appalled that I was willing to throw away the brilliant future they'd arranged for me. Every change I tried to make in my life was defeated. One morning, when you were seven, I got in my car to drive to the office. The next thing I knew I had run out of gas on a highway in North Carolina. To this day I don't remember that drive."

"You had a breakdown," Kelsey said. It was the first time she'd spoken since they'd entered the room. Cole could see that she was fascinated by the story, that it was as new to her as it was to him. Though he assumed Paul had discussed it with Lauren, it was obvious that Kelsey hadn't known the details.

"I suppose that's what it could be called," Paul agreed. "I only knew that at last I was free and that I couldn't go back. I kept driving. I won't tell you how I lived for the next year, but by the time I pulled myself together enough to try to rebuild my life, Belinda had divorced me for desertion and my family had forbidden my name to be spoken again.

"I wanted to see you, Cole. I missed you very much, thought of you every day. But I was in no shape to care for you even if by some miracle I could have gotten you. I knew Belinda loved you in her way, that you'd be well taken care of, though your life would always be subject to their wishes. I wanted to be around to help you see that there were alternatives, but again, I was thwarted over and over in trying to see you. I waited until I knew you had graduated from college, old enough to make the decision to see me on your own, and I moved back here in hopes of reestablishing some sort of relationship with you. I didn't want to live the rest of my life alone. But it was too late by then. You refused to have anything to do with me when I tried to contact you."

His throat tight, Cole could only nod.

Paul sighed. "Nothing I've told you was meant as an excuse. I was wrong. I was weak and cowardly. I should have stayed and fought for the right to run my life as I chose, to see my son when I wished. My freedom should never have been won at the price of hurting you or my family."

"Have you been happy since you left?" Cole heard himself asking without actually planning the question.

"Yes, I have," Paul confessed. "After that first year of confusion, I began to focus my energy on making a success of myself, on my own for the first time in my life."

"As I understand, you succeeded quite well. It couldn't have been easy to start from nothing and make a go of it."

"It wasn't. Seemed I had quite a flair for computers, and happened to be in the right place at the right time for the beginning of the computer boom. Other than my regrets about you, I had no reason to complain. And eventually I met Lauren. She has shown me what a real, loving marriage can be like. I know now that this is what I always wanted, what I always needed. I'm sorry you were hurt by my leaving, Cole—more sorry than I can ever tell you. But I wouldn't go back and change anything if it meant I'd have never known Lauren. Can you understand that?"

With Kelsey's hand clasped tightly in his, Cole nodded. "I suppose so."

Paul looked at him searchingly. "You're happy with your life, son? You enjoy your work with Grayson?"

"Yes," Cole answered simply. "I chose this career. I'm good at it, and I enjoy it. And I get along well with both the Graysons and Saxons. Perhaps I have been indulged more than you were—I've had little trouble having my own way."

Paul nodded, a touch of humor in his expression. "You were always very strong willed. Even as a baby. That gave me hope for you." He glanced at Cole and Kelsey's linked hands. "Lauren says the two of you are quite an item."

Cole almost smiled when Kelsey blushed rosily. "Kelsey is very special," he said tactfully. "I recognized that the first time I met her."

"Then you must have inherited something from me, after all," Paul replied with some satisfaction. And then his smile faded. "Grayson isn't going to like it. He hates me. He'll never approve of you being involved with a member of my new family."

"He isn't pleased," Cole admitted, conscious of the way Kelsey had stiffened at the words.

"He has a great deal of influence over your career," Paul warned. "I've heard that he'd intended to step down soon and turn the command over to you."

"We've discussed the possibility."

"And if it comes to a choice between Kelsey and being CEO of Grayson Shipping?" Paul's eyes were sharp now, his voice stronger.

"It won't," Cole said flatly, as he had to Paul's father in response to the same question.

"You're sure?"

"My grandfather has too much pride to risk taking me on in a public fight for control of the company."

Paul's expression mirrored both approval and a touch of respect. "You'd fight him?"

"If it were necessary, with every last ounce of my strength," Cole answered firmly. "It won't be necessary."

Paul smiled faintly. "You're a stronger man than I was, Cole. Maybe the combination of Grayson and Saxon blood is what it takes to overpower either of them. I think you can do it."

Noting that his father was growing even more pale than he'd been when they'd entered, Cole gave Kelsey an almost imperceptible nod toward the door. "You're tired," he told Paul. "And you've said what you needed to say. Get some rest now and I'll see you again after your surgery."

"You will?"

Cole nodded. "I can't promise you that I'll ever completely forgive the pain you caused me when you left the way you did," he said slowly, choosing his words with care. "I know I'll never be able to forget it. But I can tell you that I understand better now, and that I think it's possible to put that past behind us. To start over as adults.''

"I only hope we'll have that chance,'' Paul murmured, blinking back tears he obviously knew would only embarrass his son.

"We will.'' Cole spoke with a confidence he couldn't quite feel. And then he offered his father a smile. "After all, you're a Saxon.''

Paul chuckled weakly. "Yes. The one thing I have always been is a Saxon.''

Cole still wasn't sure what to call him. So he said nothing more as he waited for Kelsey to kiss Paul's cheek and then rejoin him. Paul detained him at the last moment. "Cole, don't forget your promise. You'll watch out for Lauren and the baby if I don't make it. Don't let the family bully her.''

Cole managed a smile. "I'll take care of Lauren and Jared. The only one they have to worry about bullying them is me.''

Paul gave a snort of laughter. "I'm not worried about that. Lauren can handle you. And the boy's going to be enough like you to hold his own.''

"I'm sure you're right.''

"Cole.'' This time one tear did escape, to make a slow path down one pale, hollow cheek. "Thank you.''

"You just concentrate on getting stronger,'' Cole returned gruffly. "Your family needs you.''

He and Kelsey stepped out of the room just as a frowning nurse arrived to hasten their departure.

Cole started down the hallway toward the waiting room, then suddenly stopped and pulled Kelsey into his arms. Pulling her close, he hid his face in her hair. She didn't even hesitate before putting her arms around him, holding him just as tightly. They stood that way for several long minutes, ignoring the curious glances of hospital staff and visitors stepping around them in the hallway.

* * *

It was less than an hour later when Kelsey and Cole walked together to the hospital parking lot. She turned automatically in the direction of her car, only to be brought up short by his hand on her arm. "We'll take mine," he said, tugging lightly in the opposite direction.

She started to protest. "But—"

"I'll bring you back later for yours. You'll want to come back anyway, won't you?"

"Well, yes, but I really think I should take my car now." She knew Cole intended to take her somewhere to finish the talk about their relationship. Since she hadn't changed her mind about ending it, despite the emotional scene in Paul's room, she wasn't sure Cole would be around later when she was ready to return to the hospital.

She knew full well he wasn't going to like what she had to say.

A muscle flexed in his jaw. "We'll take my car."

The words were spoken quietly, without a change of expression other than that barely perceptible muscle twitch. Still, she decided that perhaps they would take his car, after all. She could always catch the bus later if necessary, she told herself.

She had expected him to drive straight to her apartment. She almost groaned aloud when she realized he was taking her to his house, instead. He really wasn't going to make this easy for her.

Entering Cole's home was like walking into a museum—or stepping into the past. Kelsey was immediately entranced by the sparkle of crystal overhead, the gleam of wood floors and trim, the richness of marble and brass. Rugs, furnishings and accents were either authentic period pieces or excellent reproductions.

It should have been intimidating, even cold. It wasn't. She had no trouble imagining a family living in this beautiful home. She looked around the cozy parlor he led her into, picturing a Christmas tree in a bow window here, a grouping of children's portraits there. "Cole, it's wonderful," she whispered.

His expression softened. "I'm glad you like it. I'll take you through the rest of it later, after we talk. There are several bedrooms, a large master suite. It's a home made for a family."

Unnerved by his words, she cleared her throat and avoided his eyes, still studying the parlor furnishings. "Do you ever include it on historical tours?"

"Rarely. I allowed myself to be persuaded to do so last Christmas. It was decorated by professionals for the season and open to special tours for only one weekend. I stayed at the corporate apartment for those two days."

"It must have been breathtaking," Kelsey murmured, dreamily picturing garlands and ribbons and wreaths. "You have a lovely home."

"As I said, it's a home for a family, not for a man alone. I need someone to share it with me," he said deeply, moving close enough to cup her cheek in his warm, broad palm. "I need you, Kelsey."

Her breath caught painfully as she stared up at him. Surely he wasn't suggesting—*surely* he wasn't talking about marriage! He couldn't possibly want...

And then he shattered what little composure she had left with three huskily murmured words. "I love you."

"No!" The word was driven from her in a rush of panic. She pulled away from him, her movements jerky as she took two steps back, her arms crossed defensively at her waist. "You don't... you can't... it's just..."

Closing her eyes in self-disgust, she took a deep breath before opening them again and starting over. Cole looked stunned by her overreaction, but he stood very still, allowing her to say what she had to say.

She gestured around her, at the elegance and visible wealth surrounding her. "Do I really look like I belong here?" she asked, trying to make him see reality.

"You belong with me," he answered flatly. "And, yes, as a matter of fact, you look perfect for my home. I've been imagining you here ever since the first night I met you."

She swallowed a moan of exasperation. "Cole, you have to understand. It's happened too fast, too intensely. We've only known each other two and a half weeks and so much has happened to you during that time. Anyone would be confused by now. It's so easy to mistake what you're feeling when there are so many strong emotions to sort out at once."

His eyes narrowed, giving him that dangerous, daunting look of the man she'd once chased through an office building. She tightened her arms and barely suppressed a shiver.

"You really think," he asked silkily, "that I'm confusing my feelings for you? That I've simply been carried away by emotionalism?"

She swallowed before speaking carefully, knowing he was very close to an explosion. "I know you're not the type to confuse your emotions, not usually, anyway. But these past few weeks have hardly been typical."

He inclined his head in that regal, just-short-of-arrogant manner that said so much about him, about his upbringing. "I'll admit the past weeks have been eventful. As you said, I've gained a brother and young stepmother and saw my father again for the first time in twenty-six years. I've learned some truths that have been kept from me since my childhood. And I fell in love for the first time in my life. Don't tell me I'm imagining it or mistaking the feeling for something else, Kelsey. I'm not. I love you.

"I've discovered a few things during the past weeks," he continued, when she would have tried again to argue with him. "I've learned how destructive pride can be. How senseless it is to hide one's feelings. I've looked at my mother and have seen a woman who lost the man she loved because she didn't know how to tell him, didn't know how to give him the loyalty and support he needed. My grandparents lost their son because they couldn't accept him as he was, couldn't love him unconditionally. My father lost his son and was cut off from his family because he couldn't stand up for what he needed, was afraid to fight for what he wanted. I'm not going to let that happen to us.''

She wanted so desperately to believe him. To throw herself into his arms and beg him never to let her go. But she couldn't do that to him, couldn't put herself through the pain that would surely follow. ''Cole, I'm sorry. It just won't work.''

''Because of my family? You still think they'll try to keep us apart?''

''I *know* they'll try. You can't deny they're unhappy with our relationship. I saw the way your grandfather Saxon frowned when you kissed me. I heard the anger in your other grandfather's voice when he found us together at your office. And I saw the pain on your mother's face when she looked at Paul's son. I won't tear your family apart again.''

He exhaled sharply and ran a hand through his hair. ''Why won't you trust me?'' he demanded. ''I told you they'd come around, and they will. My mother has already said she's willing to try. I told you that last night.''

''I know what you told me,'' she replied in frustration. ''She's willing to have me in her home because she doesn't want to lose her son. But do you think she'll ever really accept me? Don't you know that every time she looks at me she'll remember that my sister is married to her ex-husband? If it's true she loved your father and was deeply hurt by his desertion, do you think she'll ever be comfortable knowing that my nephew is his son? My sister and her child are very important to me, Cole. I won't push them away because their presence is awkward to your family.''

"Nor would I ask you to," he said evenly. "Your nephew happens to be important to me, too. He's my brother. I've already informed my mother that I intend to be a part of his life. It won't be easy for her at first, but she's always been able to adapt to circumstances. She'll learn to accept this."

"And her father? He has the power to destroy your career. Do you really think I'd allow that to happen?"

Searching her face, he answered slowly. "You heard what I told Paul about that. My grandfather will not take away the position I've trained for most of my life, the promotion I have fully earned. Nor, frankly, will he be willing to risk pushing me out of his life. Paul was only his son-in-law. I am his only grandson. He won't jeopardize our relationship. But this isn't really about my relationship with my family at all, is it, Kelsey?"

She frowned. "I don't know what you mean."

"You're afraid of them. You're afraid to stand up to them and make them accept you."

"I'm not..." She stopped and moistened her dry lips. "Well, maybe I am intimidated by them," she admitted finally. "I've met them, remember? They're so arrogant, so powerful, so stern. Do you really think I want to push my way into their lives, force them to treat me with simple consideration?"

"I didn't promise it would be easy," he said. "But then it wasn't all that easy to reach me, was it? I didn't notice any lack of courage on your part then."

"That's different," she muttered, wringing her hands at her waist. "I was trying to help Paul."

"In other words, you're only willing to fight for what other people want? Not for yourself? Don't you have wishes of your own, Kelsey?"

Of course she had wishes, she thought despairingly, looking at him in tormented silence. She wished things were different for them. She wished they'd met at another time, another place. She wished life didn't have to be so complicated, love so painful. And most of all, she wished she could trust him not to change his mind about loving her when things settled down and he'd shifted back into his regular routine of challenging work and wealthy, beautiful people. Couldn't he understand that she didn't belong in his world?

"Can't you at least tell me how you feel about me?" Cole persisted. "Has it all been a game to you, a no-holds-barred campaign to convince me to give in and see Paul? *Did you go to bed with me to further your arguments, Kelsey?*"

Chapter Fifteen

Kelsey felt the blood drain from her face even as her heart flinched from the blow Cole had just dealt it. He looked so angry, so cold. So withdrawn. "Cole," she whispered, her voice strangled. "Surely you don't believe that."

His face softened with his smile, bringing the threat of tears to heat the back of her eyes. He lifted a hand to her cheek in that gesture she'd grown to love so much. "Of course I don't believe that," he murmured, his thumb stroking her lower lip. "Do you really think I could have spent this much time with you without knowing that you're totally incapable of such despicable subterfuge? You're the most honest, generous, loving person I've ever known. And I think you've been with me because for some reason you grew to care about me."

The tears welled, blurred her vision. She blinked them back, determined not to cry. "Cole, I—"

"You're afraid, Kelsey. You're afraid to trust your feelings—and mine. You're afraid my family will try to come between us, that they'll hurt you. You've been hurt in the past—by your mother's death, your father's absences, your sister's unhappiness. You've protected yourself since by always staying in control, working in a job where you can satisfy your loving, generous nature while still maintaining a professional distance. And now you find yourself facing a situation you can't control, one that requires total involvement on your part. This time you're the one who'll be left disappointed if something goes wrong."

She stared at him in open-mouthed astonishment, finding it hard to believe he was saying those things. He was wrong. Of course he was wrong. So how did he make those incredible things sound so rational? "No," she said. "That's—absurd."

His expression didn't change. His eyes were still warm, loving, understanding. She almost closed her own to block him out, to give her the strength to hold out against him. It was all she could do not to throw herself at him.

"I'm not going to push you, Kelsey. I love you. I've never been more sure of anything in my life. I want to marry you, to build a family with you, to share your life and your causes. I'm willing to fight for what I've found with you, willing to face anything to hold on to it. But I know I can't do it alone. I know you have to be as fully committed as I am.

"I think you love me, Kelsey. I think you're brave enough to admit that this time you're the one with a dream, a special wish. And I think you're strong enough to go after that goal with the same never-give-up determination you use when you're working for your kids. But first you have to acknowledge that you're not invulnerable, that you can't always do everything alone. You have to admit that you need me, as much as I need you."

She chewed her lower lip, unable to meet his eyes. She wanted so badly to allow him to convince her that he was right—but fear still held her in its grip. Fear of admitting her love for him, her need for him, fear of facing his family, fear of causing more turmoil in his life. Fear of losing him. Of losing herself if she did.

"Come on. I'll take you back to your car. You need time to think about what I've said. I know myself too well to believe I can be with you and not pressure you to give in," he said with a wry twist to his mouth. Surprisingly enough, he still didn't look angry. But the set of his jaw told of a deeply ingrained determination to win, to have his own way in the end, no matter how long he had to wait.

She allowed herself one wistful glance at the gleaming, curved stairway in the foyer as he led her toward the front door. "I would have liked to have seen the rest of your house," she said.

He gave her a fleeting, crooked smile. "I'll show you the rest of the house when you're ready to move into it with me."

She narrowed her eyes and lifted her chin at the undisguised challenge in his words. "I thought you weren't going to pressure me."

"If you'll remember, I said I *would* pressure you as long as you're with me. Which is why I'm being so damned noble and self-sacrificing and not carrying you up to my bedroom."

How she would have loved to be carried up that magnificent stairway to his bedroom, she thought longingly. But that was hardly any way to bring an end to this impossible relationship, she reminded herself sternly.

Kelsey was still dazed by Cole's actions by the time she arrived at her apartment later. As he'd promised, he'd left her at her car with a kiss and a reminder that she had his number when she was ready to call him. Not if. When.

Was he so very certain he'd have his way in this conflict, as he apparently did in most others?

She really should be furious at his arrogance, she thought, dropping onto her couch with a huff, her feet curled beneath her, arms crossed defiantly. How could he so smugly assume that he was so important to her, she was willing to put up with whatever his obnoxious families wanted to dish out just to be with him? And why was she beginning to suspect he was right?

It would be so much easier to stand firmly against him if he'd gotten angry, if he'd shouted and ranted and ordered her to forget her reservations and give in to his demands.

But he hadn't. Instead, he'd been gentle and patient and even understanding, though she still thought his analysis of her behavior was way off target. It was so unfair of him to refuse to be predictable. Every time she thought she knew what he'd do, he caught her off guard by doing something else entirely.

Frowning darkly, she thought of the two Cole Saxons she'd come to know during the past weeks. The businessman—hard, ruthless, impatient, unyielding, domineering, quick-tempered, unapologetically rude. All true of him.

And then there was that other Cole—the one who'd sent a sick boy to Graceland and taken another fishing, who'd bought a computer for another child to be given anonymously. The one who'd fallen under the spell of a slobbery baby grin, who'd bought baseball gloves for future games of catch. The Cole who'd taken charge of a screaming baby when he could see that Kelsey was close to breaking, who'd called in a favor to give her an autographed book because he'd known diamonds would make her uncomfortable.

The man who'd made love to her so tenderly, so totally, so beautifully. Who'd made her love him with only a smile and a gentle touch on her cheek.

She hadn't realized she was crying until a fat tear dripped from her cheek to splash onto her hand.

Swiping unsteadily at the stream of tears following that one, she found herself remembering Cole's accusation that fear was the only thing standing between them. Her fear.

She'd told herself, and him, that she was trying to protect Cole by ending their relationship. She hadn't wanted him hurt by another rift in his family, hadn't wanted to jeopardize the career he claimed to love by coming between him and his grandfather. But Cole had dismissed those possibilities with a confident wave of his hand. Apparently, he wasn't particularly worried about them. He, of course, knew his families better than she. If he thought he would be accepted even though Paul had not been, he was probably right. Even Paul had pointed out that Cole was the stronger of the two.

Which left Cole's theory that Kelsey was more afraid for herself than for him. She didn't like it—but she thought perhaps he was right. She wasn't just afraid. She was terrified.

The thought of having dinner with his mother made her hands tremble. The idea of forcing his grandparents to accept her made her stomach turn. Never in her life had she forced herself on anyone—unless, of course, it had been necessary to provide a wish for one of her special children.

This time you're the one who'll be left disappointed if something goes wrong, Cole had said. But in that he'd been mistaken. She wouldn't simply be disappointed if something went wrong, if her relationship with Cole couldn't survive the obstacles ahead of it. She would be devastated.

Nothing in her life had ever compared with the magnitude of her feelings for Cole. Nothing had ever been more important, more perilous. Nothing else had had the potential to shatter her the way losing him would after she'd risked everything to have him. And if it hurt this much to end it now, how much more horribly could it hurt after sharing even more time with him?

Maybe Cole was right. Maybe she was a coward.

But couldn't he see that her fears were not without basis? That the odds against them really were enormous? Couldn't he see that she was simply trying to protect herself—both of them—from inevitable pain?

She hid her face in her hands and gave in to the tears. Lonely. Hurting. Wishing...

Lauren and Jared arrived at Kelsey's apartment Sunday afternoon just as a summer storm erupted. Grimacing at the driving rain waiting to drench her as soon as she stepped back outside, Lauren gratefully accepted the umbrella Kelsey loaned her. "I'm glad the rain waited until I got Jared inside, anyway."

"I guess he and I won't be going on any walks today," Kelsey said with a sigh, already feeling the restlessness of cabin fever setting in. She wasn't looking forward to being restrained to several more hours of nothing to do but think longingly of Cole.

"Doesn't look like it." Hovering at the door, Lauren paused long enough to ask, "Did Cole call this morning?"

Kelsey had told her sister about the confrontation the day before, about her determination to break off the affair and Cole's equal determination for it to progress even more seriously. Lauren hadn't said much but had offered sympathy for Kelsey's distress. Kelsey suspected that Lauren fully expected Cole to come out the victor in this particular battle.

"No, he hasn't called," she answered peevishly. "And it wouldn't change anything if he had. I'm not getting involved with him, Lauren."

Lauren's eyebrow twitched. "I would say you'd already gotten involved with him."

"I thought it was just an affair. I never dreamed he'd start talking about marriage," Kelsey wailed, resisting an impulse to wring her hands.

"Just an affair," Lauren repeated with a faint smile. "Listen to yourself, Kelsey. You've never been interested in just an affair. You've been in love with Cole Saxon from the beginning."

Kelsey winced. "Maybe I have," she admitted grudgingly. "But I—well, I guess I just got carried away with the feelings at first. I didn't realize, didn't allow myself to think about how difficult it would be. I hadn't been subjected to his family then. I guess I thought Paul had exaggerated about them. Now I know he didn't."

"His parents are trying to make amends."

Kelsey nodded to concede the point. "But why?" she asked gravely. "Because they're sorry about the way they treated Paul? Or because they don't want you to keep the newest little Saxon away from them?"

"There is that possibility," Lauren admitted, glancing thoughtfully at the crib. "I have to admit I've considered it a great deal. If they think I'll allow them to try to control Jared's life, they're wrong. I'll never let them see him if I sense that's the motive behind their sudden attention. It's the same with Cole," she added. "Though I've begun to doubt that he'll interfere with my decisions for Jared, he'll still find himself with a fight on his hands if he should ever try."

"He won't," Kelsey answered unhesitatingly. "I think Cole wants to be a part of Jared's life, but he would never try to interfere with the way you raise him. Not as long as he thinks you're doing a good job of it," she added with a wry grimace, knowing that if Cole ever thought Jared was being mistreated or neglected, he'd step in with his usual arrogant authority. Fortunately, Lauren would never give him cause to believe Jared wasn't receiving the best of care.

Lauren imitated the ironic expression. "Right. The thing is that I've married a Saxon. True, he was cut off from the rest of the family when we met and hasn't had any contact with them since. But I've always sensed the need in him to be reunited with his family. I've always expected to find myself faced with them someday, though I'd hoped Paul would be well and healthy and standing as a buffer between me and them. I've always known that, when and if the day came, they wouldn't approve of me, they'd think I was too young for him, or not from a suitable background or not sophisticated enough to blend with their crowd. But I love Paul and being married to him has been worth anything we have faced or have yet to face. No one ever promised love was easy, Kelsey. No one ever said it came without risks."

"I never thought it did," Kelsey answered defensively. "But I never thought it would be quite this complicated, either."

"Yes, well, life has a way of hitting us with bizarre surprises," Lauren remarked, tightening her grip on the umbrella and glancing out the window beside the door. "The rain seems to have let up a little. I'd better make a dash for the car before it gets heavy again."

"Drive carefully. The roads will be slippery."

"I'll be careful. See you later."

"Yeah," Kelsey murmured, after the door had already closed behind Lauren. "Later."

And then she turned toward the baby sleeping in his crib in an otherwise hauntingly empty apartment.

They'd been warned that Paul's operation would take hours. There'd been no way to prepare them for how harrowing those hours would be. Lauren sat utterly still, her hands clasped as if in prayer, her face pale and set. Jared was again being cared for by volunteers from her close-knit church group so that Kelsey could be with Lauren during the ordeal. Lauren's minister, a gruff, good-natured man with gentle, smiling eyes, stayed with her for a while, leaving Kelsey to pace restlessly through the hallways, unable to be still for long.

Cole was there, as were Paul's parents. They stayed pretty much to one side, out of the way, tensing every time a doctor approached the waiting room. Kelsey felt Cole's eyes on her often, though he'd kept his word about not pressuring her verbally. Those long, searching looks only added to her tension. She tried to avoid his eyes, though so often her own were drawn to him.

The operation had been underway for perhaps an hour when Cole rose from the sofa where he'd been almost since arriving. Kelsey tensed, certain he was going to approach her. Instead, he gave her a long, impossible-to-read look and left the room with only a murmur to his grandmother.

Where was he going? she wondered. What was he doing? What was he thinking? Why wasn't he sitting beside her, holding her hand?

She moaned quietly at her own inconsistency. No matter how firmly she told herself she couldn't have him, she still wanted him.

His grandparents sat silently, stiffly in their chosen corner. They'd greeted Kelsey when they'd arrived, spoken to Lauren a few times since—usually about Jared—but had been very quiet on the whole. They looked worried. Kelsey couldn't help wondering if they were both thinking of the years they'd lost with Paul, the possibility that there'd be no opportunity to even partially make up for those wasted years.

Where was Cole?

He returned after being gone for twenty minutes. His face was pale, his eyes grim. Kelsey instinctively started to go to him, to find out what had happened to upset him. She stopped herself at the last moment from doing so, though she searched his face anxiously. Seeing her watching him, Cole made a visible effort to soften his scowl. He veered from his path toward his grandparents to approach Kelsey, stopping a few feet from the couch where she perched.

"You okay?" he asked, his voice low.

She nodded. "Are you?"

"I could be better," he admitted. She sensed the meaning in the words.

She almost reached out to him; and then she noticed that his grandfather was watching them with a frown of disapproval. Her fingers curled in her lap. "So could I," she murmured, looking away from him.

"Kelsey." He moved restlessly, then exhaled deeply. "Do you need anything? Coffee? A soft drink?" he asked, though she knew that wasn't what he'd wanted to say.

"No. Thank you."

She sensed his nod rather than saw it, since she still couldn't quite bring herself to look at him. She heard him move on to Lauren with the same offer of refreshments. Lauren, too, refused, though politely.

Cole sat beside Lauren. From the corner of her eye, Kelsey saw him cover her sister's hands with his own.

Cole's kindness brought a lump to her throat, and propelled her to her feet. "I need to stretch my legs," she blurted to anyone who happened to be listening, and then turned and literally bolted from the waiting room.

She didn't know where she was going when she started out, only that she needed to be away from the tension for a while. Away from Cole. She wasn't particularly surprised when she found herself headed toward the children's wards.

The nurses greeted Kelsey with warm smiles and concerned questions about her brother-in-law, since most of them knew about the operation. The patients, many of whom she knew by name, gave her grins and loving hugs.

"Jennifer, what are you doing here?" Kelsey demanded, spotting a familiar face in one of the rooms.

The girl made a face. "Strep infection," she said with a weary acceptance too old for her twelve years. She gestured toward the IV bottle hanging beside her bed. "Antibiotics."

Knowing how dangerous any sort of infection could be for a child whose immune system was as disease-depleted as Jennifer's, Kelsey hid her concern behind a smile. "How is Blaze?" she asked.

Jennifer's plain face lit up. "He's the most wonderful horse in all the world," she answered happily. "The woman who stables him for me called this morning to tell me he misses me. I told her to tell him I'll be back to see him later in the week. And I'll be bringing him a carrot. He really loves carrots."

"Does he?" Kelsey loved it when she could see for herself the pleasure her work wrought. Already some of the tension was leaving her. She'd needed to be with her kids.

She visited a few minutes more with Jennifer before moving on. She found Al and Linda MacKenzie conversing quietly in the hallway outside Ronnie's semiprivate room. "How is he today?" she asked them, taking Linda's hands in her own.

"Not good," Al answered simply. "He took a turn for the worse during the night."

"I'm so sorry." The words were always inadequate at times like this. Kelsey had never found more expressive words to replace them.

Al only nodded. "He sure does love looking at that sailfish," he said with a hint of a sad smile. "Bet this is the only hospital room with a sailfish hung on the wall."

"He enjoyed visiting with Cole earlier," Linda added. "He's resting now from the visit, but it meant a great deal to him. He's grown very fond of Cole."

"Cole was just here?" So that's where he'd gone.

"Yes. He was upset that Ronnie's losing ground so quickly," Linda answered, reaching for her husband's hand. "He seems to think he should be able to do something for us, something to make everything right again."

"He's like that," Kelsey agreed quietly. "Cole's so accustomed to being in control. It's hard for him to accept that there are times when his money and his influence aren't enough."

"He may be a rich, powerful man," Al said gruffly, "but he's been good to us. Good to Ronnie. That's all that matters as far as we're concerned."

"He's a good man," Linda affirmed. "We're very grateful to him, and to you, for giving Ronnie so much pleasure when he—" Her voice broke.

Al stepped in smoothly. "You tell him we appreciate all he's done," he said. "No one could have asked for more from him. He needs to know he did all he could. A man starts expecting too much from himself and he ends up in trouble. I know. When Ronnie first got sick, I thought it was up to me to somehow make him well. I thought it was my job as husband and father to protect the family from anything that could go wrong. I almost lost it when I realized there wasn't anything I could do but stand back and let the doctors do their best. If it hadn't been for Linda, I don't know what I'd have done. A man needs a woman to love him when he's given all he can and knows he's still got to keep going."

"I'm not sure Cole needs anyone," Kelsey murmured, speaking more to herself than to the MacKenzies. "He's so strong, so self-reliant."

"That's the kind that needs love the most," Linda replied, looking at her husband. "Someone to let them know it's okay at times not to be strong, not to be invulnerable. Someone to hold them when they just need to be held."

Realizing the direction the conversation had taken, Kelsey flushed and quickly turned the subject back to Ronnie. She promised to stay in contact with them, asked them to please call if there was anything she could do, told them how very much she hoped and prayed for a reprieve for them. And then she told them she had to get back to her sister.

Al pulled Linda into his arms as Kelsey turned to leave. The last glimpse she had of them as the elevator doors closed showed them still locked in that tight embrace, Al's head bowed protectively, yet somehow vulnerably, over his wife's. And Linda held on to her husband with hands that sought comfort even as they offered support.

Kelsey's heart ached dully in her chest. "Oh, Cole," she murmured, allowing herself one moment of soul-deep longing.

Paul survived the operation. Kelsey was standing by her sister when the doctor offered a cautiously optimistic prognosis for recovery. Lauren sagged as though relief had gone straight to her knees. Kelsey grabbed her arm in support at the same moment Cole put an arm around Lauren from her other side.

"You need to rest," the doctor ordered sternly, "or we'll have you as a patient, too. It's going to be awhile before you can see him. I want you off your feet during that time, you hear?"

Lauren nodded, though her eyes were still dazed. The doctor made arrangements for Lauren to be taken to an empty room where she could comply with his instructions until she was summoned for a visit with her husband. Having known her for years, he escorted her there himself, talking softly as they went.

Kelsey watched them walk away, then started when Cole placed a hand on her shoulder. "I'm taking my grandparents home," he said, studying her intently. "They're exhausted. Do you need anything before I go?"

"No. Thank you."

As though he couldn't hold back any longer, Cole tightened his grasp. "Kelsey, come with us. Get to know them. Let them get to know you."

Kelsey glanced quickly from Cole to the two older people standing impatiently behind him, Phillip's expression inscrutable. "No. I'm sorry, I can't."

Cole sighed irritably, nerves obviously raw from the long, tense morning. "Damn it, Kelsey. You're not even giving us a chance."

She bit her lip and looked away.

He gripped her shoulder in silent protest and then released her, stepping away. "You know how to reach me," he muttered, before turning to his grandparents.

Yes, she thought, watching them leave. She knew how to reach him. But she wouldn't. She simply couldn't take the risk.

Chapter Sixteen

Kelsey Campbell was a coward. It wasn't a pleasant realization. Wasn't something she liked seeing when she looked at her mirror first thing every morning after another sleepless, miserable night. But it was long past time for her to stop denying it and admit the truth.

She'd called herself wise for ending a relationship that had seemed doomed to failure from the onset. She'd tried to feel noble for sparing Cole the pain of a second family altercation. She'd even told herself it took a great deal of courage to have told him goodbye when she wanted nothing more than to be with him.

She'd lied. She'd run away from him for no other reason than that she was a craven coward, afraid of being hurt. He'd been right. She'd have fought to the last breath to accomplish a goal for one of her kids. But when it came to something she wanted for herself, she hadn't had the nerve to risk trying and possibly failing.

Her hands wrapped so tightly around the steering wheel of her car that her knuckles ached, Kelsey stared fiercely through the windshield, only half her concentration on her driving. She thought of the courage the three people who meant the most to her had shown at various points of crisis in their lives.

It had taken spirit for Lauren to elope with Tom so many years ago. It turned out to have been a major mistake, but at least she'd made an effort to attain something she'd badly wanted. And four years later, though battered and humiliated, she'd broken away from Tom and rebuilt her life. It had taken more courage than even Lauren had known she'd possessed to take a risk on another man, in a match that seemed even more unlikely than the first. A man twenty-five years her senior. A man who'd been disowned by two of the most influential families in Savannah. A man who could well have made her a young widow had the operation three weeks ago not been successful.

Paul had made a mistake twenty-six years earlier by walking away from his job and family the way he had. Even he admitted that now. Yet it hadn't been easy for him to sacrifice everything in order to find the happiness and self-fulfillment he'd craved so desperately.

Cole had taken the risk of falling in love with Kelsey. A woman guaranteed to be considered unsuitable by his families. A woman whose presence in his life would prove awkward again and again, would bring pain to his mother. A woman who, by antagonizing Cole's grandfather, could even endanger Cole's chances at becoming president of his company. And he'd taken a chance at being reunited with the father who'd hurt him so deeply once, whose loss would now hurt so deeply again.

But when it had been time for her to take risks, to fight, if necessary, for her own happiness, Kelsey had been a coward.

A traffic light ahead turned yellow, then red. Kelsey braked automatically, hardly aware of her actions.

It had been three weeks since the surgery. Paul was recovering steadily, Lauren was glowing with happiness at being granted more time with her husband, Jared was healthy and happy. Through determination and hours of persistence, Kelsey had fulfilled one wish that others had sadly deemed unattainable, making a very sick little girl blissfully happy for now. And yet it had been the most miserable three weeks of Kelsey's life.

She missed Cole. It was hard to believe how terribly she missed him. It only made it worse that she'd seen him several times during those weeks, always in the hospital when they'd both been visiting Paul or Ronnie. Each time Cole had nodded, spoken politely but distantly and walked away, though his smoldering eyes had told her how difficult it was for him to do so.

Completely won over now by Paul's elder son, Lauren spoke of him often. Paul seemed pleased by his cautiously established new relationship with Cole. Each time Cole's name was mentioned, Kelsey's heart twisted.

Nights were the worst. Long, empty, lonely nights haunted by memories of being in his arms, loving him, falling asleep tucked snugly against him.

A ragged moan escaped her just as an impatient blare from behind signaled that the traffic light had changed to green. Blinking the road ahead into focus, Kelsey pressed the accelerator.

She made a right turn; her heart started a slow, heavy pounding in her chest. She couldn't grip the steering wheel any more tightly, but her palms had gone damp against the worn wheel covering. Sometime during the endless night before, Kelsey had decided to stop being a coward. She had realized that nothing—*nothing*—could be worse than living without Cole.

* * *

Her hand was shaking so badly she missed the doorbell button twice before she managed to press it. She smoothed her still-damp palms down the legs of her jeans, staring hard at the heavy, carved door in front of her, waiting for it to open, afraid it would not. *Be home, Cole. For once, be easy to reach. Don't make me chase after you again, damn it.*

But she would, of course, if necessary.

She wasn't sure whether she was relieved or terror-stricken when the door opened. She stared up at Cole's startled face as if she hadn't quite realized whose doorstep she stood upon.

He hid his surprise almost as quickly as she'd seen it. "Hello, Kelsey," he said as casually as if he'd been expecting her all along. "What are you doing here?"

Clenching her fists at her sides, she took a deep breath. "I came to see the rest of your house."

It was immediately apparent that he understood the message behind her rather inane answer. His silvery-green eyes lit with a flare of satisfaction, his hard mouth quirking into a smile. "It's about time," he said simply.

She'd half expected to be crushed in his arms. Or, failing that delightful possibility, to be interrogated about her reasons for changing her mind. She really hadn't thought he'd accept her surrender with such smug contentment, as if there had never really been any question of her doing anything else. "You're so arrogant," she breathed, her hands on her hips as she glared up at him. He hadn't even invited her inside.

He inclined his head, his smile deepening. "Yes. Want to change your mind about seeing the house?"

Determining to be as casual as he seemed to be, she crossed her arms and tilted her chin to a cocky angle. "No. You see, I've decided I'm just what you need. I'm going to turn your life upside down, you know."

"Yes, I know." He didn't seem particularly disturbed by the prospect.

"I'll nag you incessantly to donate to my kids."

"I don't think I'll be such a hard touch, do you?" he asked humorously. "Though, of course, even my resources have limits. As you once pointed out, I can't personally finance all the dreams."

"I'll expect you to help me hit up your wealthy friends for donations."

He crossed his arms and leaned comfortably against the doorway, still not bothering to invite her inside. "I can try," he said meditatively. "They may well start running when they see me coming, but it won't be the first time I've encountered that reaction."

"I put in very long hours for my job. Weekends, holidays, evenings. When I get started on a project, I tend to be consumed by it until it's concluded."

"I'm known as a workaholic, myself. We probably both need to learn when to delegate work to leave time for each other occasionally."

She fought the smile that wanted so badly to escape. It was going to work, she told herself exultantly. She and Cole were going to be magnificent together. Why had she ever doubted it when apparently he had not?

"I'm not going to let you fall back on your old ways if we go ahead with this," she warned, trying to sound menacing. "I'm serving notice right now that there won't be any other women wearing diamonds you purchase."

"Any diamonds I purchase will be for you," he assured her.

She flushed, not wanting him to think she'd been asking for gifts. But then, deciding he hadn't, she continued rapidly. "I'll work on your family. I'll charm the socks off them if I have to. I'll be so nice to them they'll be ready to adopt me or elect me president. But I'd better not go to all that trouble only to have you decide you've changed your mind. If I move into this house with you, it's for life. Exclusive, permanent, mutual. You got that, Saxon?''

"You have me thoroughly terrorized," he assured her. "I wouldn't even think of changing my mind. I just have one question."

"What?" she asked suspiciously.

"What do *I* get out of this?"

She smiled. "Someone who wants you to the point of insanity. Someone who knows and loves every side of you. Someone who'll be there for you whenever you need to not be strong for a little while. Someone with whom to laugh and cry and raise babies and grow old together."

"You?" he clarified lightly, though his eyes burned even more brightly. She could almost feel the warmth of them as they caressed her face.

"Me," she answered, no longer smiling. The whimsical conversation had suddenly become totally serious.

Cole's voice turned husky. "Sounds like I'm getting the better part of the deal."

"Do you love me, Cole?" she asked softly, her eyes locked with his.

"More than life itself," he replied without hesitation.

"Then I'm perfectly happy with my side of the bargain," she whispered. And she was no longer afraid. How could she be? Cole loved her.

Cole cleared his throat and moved away from the doorframe. "Would you like to come in?"

"I'd like that very much," she answered, stepping forward.

He held out his hand, and she placed hers in it. She couldn't wait to be inside, alone with him, to have the privacy to throw herself in his arms and . . .

She came to an abrupt stop as she stepped into the foyer only to find herself face-to-face with Cole's mother.

Cole's fingers tightened reassuringly around hers when he felt her quiver. Kelsey was struck momentarily speechless. The woman was dressed to attend a palace reception, she thought with a silent moan. Suit by Givenchy, shoes by Gucci and neat little white gloves by— Where *did* one buy little white gloves these days? Kelsey wondered, miserably aware of her own hot pink T-shirt and whitewashed jeans. Her white canvas sneakers didn't even have a trendy brand name, she thought incongruously. She'd bought them on sale at a discount store. Four ninety-eight.

"Hello, Mrs. Saxon." Kelsey just managed not to wince at the stilted sound of the words that escaped her.

The older woman smiled at her. "I think we'd all be more comfortable if you call me Belinda, don't you?"

Kelsey didn't think that at all, but she certainly wasn't going to argue. If Cole's mother wanted to be called Belinda, she would call her Belinda. Now if only she hadn't overheard any of that ridiculous exchange between Kelsey and—

"I understand you and my son have become engaged," Belinda said, shattering Kelsey's faint hope. The hint of genuine amusement in her voice made Kelsey suspect that Belinda had heard every word.

"Yes, I... believe we have," Kelsey managed faintly.

Cole's hand tightened even more snugly around hers, though he didn't speak.

"Welcome to the family, Kelsey," Belinda said, nodding with courtly acceptance of the situation. "Cole's been telling me about your fascinating work with children. You'll have to give me more details so that I can discuss contributions with my friends. We're always interested in worthwhile charities."

"Thank you, Mrs.—er—Belinda. Any contributions you'd like to make would be greatly appreciated."

"Well," Belinda murmured, looking from Kelsey's flushed face to Cole's amused one. "I'd best be going. I'm sure the two of you have a great deal to discuss."

"It was very nice to see you again," Kelsey fibbed graciously. Why wasn't Cole saying anything?

Belinda smiled again. "Thank you, Kelsey. I found the past few minutes quite... illuminating."

Kelsey blushed even brighter, resisting an ignoble urge to hide her face in Cole's shoulder.

"Drive carefully, Mother," Cole said, speaking at last. "And thank you." He didn't bother to clarify the reason for his gratitude. All three of them knew he was thanking her for accepting Kelsey graciously.

"Yes, of course." Belinda reached for the doorknob just before Cole could open the door for her. "By the way," she murmured, pausing at the threshold. "How is Paul?"

"Much better today," Kelsey replied somewhat warily. "He may get to go home in a few days."

"I'm happy to hear that. Give him a message for me, will you?"

"What message, Mother?" Cole asked, as guarded as Kelsey had been.

"Tell him there's no reason why we shouldn't both attend our son's wedding. I believe we're civilized enough to handle it gracefully, don't you?"

"Yes, I know you are. Again, thank you, Mother."

She answered with the regal nod that Kelsey recognized, having seen Cole make the identical gesture. And then she turned and walked out the door with elegant dignity.

Kelsey turned to Cole the moment they were alone. "You," she said ominously, "are going to die. Slowly. How could you let me make a fool of myself that way?"

"I couldn't stop you," he answered, not quite successfully stifling a chuckle. "You seemed determined to have your say."

"Cole!" she wailed. "You *knew* she was listening, damn it!"

"Yes," he admitted. "And I knew she would be charmed by you. I was right, of course." He didn't add "as always." He simply left the words implied.

She looked at him with narrowed eyes. "I don't know how," she said softly. "I don't know when. But someday, someway I *will* repay you for what you just put me through."

"I'll look forward to it," he assured her absently. "Now will you please come here and kiss me before I do something violent?"

She threw herself at him without hesitation, unable to wait another moment to be in his arms.

"Oh, God, Kelsey," he murmured shakily, holding her so tightly her breath locked in her lungs. "If only you knew what I've been through in the past three weeks. I was beginning to think I'd lost you for good."

So he hadn't been quite as confident as he'd appeared a few minutes earlier. She was glad. Smiling, she pulled his mouth to hers.

"Cole, I love you so much," she murmured several long, heated minutes later when he lifted his head long enough to allow her to speak.

"And I love you." He nuzzled her cheek, his voice low, seductive, his hands holding her close. "Dare to dream, Kelsey," he murmured, his breath warm on her ear.

She tightened her arms round his neck. "I already did. And you've made it come true."

"Then how would you like to see the rest of the house? Starting with our bedroom."

"I'd like that," she assured him huskily. "I'd like that very much."

The words had hardly left her mouth before he swept her off her feet and into his arms. And then he proceeded to fulfill all her fantasies by carrying her up his curving staircase and straight to his bed.

Epilogue

Lauren opened her door in answer to Kelsey's ring. "It's about time you got here," she scolded, though she was smiling. "Cole was about to come looking for you. And I was afraid you were going to miss Dad's call. He should be calling soon, according to the card he sent last week."

"I had to make sure all the Christmas gifts were delivered to the kids in the hospital," Kelsey reminded her sister, shrugging out of her coat.

Lauren reached for the coat with her left hand and patted Kelsey's stomach with her right. "You're going to have to start taking it easy before long, you know. My niece or nephew needs rest."

Kelsey only laughed. "Get serious. The kid's a Saxon, remember? You don't get any tougher than that."

"Tell me about it," Lauren answered with an exaggerated sigh as a loud squeal erupted from the den behind her, followed by a series of high-pitched electronic beeps and buzzes. "Sounds like Cole and Jared are having another laser battle. I can't believe you actually allowed Cole to buy those noisy, battery-operated laser guns for my son."

"I wasn't with him when he bought them," Kelsey replied with a grin. "But do you really think I could have stopped him if I had been?"

Lauren smiled wickedly and turned a pointed glance toward Kelsey's stomach. "Just remember I owe you one."

Kelsey groaned and followed her sister into the battleground.

A huge, gaily decorated Christmas tree dominated one corner of the comfortably furnished den, colorfully wrapped presents piled high beneath it. Beside it, on a low sofa, Phillip and Eudora Saxon sat side by side, watching their grandsons at play with amused indulgence. They greeted Kelsey when she entered, Eudora quite warmly, Phillip more reserved, as usual, but still pleasant enough. He'd long since accepted that Cole's love for Kelsey was of the permanent variety, despite Phillip's discomfort with the somewhat awkward logistics of his son's and grandson's marriages to sisters. The anticipation of his first great-grandchild had gone a long way in sealing his approval for Kelsey.

Paul stood at the bar, pouring eggnog into tiny glass cups. He looked up when Kelsey and Lauren entered. "Hi, Kelsey," he greeted her. "Want one?"

"Of course," she answered with a smile. Out of long-established habit, she studied him closely, but saw only a healthy man in his fifties. He was thin, but then he always had been. His hair was more gray than dark, but still abundant. And those silvery-green eyes his sons had inherited were as sharp and lively as ever. He had been able to resume a reasonably active routine since his surgery, though he was still very careful with diet and exercise and was checked regularly by a doctor. So far, he'd been assured there was no reason to believe he wouldn't live to a comfortable old age as long as he took care of himself. And Lauren would certainly see to that.

"Bang, Kelsey! I got you!" a gleeful young voice announced from behind a chair on her right.

She looked around to spot her three-year-old nephew grinning at her from behind an enormous blue plastic laser gun that flashed with multicolored lights. "Don't tell me you've already opened presents," she wailed teasingly. "I thought you were going to wait for me."

"This is all I could open," Jared assured her gravely, coming from behind the chair to give her a hug. "Cole couldn't wait."

During the general laughter that followed, Kelsey searched out her husband. He rose grinning from behind another chair, his expression endearingly sheepish. She couldn't help thinking of the unsmiling, work-absorbed man she'd first met just over three years earlier. How much happier he looked now than he had then.

"I only allowed him to open them so he'd have something to keep him occupied until it was time to open all the presents," Cole assured her, making a futile attempt at looking dignified.

"Sure you did," Kelsey said skeptically. "Not because you wanted to play with them yourself, or anything."

"Of course not."

The others in the room laughed again, proving that not one of them believed him. Not even Jared.

Kelsey settled on a love seat with Cole just as Paul brought two cups of eggnog to them.

"Thanks, Paul," Cole said easily, accepting his. "This looks good." Cole and Paul had long since established a comfortable relationship. It wasn't exactly that of father and son; twenty-six years of separation had strained that particular connection. During a recent discussion of their hus bands, Kelsey and Lauren had decided that the two men had become friends. Just as everyone was satisfied with Cole's older-brother relationship with Jared, so they accepted his friendship with Paul. It was, after all, more than anyone could have expected three years earlier.

Peaceful contentment fell over the room as the adults sat sipping their eggnog, Paul on the arm of Lauren's chair, Jared curled quietly—for the moment—in his mother's lap. The elder Saxons seemed pleased to be spending Christmas Day in their son's home for the third year in a row. Kelsey and Cole had followed their usual tradition of spending Christmas Eve with the Graysons, saving today for the Saxon side of their family. A little tired from the usual holiday bustle, Kelsey nestled into the curve of Cole's arm, an embrace that had become increasingly protective during the past five months.

Kelsey was the one who broke the rare silence. "By the way, Cole. You know how badly Christmas depleted the foundation funds?"

Cole groaned. "Kelsey—"

"We should have enough coming in to replenish in a few weeks," she assured him hastily. "But we're terribly short now, and we have two children who really need to visit Walt Disney World soon, if they're going to be able to go at all. I was sort of hoping . . ." She let the sentence trail off, knowing it wasn't necessary to complete it.

Cole sighed deeply, then glanced at his father and grandfather with sudden calculation. "Tell you what," he suggested smoothly. "Grayson Shipping will contribute a third of the amount you need if the Saxon law firm and CompuComm will supply the rest."

Both having been hit up regularly for Kelsey's beloved cause, Phillip and Paul groaned in unison, sounding very much like Cole had only moments before. But both seemed equally resigned to opening their checkbooks yet again.

"Just wait until after the first of January, will you?" Paul requested. "At least that way it'll come out of next year's donation budget."

Kelsey nodded happily. "That's no problem," she assured him.

"All right, I'm glad that's settled, but I want no more business conducted today," Lauren announced sternly. "It's Christmas, remember? So what would you like to do first—eat or open presents?"

"Eat," Kelsey, Paul and Phillip answered promptly.

"Open presents," Jared and Cole declared at the same time.

Her head on her husband's shoulder, Kelsey giggled during the ensuing noisy discussion. Glancing around the room at the smiling faces surrounding her, she reflected with deep satisfaction that this was one family whose dreams had all been granted three years earlier. Including her own.

Oh, how she loved watching dreams come true!

*   *   *   *   *

FOUR UNIQUE SERIES
FOR EVERY WOMAN YOU ARE . . .

Silhouette Romance®

Love, at its most tender, provocative,
emotional . . . in stories that will make you laugh and
cry while bringing you the magic of falling in love.

6 titles per month

Silhouette Special Edition®

Sophisticated, substantial and packed with
emotion, these powerful novels of life and love will
capture your imagination and steal your heart.

6 titles per month

SILHOUETTE *Desire*®

Open the door to romance and passion. Humorous,
emotional, compelling—yet always a believable
and sensuous story—Silhouette Desire never
fails to deliver on the promise of love.

6 titles per month

SILHOUETTE·INTIMATE·MOMENTS®

Enter a world of excitement, of romance
heightened by suspense, adventure and the
passions every woman dreams of. Let us
sweep you away.

4 titles per month